THE DESERT PLAYER

Scott Chalmers

Cover design by: Samantha Chalmers
©[John]/Adobe Stock
©[Kevin Carden]/Adobe Stock

Printed in the United States of America

Dedicated to all my golfing buddies through the years:

Pop, Jao, Granddo, Mr. W., Alex, Tay, Harps, Pat, Eamer, Charlie, Tom, TBaldo, Theo, Cleats, Cav, TonyO, Dobs, Matt, George P., Joe F., Jablonk, Jay Barbs, George Speech, Joe S., Fitz, Chris G.

"...out here, in the desert, if you want to be a player, a real player, you don't accept a challenge by hitting to the middle of the green. If you've got guts, I mean the guts to be a real player, you wouldn't have played ten yards off the green, and then patted yourself on the back for being mediocre."

"A player never talks about golf like you do. When a 'player' says someone can 'play', they don't mean they can hit the ball well, putt, or know how to score. They mean they know how to win money. The best 'players' win money. That may mean they can't break eighty-five or that they can't get the ball off the ground. But if they collect at the end, in the eyes of a 'player', they can 'play'."

BEN NEWELL

CHAPTER 1

The view was magnificent. It was much better than any of my memories of standing in this spot thirty-six years earlier. The fairway running away from me was a deep green and stood out in contrast to the tans and browns of the surrounding desert. With the mountains in the background and the morning sun fighting through dark clouds, I was looking at a perfect cover for any golf resort magazine.

"We just replaced the old windows," a kid, maybe twenty years old, said. He walked over and wiped down the table I was standing next to. "There used to be three windows, so now with just the one huge picture window it opens up the view of the first fairway."

I looked at the entire wall which was a dark cherry, with intricate molding around the window that bordered crown molding running along with the ceiling. The patio outside the window was designed with beautiful stone inlays around two fire pits surrounded by chairs and natural-cut limestone benches. As I turned to look at the barroom itself, I shook my head. I thought I was standing in a stuffy, old British gentleman's club from the early twentieth century, not the barroom I remember where we sat on broken wood stools and leaned on a peeling laminate countertop from the fifties.

"It has changed quite a bit from the last time I was here," I told the kid.

"When was that?"

"Oh, probably 1983, maybe 1984."

"Way before my time," he said. "They put a lot of money into the place." He moved on to wipe down another table. "I know the bar used to be in the corner, not along the entire back like now. Some old pictures are hanging on the walls of the hallway out by the pro shop if you want to take a look."

I nodded. "I'll check them out." Pointing out the window, I said, "The course also looks different. I don't ever remember it being nearly this green."

"They put a few million into the irrigation, and the head greenskeeper was hired from a private club back east. He turned this place around. Pete Dye's company rebuilt all the greens. Word is they want to get a PGA event here. They're in the running for some local qualifying events, and maybe a state Open in three years."

I nodded as I looked around, not sure how this was the same place. "Well, I guess that's good for them. When I played here this was a pit in the desert."

The kid walked back toward the bar and said, "I hope it happens because that means this place will be full, and that means better tips."

I started to tell him that maybe he should have a better plan for his future than waiting for "better tips", but I caught myself. I, more than anyone, should know that your life can change on a dime. Maybe if I had maintained more conservative and stable goals when I was his age, I wouldn't have the nightmares that often visit me.

But, then again, I also would not have been standing in the clubhouse of Desert Bridge Country Club. When I walked out of this room and left the desert thirty-six years ago, I was told never to return, and I swore I wouldn't. Hell, I even get nervous whenever I fly over Las Vegas. Now, here I was.

A voice called out from the hallway behind me. "Will! Start the ice machine. And go down to the cellar and bring up a case of Jack."

"Will do, Milly," the kid replied.

I looked over my shoulder. "Did you say, Milly?" I asked.

The kid started to walk to the entrance of the kitchen. "Yea. Milly."

"Miller Halverstrom?" I asked.

"One and the same," he said as he walked out into the kitchen.

My heart rate jumped. During the two days it took me to drive from Austin to Vegas, I convinced myself that after all the years there was no chance I would run into anyone from the past. Now, after only ten minutes, I realized I was wrong. I looked at the exit and took a deep breath.

"Remember it's been a long time," I said under my breath. I ran my fingers through the new beard I grew for the trip.

"Hello," a voice said from behind me. "The bar isn't open yet, but if you want I can get you something from the kitchen."

I shook my head to get back to reality. "Thirty-six years," I whispered to myself.

I turned around and there stood Milly. I did my best to conceal any reaction. He looked like what you would expect: a nearly four-decade-older version of the man that was a fixture at the course and witnessed most of the events that shaped me into the man that I am today. Thinking that eye contact would help him recognize me, I looked down at the floor.

"Some coffee would be great. Decaf, if you don't mind," I said.

"Coming right up," he said, retreating into the hallway.

I laughed to myself. If Milly recognized me, he certainly didn't give anything away. I walked over and sat at one of the oval oak tables. Out of habit, I put myself into the corner of the room with a clear sight of each of the doors. Taking out my phone, I sent a quick text to my wife that I was safe and sound at the golf course. She immediately replied with a smiley face and again made fun of me for growing the beard. It was her attempt to calm my nerves. Putting the phone down, I leaned back and took a deep breath. I was glad the room and the club were so different. It helped to ease my mind and keep the ghosts at bay. During the entire drive up from Austin, I continually told myself there was nothing to worry about. Even with Milly still here, I knew the idea I would be recognized was my mind playing tricks.

A loud bang grabbed my attention. The kid burst out of the kitchen carrying a couple of liquor cases.

"I almost lost it," he said with a laugh. "Milly would have my ass if I dropped a case of JD. He'd probably make me lick it off the floor."

I guess Milly had changed. When he poured drinks and handed out beers back in the day, I could never figure out how he kept any control of the bar. The room was always packed, Milly was always serving, and I never remember anyone paying.

"He told me that he would be right out with your coffee. He had to make a quick call."

My heart rate jumped and I sat straight up in my chair.

"Call?" I asked. I looked again at the exit and grabbed my phone.

"Yeah, I could hear his wife from the other side of the room laying into him. Something about forgetting to pay a bill."

I forced myself to take a breath. After a second I shook my head and laughed. "I've been right where he is."

The kid dropped the cases behind the bar and headed back into the kitchen. My wife texted asking how I was feeling. When

I told her that I was seeing ghosts and monsters around each corner, she sent back a single, all-caps message:

'36 YEARS!!!'

She was right. When Milly walked out with my coffee I looked him straight in the eye and thanked him.

"I hope you don't mind if I camp out here," I said. "I'm meeting someone, but I don't know when. It could be a while."

"Not at all," Milly said. "There's a storm about to hit so the golfers will start filling this place up. If you want anything stronger than coffee before noon, just ask. I can break a rule once in a while, and I don't think anyone will come down on me if I serve a drink before the club says I can."

"Don't worry," I said. "Coffee is good for now."

Same old Milly. Mr. Law Abiding Citizen on the outside but is never afraid to skirt the law if need be. Of course, I wasn't judging him. I was no saint either.

"Take all the time you need," he said, walking back to the kitchen.

"Okay," I said. "I'm not sure when he'll be here."

Or if he'll be here.

How could I drive all this way and sit here without talking to Milly? He was the voice of reason in all the craziness during my time in Las Vegas. He was the man that I was told knew everything. I decided I would go find him and say hello. I stood and took a few steps toward the kitchen but stopped. The patio door opened and an older gentleman stepped in. My heart stopped as he held the door open. When a woman walked in, I realized it was not him. I looked again at the kitchen and returned to the table. I would talk to Milly after he arrived. If he arrived.

It started to rain. Yes, it does rain in Las Vegas. Looking out at the patio, I saw that there was heavy rain. Over the loudspeaker, a voice said that all the golfers were to leave the course due to lightning in the area. After five minutes, the bar filled up with players to wait it out. I stayed in the corner listening to the groups of people around me, mostly talking about golf and sports in general. Being able to watch and listen allowed me to keep my thoughts on the present. My wife thought this trip, and having time alone in the car, was going to allow me to sort through all the conflicting stories in my head. I wanted anything but that. In fact, during my drive up I almost blew out my eardrums because the louder the music played, the easier it was to drive out the memories.

A group of four men walked over and sat at the table with me. They were all in their forties and, despite the rain, were having a good time. Four friends, happy to be with each other, playing the game they loved.

I remember that love. The way walking onto the first tee could scrub all the problems out of your head. How the anticipation of hitting a ball with a club with friends was enough to make life worth living, if only until you walked off the eighteenth green.

One of them asked if I was waiting out the rain. After I shook my head, he drew me into a conversation about the course. As hard as I tried to stay out of it, he kept me engaged. When I told him I played the course a long time ago after I left college, he centered right on my pain, asking me about the course's history. It was almost as if he knew who I was.

My wife's voice sounded in the back of my head, telling me I had nothing to worry about. I always had a fear that bells and whistles would start to go off if I crossed the Vegas city line. Yes, it was probably me being paranoid. But I did think it ironic this guy was probing my past, almost as if he read my mind.

"You look like you're about sixty, so that would be about 1980, or so?" he asked. "I heard this place was a dump back then and most of the games here were big-money because no one cared about the police. Are all those stories true? Did you get in some of those games? I heard it was common for big-name guys to come here and play for really big amounts."

I looked him in the eye. He was asking an innocent question to a guilty man.

"I'm sure most of the stories are exaggerated," I said. "But, yeah, some money games were going on."

The man reached over and shook my hand. "Matt Wilson," he said. I think he believed that if he introduced himself, I would open up to him. He was curious and knew I had answers.

"Mark," I said. "Nice to meet you. Do you have an interest in the topic?"

"I love everything about golf history," he said. "There is so much history in the valley. Ask these guys, I can't get enough."

I looked at his friends and they all nodded, but with their quick eye rolls, I realized they were not as passionate as Matt was.

I smiled and one of the men said, "Matty's wife might be better to comment on how much he loves the game."

There were laughs around the table. One of the other men said, "His boy, Josh, has no choice. He was born with the Masters playing on the TV in the delivery room."

Matt shook his head. "That is not true. The Duke took to the game all by himself."

"The Duke?" I asked, realizing they were drawing me into their conversation.

"It's my boy's nickname. He reminded me of the video game character Duke Nukem."

Again, the men all laughed. I joined them, more to move the

conversation to an end. I had no idea who Duke Nukem was. Matt was not done though. "Is it true that there were million-dollar matches here, and that the mob used to have guys here all the time?" he asked.

"Not that I know of," I said, taking a sip of my cup of decaf. "Most of the players here were local. I never heard of million-dollar games. Most of the stuff I knew about was small stuff with friends. The clubhouse was just a small old house. The course was always dry and fast. I liked to play here but because it was under the radar of the hotel and casino crowd."

He sat back unable to hide his disappointment. "C'mon, I looked at the photos on the wall in the hallway. There are some PGA players in those photos. Why would they be here?"

"Well," I said, "I doubt anyone that played on the tour that was tied up in a big-money game would allow themselves to be photographed."

He nodded. "I guess," he said, his voice trailing off and his disappointment obvious on his face. I thought we were done but then he sat up to the table. "Think about it though. Having a putt for a half-million bucks. Back then. That would be like ten million today, and not from a tournament purse but from your pocket."

I did my best to keep a straight face. I thought about changing the topic to get him away from my past, but I let him go on. I looked out the window, hoping to see the sun so that these guys would leave, but it was still raining.

He kept pushing. "Mark, you had to hear about some of those games, right? If you were here back then? Have you ever seen any of the greats? I hear Evel Knevel was a hustler."

One of his friends said, "What? Evel Knevel? C'mon, Matty."

"He's right," I said, and immediately wished I kept my mouth shut.

"Yeah," Matt said. "The best hustlers were guys that you would never think of, or heard of. Mark, who was the best? Who was the best Tour player you ever saw play for big-money here? Was it Trevino, did you ever see him? Or how about Ray Floyd?"

I sat back again and looked at the door. I felt like I was on trial and had to think out my answers to the word before speaking.

"The best? I don't think there is a best when it comes to big-money. Some of the big-money guys were hustling, and others were trying to make it in the game and wanted the experience of playing under pressure. Kind of like preparing for the future. But the best, I don't know if there's a way to figure that out."

Matt looked at me and nodded. After a second, he said, "How about Ben Newell? Have you ever heard of him?"

My heart stopped and I felt sweat immediately form on my forehead. If I was on the stand, my reaction would have convinced any jury that I was guilty. I tried to take a breath but I ended up coughing.

"Ben Newell?" I asked, trying to remain as detached as I possibly could.

"I heard that he was the best," Matt said. "Not just the best at gambling. I heard that guy could have been one of the greats. Better than Nicklaus."

Again, I tried to control my reaction. "Where did you hear about him?"

"There was an article a few years ago on the internet about this place," he responded. "That's why we came to play here. I think the writer called this place just, 'The Bridge'. Not 'Desert Bridge'. That's where I heard there were lots of big-time gamblers that would play here. The article said this guy Ben Newell was the best."

"Shouldn't believe anything on the internet," one of his friends said.

"Well, there were some great players," I said, trying to change the topic. "And the money games happened, just not for thousands. But at this place, I used to like it because it was always empty. Especially when it was hot."

The same friend said, "Matty, I can't see how any of these gamblers were better than Trevino or Nicklaus. If they were, why didn't they play on the tour?"

"Are you kidding?" said Matt. "Trevino was a money player. He used to play for pennies when he was young so that he could eat. Or something like that."

"One of the great quotes of all time came from Lee Trevino," another friend said. "I guess someone asked him about the pressure of playing in a tournament for a big purse. He said, 'Pressure is playing for ten dollars when you don't have a dime in your pocket.'"

All four men laughed, and I did too.

Over the loudspeaker, a voice told everyone that the lightning warning was over and that they were free to return to the course. I looked out the window and sure enough, the rain was now a drizzle. When the announcement was done, the entire room stood and like doors opening at a store on Black Friday, everyone rushed to leave the bar and get back on the course.

Matt reached over and again shook my hand. "It was nice meeting you, Mark. Best of luck."

"You too," I said with a smile. "Have fun out there. Don't let the pressure get to you."

"Hey," he laughed, reaching into his pocket. He dropped a five-dollar bill on the table. "No pressure on me. I got more than a dime in my pocket."

He turned and joined the cavalcade of golfers heading out of the barroom. I nodded to him and looked at the clearing sky. Smiling to myself, I said, "Pressure isn't playing for ten dollars when you don't have a dime. Pressure is playing for a million when there's a gun pointed at your head."

I reached into my jacket and took out the envelope. The edges were browned and years ago, folds turned to tears. It was now held together with tape and protected inside a clear plastic bag. I held it up and looked at it. For what must be the thousandth time I wondered what was inside. I hoped that today I would be able to find out.

As I stared at the door and waited, my mind went back. Back to the beginning. Back when my life was simple. When the important things were going to school, my mom, my friends, and....

CHAPTER 2

….Golf.

It was my first love. The moment I picked up a club and hit the ball, I fell hard for the game.

Golf started for me when I was thirteen. It was the immediate focus of my life. When I first played, it was on a public course in my hometown called Saddle River Country Club. I played with a couple of friends from my neighborhood. My set of clubs was given to me by my grandfather. The irons were a set of MacGregor Tommy Armour Silver Scots from the fifties. The woods, yes actual Persimmons back then, were a Tourney Driver, a Top-Flight two-wood, and a Pederson three-and-a-half-wood. My putter was an original Ping Anser with the Phoenix address.

I played with golf balls I found scouring the woods with friends off of the fairways at Water Edge, a private course, which was across the railroad tracks that ran behind my backyard. The golf ball hunts were a major part of those teen years and were governed by certain rules. Rule one was that the first to see the ball owned it unless the ball had a logo. All logoed balls went into a pile that we would divvy up after. Rule two was that if you saw a ball, you had to make every effort to get it, even if that meant climbing through prickers, under or over fences, or into mud or water. The last rule was any ball that was hit into the woods while we were searching, would be thrown back into the fairway. We would explain to the player how lucky they were to have hit a tree and gotten a favorable bounce out of the woods.

Looking for balls became an art. We knew the best side of the hole to search and how to find balls plugged into soft soil or deep grass. We went once a week and on a good day, we could find over a hundred balls. One day we went into a pond that sat between two holes and pulled out over three hundred and fifty. After searching, we would get together and compare what we found. Some balls were traded, and the old ones went into a pile that we would hit back into the woods or at the freight trains as they moved down the tracks.

We always found Blue and Red Maxflis, Tourneys, Pro Staffs with the truncated cone dimple, and Top Flights. Anytime you found a Titleist, it was as if you found gold.

As a teenager, being with my friends on the course with no adults and trying to learn this difficult and complex game took over all my waking moments. If I wasn't chipping in the front yard, I was practicing putting on the carpet in our family room. Saturday and Sunday afternoons were reserved for watching golf on TV. Back then you only got to see the last four or five holes during the coverage. For me, it was as if I was looking at my future. If there was any daylight left after the tournament ended, I would be in the front yard recreating what I just watched using plastic golf balls. I treated any paved surface like a water hazard and the various trees in the yard were my targets.

The first time I played we were only able to get in sixteen holes before it got dark. I shot a ninety-six for those sixteen holes. I broke one hundred the second full round I played, and by the end of that summer, right as I was starting eighth grade, I broke ninety.

I wanted to be around the game for my entire life. I wanted golf to be the thing that shaped who I was, how I was, and why I was. Looking back, all of that became true. I guess it can be said that anyone's path in life can be forged by a random act that, at the time, you don't know is random or an act of any significance. Looking at my life, it's no secret that living in Las Vegas after college was the single most influential event in my life. It was the game that led me there. There were three random acts, each around the game, that played a part in leading me to Vegas.

First, I met a friend at a golf camp when I was fourteen. Second, I hit two shots, one great and one horrible, in a tournament that meant nothing, in front of a man who I thought was some asshole's uncle. Third, I had a run-in with two idiots thinking they would try and be cool in the middle of the night. All of these events were around the game I loved: golf.

The summer before my freshman year at high school I went to a week-long golf camp. While my time was more about chasing girls from the tennis camp at the same facility than it was about golf, for the first time I learned about the game. It was also my first step to Las Vegas. At camp, I met Kenny West who was my age and also learning the game. We were together the entire week and since we only lived a few towns from each other, for the remainder of my high school years he would often join me and my friends when we played the public layouts.

When I went out for my high school team in the spring of my freshman year, I was surprised to make it. I even played some varsity matches and got my letter.

I wasn't good though. I was a good athlete that could hit the ball and once in a while come close to breaking forty in our nine-hole school matches. Most of the time though I played bogey golf. The summer after my freshman year I played a lot of golf but got no better. That was until I met Mr. Wittich, the local golf pro at Water Edge Country Club. He was a friend of my high school golf coach, and he allowed me, a non-member, to use the club's practice range and green. Once a week he watched me hit balls and, in his crotchety way, offered some ideas and changes to improve my swing. After I started to get better, his suggestions became demands. He was a tough, former marine that knew my swing. He never really said what he wanted me to do, it was more grunts, short sentences, and shakes of the head. When he wanted to show something, he would grab my hands, arms, shoulders, or hips, and force me to move the way he wanted. It took me a few lessons but I got used to his ways.

In the fall of my sophomore year, I continued going to the range once a week. Once Mr. Wittich taught me the meaning of tempo, his lessons started to pay off. In the last week of November, just before everything shut down for winter, I played eighteen holes with some of the guys from the team that were members at Water Edge. I shot seventy-four.

That spring, I became really good. At least by my definition. I broke par for nine holes for the first time in a match and did it again several times after that. I played in my first junior event that summer and did well enough that I qualified for the State Amateur. Even though I was horrible at the State Am and missed making the cut for match play, I loved the experience. That fall, when I started my junior year, I won a small local junior event. I shot a seventy-one and won by ten. While it wasn't anything to go nuts over, it was my first winner's trophy.

It was after my junior year golf season that my coach started to talk about college. He thought I was good enough to play, and since I was starting the process of visiting schools with my mom, he wanted me to talk to the Athletic Department and the golf coaches at these schools. Most of the schools that said they were interested in me were smaller and had what could best be described as "low-focus" golf programs, which was fine by me. I had no vision of playing on the PGA Tour or being able to play for a national program at a Division 1 school. I just thought that playing in college would help me start a career associated with the game.

As the summer started, Mr. Wittich told me that I needed to get a different set of clubs. He helped me buy a set of Ram Accubar irons and a set of Ram Persimmons woods. I kept the Ping putter in the bag. As I learned how to get the feel of the new clubs, he started to work on different parts of my swing. In the first two weeks of summer, he worked with me harder than at any time before. I was hitting balls all day long and I could feel the difference.

With my new clubs and my ever-improving swing, I won the first summer tournament that year, the County Junior. I won by three strokes. I then played a fun round with some friends on the weekend of July Fourth and shot a sixty-seven on a pretty good course. In the last week of July, I played in the first round of the State Open qualifier. For the thirty-six holes, I ended up two under to qualify. When I saw Mr. Wittich a few days later, he nodded and said, "I think you may be a good golfer." Coming from him meant the world to me.

The next week, my road to Las Vegas continued.

It was a tournament that no one had heard of. It was sponsored by one of the automakers, and state qualifiers would go to Houston to play in the national finals. I signed up more for the opportunity to play Sanders Bay, one of the finest private courses in our state. Also, because I won our county junior championship, I got in without having to pay the twenty-five-dollar entrance fee. It didn't matter to me that if I did qualify, I would not be able to go to the finals. My cousin was getting married the same weekend as the finals in Houston. So, for me, there was no pressure. Just a chance to play a great course for free.

To make things better, I was paired with my good friend, Kenny West. He also would not be able to go to Houston if he qualified, so both of us were relaxed and looking to play for fun.

One interesting thing about the day was the third player in our group. He was from the farthest part of the state. I didn't know him and neither did Kenny. After two holes we knew what he was though. He was a whiner. On the first and second holes, he was making excuses. When his tee shot on the par-3 third flew the green, this guy started to blame the company that printed the yardage on the scorecard. After missing a short putt on the fifth he turned and threw his putter from the green to the next tee. If either Kenny or I were taking this round seriously, we would have gotten in his face. But both of us let it slide and tried to not laugh at him.

On the sixth hole, two men showed up on the course and started to follow us. One was the whiner's father. Kenny and I assumed the other man was an uncle or a friend of the father. Whoever he was, he was being treated to one of the most embarrassing displays of course etiquette I had seen. By the time we made the turn, this kid was five over and made more enemies than pars. On the back nine, I could have choked him when he tossed his putter toward his bag and nearly hit me. I kept my mouth shut, but to let him know I wasn't happy about being a target, I asked him three times to make sure I recorded his correct score. It was a double bogey.

As for me, I was playing the best tournament round of my life. I made the turn at three-under and made a bomb of a putt on the tenth to save par. After a bogie and a birdie on the next two holes, I made the best swing of my young golfing life. It was the second shot on the par-4 thirteenth. I had driven into the left rough and had no open shot at the green. My only hope was to hit a thirty-yard draw keeping the ball low enough to stay under the branches ten yards in front of me. I then had to get over some other trees blocking the right side of the green.

No problem, I thought. I can't play in the finals even if I qualify, so why not go for it? So that's what I did. I hit a five-iron so pure that I never felt the contact. Because of the trees, I lost sight of my ball, but when I ran to the fairway to see where I ended up, I saw a ball ten feet below the hole. Looking at where the other guys were, I realized it was my shot. Until many years later, it was the best shot that I witnessed firsthand.

I made the putt.

Golf, as anyone that plays will tell you, is a tough game to stay on top of. And for me as a sixteen-year-old, I was not nearly strong enough mentally to hold it together for a full round. On fourteen, I had the anticipated breakdown. On the par-3, with my trusty Accubar five-iron, I tried to flight it low but I hit what can best be described as a shank. The ball shot out to the right like a bird flying away from a loud noise. I yelled, 'Fore!,' and watched my ball head directly at the group playing the fifteenth hole next to us. Luckily no one was hit, and I laughed it off. I even laughed at the whiner when he shook his head at my shot. I also caught sight of the whiner's uncle, or whoever he was, looking intently at me. As I walked to my ball, he followed. Good thing he did, because he got to see firsthand my next shot, which I carried over a tree to about five feet. I made the par putt.

Kenny and I laughed and carried on to the next tee. We both know that any time you make par on a hole where you hit a shank, you have to celebrate.

In the parking lot after the round, Uncle Whiner walked up to me. He introduced himself as Charles Tipton. He was, it turns out, not the whiner's uncle, but the coach of one of the best mid-size university programs in the country. He was there to watch the whiner play but was more impressed with me. We spoke for about fifteen minutes. He told me that he saw a lot of good golf from me and that while my sixty-six was a great score, my five-iron on thirteen was one of the best shots he had seen all summer. After I thanked him, he told me that it was the second-best shot he saw me hit that round. The best? That was the approach after my shanked five-iron on fourteen.

"Toughest shot in golf is the shot after a shank," he joked. "You don't par that hole unless you're mentally strong. I like that. And I like the fact that you could laugh off a shank. You've got a great, carefree attitude on the course."

He told me he was going to reach out to my high school coach. I gave him Mr. Wittich's name so he could ask my teacher about my game. I left the course that day with a great round, my first contact with my future college golf coach, and although I didn't know it, my second step toward Las Vegas.

Things worked out for me and a little over a year later I was starting my freshman year in college, playing for Coach Tipton. I majored in business and hospitality. It didn't take me long to decide on the areas of my study. I wanted to stay close to the game. I thought that I would strive to be a teaching pro. That meant playing as much as I could, learning how to run a business, and making contacts with the right people to set myself up eventually as head pro at a resort or club.

One thing got in the way: my golf game got better. Much better. While Mr. Wittich worked on my swing, Coach Tipton worked on my head. By the time I was done with my junior year, I had finished in the top five of a few major college tournaments and won my share of regional events. I was named an All-American.

During the summer, I spent time working at Water Edge setting up carts, whipping greens, and helping run tournaments. Mr. Wittich was my full-time teacher at this point. My game was so good that he and Coach Tipton were talking to me about golf after college. Not as a teacher, but as a player. When I opened my locker at the club one day, I found entrance forms for the local PGA Tour Qualifying, and a form to turn professional. It was Wittich's way of telling me I should not be taking my talents lightly. I took those forms with me back for my senior year at school to keep my focus on these big goals. I didn't believe I was good enough, but his point was well taken.

The third major step on my journey to Las Vegas happened on New Year's Eve. I was back home working at the club, serving drinks to the members and guests at the big gala. I had exactly one drink myself, a beer at midnight. I was done cleaning up at 2:00 AM but spent an hour with some of the guys I worked with hitting balls into the dark. Even though it was twenty degrees outside, it was a great start to the new year to be able to swing a club and have fun. By the time I left the club at 3:00 AM, I was ready for bed. My drive home was all of one mile. When I turned onto my street, I could see my house at the end. I accelerated, but out of habit I slowed down at the cross street even though I had the right of way, and woke up on the front lawn of my neighbor. That is exactly what my memory is. One instance in my car, the next lying under an Azalea bush looking up at my neighbor. His exact words were, "Roll to your left. If you roll to your right you'll crush my bushes."

I was in no position to roll. My head was killing me, but more than that, my entire right side was on fire. I lay there until an ambulance came. Thank goodness I was able to talk because my mother, who heard the sirens and was standing in our front yard when a neighbor told her it was me, was going nuts. I calmed her down, and she stayed with me at the hospital for five hours while I waited for all of the tests to be run.

At 9:00 AM in the new year, the doctor came to my bed and told me that I had broken three ribs and that my hip may also be broken. I had a concussion but all in all, he was telling me I was a lucky man.

At 9:05 AM in the new year, a police officer came to my bed and told me that I was t-boned by not one, but two cars that were drag racing and hit me at an intersection just seventy yards from my driveway. Not more than a half-wedge. Both of the other drivers were fine. It was a father and son who thought that since it was so late they could start the new year racing in the neighborhood. They did so without headlights on because it was more of a challenge. I knew the kid, he was a year older than me. He was an asshole, and as it turns out, so was his father.

A lawsuit followed. Today I probably could have taken their house and they would be in jail. In 1983, I settled for twenty-five thousand dollars. I got the settlement check a week after I got my diploma. When I graduated, they announced me as Mark Travers, Bachelor of Science degree in Business and Hospitality,

Cum Laude, and a three-time athletic letter winner.

Three times, not four. I missed my last season because I could not walk more than nine holes without having to sit for an hour. My ribs healed, as did my hip. After thinking I may not play for a long time, I was on the range by the end of February. By March, I was hitting the ball great. I shot a sixty-four in April but did so riding in a cart. I could not walk for long without a great deal of pain. Of course, carts are not allowed in college matches or tournaments, and even with one, my hip would be on fire at the end of the day.

It took a few months to determine that bone spurs were irritating my hip joint. The technology of the day was not able to do much about it other than a long rehabilitation. So my chances of making a career in professional golf were on hold. I was upset, but not so much that I let it derail any plans around golf. I started down the road of being involved with the game however I could. I figured as long as I was able to play and practice, when we figured out the issue with my hip, I could give being a professional a try.

And that all led me to a phone call I received on the first day of August. I was still working at Water Edge when I got a call from Kenny West. Kenny had gone to college at the University of Las Vegas. He called me once a month to get me to come out and visit him but I never took him up on it. Las Vegas to me was not the ideal vacation spot. I thought that was the reason for this call, but I was wrong. He shared with me that he got his first official full-time job working in the accounting department of the Olympia Casino and Hotel and there was an opening for what he called a Golf Ambassador. He told me that the casino offered clients and big bettors the chance to play golf on some of the best courses in Las Vegas and, if they wanted, play with great players. In my case, Kenny said, they would be able to play with a college All-American.

When he heard that there was an opening, Kenny offered up

my name. Without asking for my approval, he told me I would be getting a call the next day from their Human Resource department. That was Kenny. Never ask permission, and never apologize. Just do it.

At first, I told Kenny no way. His response was clear and to the point: "Listen, asshole. I work behind a desk pushing papers and numbers all day, learning the ropes at the bottom. You'll be playing golf with access to a practice facility that kicks the ass of any place you've ever been to. They'll pay you to get your game ready to turn pro. I don't know anyone in the world that loves the game as much as you do. So now you get paid to play. Besides, they'll fly you out here for free to check it out."

So, I flew out to Las Vegas. When I walked outside the airport terminal, it was one hundred and twelve degrees. I felt like I was hit in the face with the blast from the engine of the jet I had just flown on. I met with a few people at Olympia answering their questions about my personal hygiene, how many times I swear in a day, my favorite pastime, and my favorite tennis player. Yes, I was asked about all of these questions.

When I finally sat with the Director of Events, I got to the real details of the job. They had several golfers, all former professionals or college players, who would play golf with guests. At times they would accompany the guests as what he called, a golf tour guide. At other times, the guests wanted to play with someone that was able to play at a high level. The goal of the program was to keep guests happy so that they would return to the casino and spend money.

The casino asked two things from their golfers. The first was to practice and keep their games sharp. The second was to be a friendly and engaging ambassador for the casino. Any spare time that the players had could, if the player wanted, be spent working various jobs in the casino. All of this for a salary of $25,000 per year and a housing stipend.

All I could say was, "Wow." I could play golf and have a chance to learn the business.

There is one catch, he told me. "We keep fifteen percent of your salary earned from May through August in an account and pay it to you, with interest, on October 1. Too many of the players we have on payroll leave in the summer because of the heat."

No problem, I thought. The month of May was a long way off so I wasn't going to worry about it.

I accepted his offer to join them for a month. If after that time we both agreed it was a good partnership, I would become a full-time employee of the Olympia Hotel and Casino as a Golf Ambassador. I flew home, and after many tears from my mother, I packed my stuff and flew back out to Vegas.

CHAPTER 3

Kenny picked me up at the airport. I had my clubs, a bag of clothes, one hundred dollars in my pocket, and no idea what I was getting myself into. Kenny handed me a two-hundred dollars check from the casino that was for my room and board over the month. I pocketed that money and moved in with him. He had a single-bedroom apartment within walking distance of the Olympia business offices. To me, his complex looked like college dorm rooms but there was a big swimming pool and an open bar each Friday night. We spent the first day, a Sunday, walking The Strip and looking at the girls at the pool. I told Kenny my mom had made me swear that I would not gamble in the casinos. Ever. He told me his mom and dad made him swear the same thing.

On Monday, August 8th, I went to work. I sat through an orientation process with ten other new hires. I knew I was in Las Vegas when one of the new hires I was with performed card tricks that I would never be able to figure out. Another person recited the house odds of every gambling game the casino ran. If I was ever thinking of breaking the gambling vow to my mother, remembering those odds would snap me back to keeping my word. Things were so much in favor of the casino I wasn't sure how anyone could expect to win money.

I was shown three videos about the company, and I met with a few people telling me about the great culture that they had in the workplace. The entire time I was thinking that I wanted to be anywhere but in an office. I wanted to play golf.

That afternoon I met Kirk Bellows, the Director of Olympia Guest Sporting and Fitness. He was my boss. He was anything but a sportsman and not fit. He was a slob. He was crass. He was loud. He was not what I expected.

His windowless office was at the end of a long hallway amongst some closets and a sitting area that looked like it had been empty for years. He sat behind a desk that was full of empty soda cans, food wrappers, horse racing forms, and newspapers. Most of the papers were opened to the Racing section and had arrows, circles, and markings everywhere. The smell of cigarettes was so thick in the air, I had to turn away toward the door to get a deep clean breath. Turning back, I saw that the only chair on my side of the desk was covered with empty shoe boxes and more racing forms. He made no move to clear the chair, nor did he ask me to sit.

"Look," he said to me reaching into the side drawer for a cigarette, "the Ambassador program makes no money for us, directly. All you have to do is make these people happy and get them back to the casino in one piece. A happy big spender is a gold mine for the casino, and my performance is based on how happy you make them. Got it?"

I nodded.

He lit the cigarette using an Olympia Casino lighter and pulled out a drawer on the other side of the desk. Inside was an ashtray that was overflowing with butts and ashes.

"I hear you're a good player, is that true?"

I nodded, again.

"You screwed up your hip?"

I nodded, again.

"But you can play? And don't just fucking nod at me."

I started to nod but caught myself. "I.., I can play," I said. "I just can't walk eighteen holes."

"Don't worry, you won't need to. It's usually too hot to walk." He looked me up and down and took a draw that seemed to burn down half of his cigarette. When he flicked off the ashes, most missed the ashtray and ended up on the floor. I again turned my head to get a clean breath and took notice that there was a fire extinguisher on the wall opposite the office door. Still staring at me, he took another deep drag. He nodded, and with smoke coming out of his nose and mouth, said, "Go down to the end of the hallway, turn right, and ask for Melissa. She'll give you all the details and get you access to your equipment. Tomorrow you're playing with one of the guys. I don't care what your score is. I just want to make sure you can play. He'll tell me."

I nodded and started to walk out.

"Three pieces of advice for you."

I stopped and turned back to him.

"First, if I hear you're screwing with the guests on the course, like laughing at them or not doing everything in your power to make sure they're happy, you're done."

He paused and I nodded.

"Second, I get as much as a whiff that you're gambling with guests in non-money rounds, you're more than done. I'll make sure you get bloodied up first. You'll be heading back east with my boot up your ass. And not my regular boot, but the one with the steel toe. I'll be damned if I'm gonna deal with the Gaming Control Board because you're trying to be some high roller on casino time."

I swallowed hard and nodded.

"And third, if you ever nod at me again, or do that in front of a guest, I'll throw your ass off of the roof of this place. Speak! Talk! Got it?"

"Yes, sir," I said.

"The name is Kirk," he said with a roll of his eyes. "We're on the same team, so none of that 'sir' crap."

"Got it, Kirk."

I turned and walked out of his office. My forehead was starting to sweat and I felt like he was looking at me through the wall as I walked away. Taking longer strides, I made it to the end of the hallway and turned right. Seeing a Men's room, I stepped in. I was able to take a deep breath and wash my face. Looking in the mirror, I saw some scared eyes looking back. This guy was maybe the most intimidating man I had ever met.

I dried my face, took another deep breath, and told myself to get over it. I stepped out of the bathroom to find Melissa. Hopefully, she was a little easier to deal with than the ogre that was my boss.

Stepping into the hallway, I nearly ran over by a woman carrying a stack of computer printouts and binders. She side-stepped me but ended up against the wall, facing away from me. I went from blubbering in front of my boss to injuring people in the hallways.

"Sorry," I said, putting out my hands to keep the woman from dropping everything.

"No," she said, balancing her pile. "I think I have it."

When she turned back to me, I realized this 'woman' was young, around my age, and beautiful.

"It was a close call, but I've got everything," she said with a full smile.

I stood, stared, and nodded. It was obvious she was waiting for me to say something, but I couldn't get any words out. I couldn't take my eyes off her.

"Well," she said, not able to hide her discomfort, "I'm going to drop these on my desk. You're new here, I can tell. Is there someone I can help you find?"

I nodded, but the face of Kirk Bellows, directly in front of me with his hot and stinking breath, brought me back to reality.

"Yes," I said. "I am looking for Melissa. Kirk sent me."

"Sure," she said, "follow me and I'll show you where she sits, but she's not there now."

I did my best to look anywhere but at her as she walked in front of me. There were a few people walking the other way in the hall and others were milling about the sea of office cubicles. I nodded at some of them, trying to act the part of the experienced businessman. It was no use though. When she stopped and put the papers and binders on top of a filing cabinet, I almost ran her over.

"Sorry," I said, quickly trying to take the focus off of my continuing clumsiness. "Um, does Melissa sit around here?"

"Yeah, she does. Right there," she said, pointing at a desk with the name tag, 'Melissa Patterson' hanging on the cubicle wall. "But as I said, she is not at her desk. Do you want to wait?"

"Sure, can I just stand here?"

"No, that's not a good place." She walked around me and pushed me a few feet closer to Melissa's desk. "Now that is a good place."

I was confused, but when I looked at her she was smiling. "Oh, got it," I said, starting to smile myself. "Funny."

"Well, look at that," she said. "You know how to smile. You should do that more often. We like to have fun here at Olympia."

"Ah, well, I guess I'm a little nervous. It's my first day."

"And," she said, "you got the Kirk Bellows introduction. Let me guess, he sat behind his desk, smoking, and stared you down."

"Um, yeah," I said. "It was a little uncomfortable." I was starting to forget that I was speaking to a beautiful girl. I felt myself relaxing. "So, seeing that this is a good place to wait, when will Melissa be back?"

"Oh," she said. She walked past me and into the cubicle. Stepping around the desk, she sat down. "Well, Melissa is back."

My embarrassment level shot back up, but she laughed and extended her hand. "You're Mark Travers. Correct? I'm Melissa Patterson and I am your corporate liaison and contact. Kirk likes to think he's the one that runs the guest activity programs, but it's people like me."

I felt myself again staring at her like an idiot as she spoke. I recovered and shook her hand. She pointed to a chair so I sat across from her. After some small talk about the organization, she explained her role in controlling my schedule. I should expect to be playing with guests daily. When I was not playing I was expected to practice. She handed me a corporate membership card for three different local courses. I had complete access to practice facilities as well as the equipment shop if I needed to work on my clubs. She would be at the course as the casino service representative, introducing guests to players and driving around making sure that they were happy.

"All of that makes sense to you?" she asked.

"To be honest, no. It's kind of too good to be true," I responded.

"Yes, Kenny told me about your situation."

"You know Kenny West?" I asked.

"Sure, I was his hiring mentor when he started in June. Every new employee gets a mentor to help with the first few weeks. When he found out we had an opening in the Ambassador program, he recommended you."

"Interesting," I said. "Do I get a mentor?"

"Yup," she replied with a smile. "You are stuck with me."

Now it was my turn to smile. Stuck is not the term I would use. "I think I'll go with 'lucky', not 'stuck'," I said.

"Cute," she said and we shared a laugh.

She stood up and asked me to follow her. We went down the hallway toward my boss's office. Thinking she was taking me back to see him, a tinge of fear shot into my head. Thankfully we stopped before we got to his office and Melissa used a key to unlock a storage room door. I rushed to follow her into the room to get away from the cigarette smell that filled the hallway. When she closed the door, we both took a deep breath of stale but smoke-free air.

Shaking her head, she said, "I can't stand it. Even when he's not in his office, which is most of the time, the whole area smells."

I laughed and looked around. I thought for a moment that I was standing in a golf pro shop. There were shelves filled with cartons of golf balls, bags of tees, ball markers, towels, sweaters, pants, golf shirts, hats, and shorts. Melissa picked up an Olympia-logoed duffle bag and walked around grabbing a few of each.

"Every time you step on a course to play or practice, you need to wear Olympia Casino logos. What size are your feet?"

"Twelves," I said.

She walked over to a wall of shoe boxes, grabbed two, and handed them to me. "Here, always wear these. You get a new shirt every week, a new sweater once a month, three dozen golf balls a week, and as many tees as you want. You're on the honor system. The key is at my desk. And don't sell any of this. Kirk will find out. The man has ears everywhere in this city. He told you about his steel-toed boots?"

"He did," I said.

"Well, he's serious. You gamble, or sell, or make him look bad, he'll come after you."

She then walked around the corner of the room and returned with a golf bag. The Olympia logo was printed on the side.

She put it down in front of me and took an umbrella that was leaning on the wall. "It does rain here, so you may need it. Remember, if any of the guests ask about golf equipment, or even ask you for your equipment, tell them to talk to me. I'll always be there."

Looking up at my head, she nodded and reached over the shelf of hats. Grabbing three, she threw two in the duffle bag and put the third on my head. When her hand brushed the side of my face, my knees went weak.

"Okay, you are now an officially outfitted Golf Ambassador. Tomorrow you are playing at 10:00 AM at Desert Oasis. Since you don't have a car, there's a shuttle that you can get from the front of the office. If you want them to pick you up where you're staying, or at the casino, just call me the day before. My number is in the folder of information you received during your orientation. You can lug your clubs around or leave them in the storage room downstairs. Since most of you guys sleep with your clubs, I usually see them being lugged around. Now, where are you staying? Are you staying in an apartment?"

"For this month, I'll be staying at Kenny's."

"Oh, good. He has a nice place. I'm talking about the complex, not his mess of an apartment," she said.

Immediately my heart sank. Was Kenny seeing this girl? I shook the thought out of my head and asked her who I was playing with in the morning. She walked over and looked at a piece of paper hanging on a bulletin board on the wall.

"This is the list of players we have. You can look but never share it. Some of these are money players and we need to keep their names protected."

"What are money players?" I asked.

"Um, well you're an Ambassador. You play with or ride around with guests. These are people that are looking for a fun time. They want to play with talented golfers so that they can maybe learn, have fun, and tell stories when they go home. The resort also sets up money matches where a set amount of money is wagered based on handicaps or terms agreed upon ahead of time. Kirk also runs that program and always sets the terms. Money players show up, play their best, and whatever the outcome of the match is handled by a casino official. The Gaming Commission gets involved and Kirk is the man around here when it comes to knowing the right people."

She turned and looked at the list of names. "Oh, this is interesting. Kirk has you playing with Ben Newell. He is a fun guy, and, well…" She continued to look at the bulletin board, moving papers around to look at sheets hanging under others.

"What's the problem?" I asked.

"Nothing," she said, "Ben usually doesn't take part in tryouts. That's what we call your first round." She stepped away from the wall. "Don't worry, he's a good guy. Just don't be surprised if he is a little late. 10:00 AM might be a little early for him. Just head to the practice range when you get there. I'll be there working a few matches and rounds we have scheduled so I'll make sure he finds you."

I said okay, standing there with my arms around all of the golf bling I was given. I kept my head as I walked out with her, and I think my goodbye to her made me look fairly normal. Inside I was nervous about this 'Ben' person that didn't like to get up early, I was nervous that the new love of my life may have been in my friend's apartment doing who knows what, and I was a little self-conscious walking out of the office looking like I had just robbed a Herman's Sporting Goods Store.

CHAPTER 4

The next morning Kenny dropped me at Desert Oasis at 9:00 AM. I was dressed in my Olympia golf shirt and shorts and carried my Olympia golf shoes. Kenny made a wisecrack about keeping my pants on when I saw Melissa. The night before he told me two great pieces of news. The first was that he was not seeing Melissa. They knew each other from college at UNLV where she was a year ahead of him. They did hang with the same group of people at work but there was nothing more between them. The second thing he told me was that she was not seeing anyone. She broke up with a boyfriend during her second year in college and has been single since.

Arriving at the course, I could not wait to see her. In my mind, we were already a couple. I just had to figure out the path to get me to that result.

When I walked into the pro shop, the woman behind the desk knew who I was. She showed me around the clubhouse and pro shop and left me in the employee locker room. The clubhouse was new and reeked of Las Vegas. It had cheesy art on the walls which were painted with bright pastel colors. Everywhere you looked there were couches and tables to sit and drink. The locker room was full of dark wood and first-class amenities. The employee locker room was not up to the same standard. It rivaled the dirty and gross high school locker room back home. I changed my shoes and locked my things in a locker that I was pretty sure would open with one firm kick.

Walking out to go the range I ran into Melissa. As I expected, she looked great. Because she was working, she was dressed in an Olympia Resort and Casino uniform consisting of a short skirt and sleeveless top. As with everything in Vegas, sex sells. But not to be overdone, she was wearing just the right amount of makeup and her smile was perfect. Instead of a Las Vegas slut, I was looking at an All-American beauty. Waving at me, I walked over to her.

"Don't act like a horny teenager," I whispered to myself.

"Good morning," she said. "Did they set you up?"

"Yes," I answered. "I feel like a member."

"They want you too. It looks better for the guests if they think you're one of the professionals here. Remember, the resort and the courses we use all make a lot of money from these guests. The fact that they will spend four or five hours on the course with you means you have to represent both."

"About that," I said. "How am I supposed to be a representative of the resort seeing that I've only been here for a day?"

She laughed and said, "Don't worry. Most of the guests want to talk about golf. You can do that. If you're not sure, point them to me."

She smiled, stepped back, and looked me up and down. "Of course, there are times when you will have to play with some women, and older ones at that. They may be interested in more than golf. In that case, you'll have to get out of it yourself. Kirk will go nuts if you sleep with the guests."

I stood there with my mouth open for a moment trying to figure out if she was kidding. Before I could say anything, Melissa said, "I'm not kidding. It has happened before. But don't worry, you're not allowed to say yes."

I laughed and took a breath. "Good, that's out of my league. As for today, will the guy I am playing with answer my questions? I need to learn the course so I'm hoping he can help me."

She paused. "Well, Ben is a unique guy. He's a nice guy, but... Well, don't listen to me, I'd rather you just meet him. You need him to tell Kirk that you can play. You need me to tell Kirk that you can handle guests. You'll be good at both, so don't worry."

Someone called her name and she went off to handle the guests that were starting to arrive. I moved off to the range to hit some balls. It had been over a week since I last played and I wanted to be able to impress this guy.

"Ben Newell," I said as I was warming up, "I wonder if he can play."

I went through each club in my bag on the range and then walked over to the putting green. I spent twenty minutes there, but still no Ben Newell. Having worked up a sweat on the range, and with the temperature around ninety, I was thinking I should head to the clubhouse and cool down.

"You Travers?" a struggling voice called from across the large practice putting green.

Looking up, I saw Ben Newell for the first time. He was sitting slumped in a cart with a hat pulled low over his forehead. His hair was dark and thick, falling out from under his hat. As I walked to him, I guessed he was sixty years old. The closer I got, the younger he got. When I finally stood next to him, I realized two things: Ben Newell was about forty years old and Ben Newell was hungover. His eyes were bloodshot red and his face was pure white.

Even with the impact of his previous night's drinking on his eyes, when he looked at me, his eyes bore right through me. They were as deep a blue as I had ever seen.

"Ben Newell?" I asked, walking up to him.

He turned away from me. "Throw your clubs on the cart," he

said, ignoring me. "Let's get this effing round over with."

"Okay", I said to myself. This was going to be awkward.

I put my clubs on the back of the cart. In the basket behind the seat were six empty cans of Pabst Blue Ribbon beer. I sat down wondering if they were consumed this morning and how long it took him to finish off the six-pack. As I hit the seat, he floored the accelerator. We lurched forward and headed for the first tee. The only communication we had was him groaning as we took a few turns. He jammed on the brakes as we got to the tee. I stepped out but he stayed in the driver's seat.

After a few seconds of silence, I grabbed my driver and took a few steps away from the cart.

"Do you want me..." I started to ask.

"Kid, just tee off, okay," he said quickly with a grunt. He pulled his hat lower on his head and slumped down in his seat.

"Sure," I said, turning around. This was getting more uncomfortable every second. Luckily the fairway was open so I did not have to wait. I teed up my ball and as I moved behind it to get a view down the fairway, I looked over at Newell. He was starting to cough and was having trouble getting a deep breath.

"You okay?" I started to walk back to him but he shot his hand up telling me to stop.

"Crap," was all he was able to say, but he did not quite finish the entire word. In his most athletic move of the morning, Newell jumped out of the cart and made a quick run for the edge of the cart path. Kneeling on the hardpan of the desert ground just off the paved surface, he let go with a loud and prolonged grumble and then vomited next to a small ground cactus.

While I stood on the tee watching him, he continued to lean forward on both hands and knees, vomiting and spitting out whatever he was able to bring up. After a minute, he pushed himself up onto his feet, struggled back to the cart, flopped into his seat, and looked at me. Grabbing a towel he cleaned the hanging spit and vomit off of his chin.

"Have you hit yet?" he asked as if nothing had happened.

"No, I was waiting for you to, well…"

"Don't worry about me, just tee off."

I shrugged and went back to the tee. The first hole was a par-5 with a bend to the right. I sent a solid drive down the right side and walked to the back to the tee to wait for Newell to hit.

"C'mon, kid," he said. "I just blew my left kidney onto the desert floor. I'm not gonna try to hit a ball. I won't make it off the tee."

"Sure," I said and walked back to the cart. The second I sat down, he floored the cart and we headed down the first fairway. Neither of us said a word. When we got to my tee shot, I stepped out and reached for a scorecard to figure out my yardage.

Newell groaned and I thought he was prepping to puke again, but he was trying to focus down the fairway. Lowering his face, and then rubbing his eyes, he grunted, "Ugh, it's bright out here. You got two-forty-five to the front, about sixty to the pin. Don't go left."

"Okay," I said. I stood behind the cart doing the math in my head.

"Don't even think about laying up. Hit the fricking ball."

His words caused my hand to go directly for my three-wood. I went through my normal routine and hit a high fade that headed for the right edge of the green. As I stood and watched, he gunned the cart and went ten feet down the fairway before hitting the brake.

"Once the ball leaves the club you can get your ass back in the cart. Your shot doesn't care if you're watching or not."

I looked at him, but his head was down and he was trying to

control his breathing. "Yes, sir," I said. I thought of a few things I could say to him. If he was a friend of mine, I would have laid into him. But, I reminded myself that this was my job.

As I sat, he again floored the accelerator.

"Where did you go?" he asked.

"How am I supposed to know," I said with a quick laugh. "You wouldn't let me watch it."

"Smartass," he said. With a loud grunt that sounded like he was choking, he worked up a mouthful of phlegm and as we drove, spit it all out. As we got closer to the green, he looked at me and said, "Don't worry, I'm starting to feel better."

"Sure you are, and you look great," I said, somewhat under my breath.

Newell laughed and looked at me. "Good," he said. "You got some balls it sounds like. That's a good thing if you want to make it here."

He drove on the cart path around the back of the green. Screeching to a stop, he said, "If you're off to the right, you can't putt from there. The grain will be right at you and it's like hitting into wire."

"You saw where my ball ended up?" I asked. "Why'd you ask me where it went?"

"I guess I'm testing you. I didn't see it though. It's too bright out. I heard it land. Hurry up, 'cause if I sit here too long, I'm gonna puke again. I don't care how you score, so don't take a year on each shot."

I hurried up to the green and my ball and started to line up my shot. Looking back over at the cart, Newell was slumped over on his side, facing away from me. I started to wonder what I was trying out for or even why the hell I was out there. I decided that I needed to learn the course, so I took my notebook out of my back pocket and did a quick survey of the green. In college, I started the process of documenting the courses that I played so that in the future I would not be playing a course blind. After a minute of writing down the contours of the putting surface, the depth of the bunkers, and the areas around the green to avoid, I put the notebook back in my pocket and chipped up to the hole. Tapping in for my birdie, I walked back to the cart and found Newell was sleeping.

Shaking my head, I slammed my putter and wedge back into my bag. Newell shook his head and sat up. Without looking at me, he said, "Let's go," and floored the accelerator just as I sat.

The remainder of the front nine was pretty much like the first hole. We barely spoke, and when we did it was mostly him complaining about his head, the sun, or how he needed sleep. When we got the eighth hole, a long par-3, Newell got out of the cart for the first time. By now, I was just playing and updating my notes. I had forgotten he was there. So seeing him reaching around his bag for a club, I was shocked. When he walked onto the tee, I stood back to let him hit.

"This is just over two hundred to the middle from here," he said, digging his iron into the ground. "What are you hitting?"

"I have a five-iron," I said.

Suddenly, Newell looked like a golfer. He was standing tall and speaking clearly.

"What's your normal carry with a five?" he asked.

"On a hot day like this? About two hundred," I responded.

"And you play a fade?"

"I can move it both ways. My normal ball is a draw."

"Here," he said, "hit this. It's my three."

I nodded and he handed me his three-iron. He was playing

Hogan Apex irons which had smaller clubheads than my Accubars. His grips were also thinner than mine so the weight and look of the club made it feel like I was holding a feather.

I teed up my ball on the left side of the tee box and took a practice swing. Since his club was so light to me, I felt like my swing would be fast and I would hit a huge draw. I wanted to be on the left side of the tee so that my right-to-left shot would stay on the green. And with the flagstick on the right side of the green, there was little chance I could get this shot close.

"No," he said, walking over and kicking my ball to the other side of the tee. "Play a fade."

I didn't say anything. I picked up my ball and teed up on the right side of the box. He was asking me to play a shot that was not normal given the weight and size of the club, nor for my natural swing. Also, with a three-iron, I had to cut down the distance. As I set up behind the ball playing the shot in my mind, he walked over and stood three feet behind me. I turned and looked at him as if to say I needed some room, but he stood still. I turned back to the shot feeling like a judge and jury were standing over me.

"Fine," I said. I moved over the ball and pictured the flight I wanted. I aimed to the left of the green to leave myself a margin of error in case I hit a big slice and let loose with an easy swing cutting across the ball. I finished with an abbreviated follow-through to keep the shot low and watched the ball start ten yards left of the green and fade into the middle. It hit thirty feet left of the pin, took one bounce to the right, and ended up twenty-five feet away from the hole.

I was happy. Even with my normal club, twenty-five feet from the pin on this hole was a solid shot. As I reached down to pick up my tee, he walked by and grabbed his club out of my hand. Dropping my club on the ground, he started to walk back to the cart.

"You're not hitting," I asked.

He didn't say anything so I followed him. As we headed for the green, his silence was getting to me. I couldn't figure out if he was just a hungover drunk or a mad scientist. Either way, he was starting to frustrate me.

When we pulled up to the green, I stepped out and said, "You want me to use your putter?"

He shook his head and smiled. "Still a smart ass." He turned himself around and looked at me. "Was that a good shot you hit there?"

I looked at my ball on the green and nodded. "Well, not bad considering you play with blades, I had to hit a fade, and I had you hunkering over me on the tee."

"So all of that means that under pressure, you think you came through?"

I thought for a second and said, "Yeah, not bad."

"Not bad?" He started to laugh and repeated, "Not bad."

"Right," I said. "It wasn't bad."

"Unreal," he said under his breath. Pointing at the green, he said, "Kid, go putt-out. Maybe you can make a par. That's, 'not bad', right?"

I stood there looking at him, trying to figure out what he was trying to get at, but I gave up and grabbed my putter out of the bag. After two-putting for par, I came back to the cart, dropped my putter in my bag, and sat down. Since I was so used to him gunning the cart the second I sat, I was surprised when we didn't move. After five seconds, I looked over at him.

"What?" I asked.

"Nice par," he said. "Not bad."

He then gunned the accelerator and we shot off to the ninth hole.

After I putted-out on the ninth and walked back to the cart, Newell was sitting on the passenger side.

"Drive me to my car," he said. "You can take the cart out and play the back nine. I've seen enough. And I need to sleep."

I didn't say anything. When I dropped him off at his car, a maroon 1970 Cadillac Eldorado that looked like it had been found on the side of a junkyard, he grabbed his clubs and threw them in the back seat.

"So, what was the point of this?" I asked.

He turned to me and said, "The point? Well, I'll tell Bellows that you can play and do a great job making the old farts that want to see a young stud hit the ball a mile, happy. That's all he cares about. Oh, and that you have the game to be a money player for him. That'll make you a little more in your pocket. Other than that, there was no point."

"You got all of that from the shot on eight?" I asked. "That's the only shot you watched. In fact, that's the only time you got out of the cart, other than puking on the first tee."

He looked at me for a second and for the first time since we met, he turned serious. His deep blue eyes were like lasers cutting right through me. "You know what I learned on eight? Two things. First, you have no idea how to be a pro. Second, you aren't anywhere near ready to be a player. You don't have the guts."

I shook my head at him and tried to think of something to say. All that came out was, "What?"

"Do I need to explain everything to you, kid?" he asked.

After I nodded, he went on. "If you want to be a pro, then never miss a chance to show yourself you can be great. Always go for the shot, so in the future you know you can hit the shot when you have to. There are guys out there right now, the ones you see on TV, that got there because of one shot, one putt, or one save that has stuck with them. They put it into their brain bank and pull the memory out when they need it. And I'm not talking about trying to pull off some miracle shot when there's nothing on the line. It's a shot you hit when someone puts you on the spot. When someone has a gun pointed at your head and says, 'hit the shot'. The confidence you get from coming through sticks with you. It's what you go back to when you have to do it again. But you? You didn't even try."

I took a deep breath and slowly let it out. "Brain bank? Wow, you take this stuff seriously. Sorry for letting you down. I thought you just wanted to see me take a swing. I didn't know…"

"Shut the hell up," he said. "More than that, you'll never be a player. I said you've got balls because you can be witty with a comeback. I do like that. But out here, in the desert, if you want to be a player, a real player, you don't accept a challenge by hitting to the middle of the green. If you've got guts, I mean the guts to be a real player, you wouldn't have been a pussy and played ten yards off the green, and then patted yourself on the back for being mediocre. You would have gone for the pin. Kid, you can play. I see that. But from what I got on the eighth, you're gonna spend your time in the desert making old women fall in love with you. That's it. When you grow a pair, a real pair, let me know and we'll see how good a player you are."

I was speechless. It was the first time all day he spoke with any passion. It was the first time all day I was intimidated.

He turned back to his car and slammed the back door shut. Walking around to the driver's side, he climbed in and drove off, leaving me with my mouth open wondering what the hell he was talking about.

Without Newell, I took my time on the back nine, going over the course as if I was preparing for a tournament. By the time I was done, Melissa was gone. I got a ride from the Olympia shuttle back to Kenny's apartment. When he got back from work, I tried to explain to him what I experienced with Newell. He laughed most of the time, but as we were having a beer at the apartment's pool, he suddenly jumped up and ran back to the apartment. Coming back a few minutes later, he told me I would soon have some answers.

"The guy that lives over us is a good player. He played at UNLV ten years ago. I played with him a few times. He's good and he knows everyone in the area. He's gonna stop down in a few."

I nodded and sat back on the lounge chair and thanked him. "Newell is screwed up," I said. "I mean, really screwed up. I'd ask Melissa but I don't think she would tell me his story."

"So," Kenny said, "how is your girlfriend?"

"She looked great today," I said, picturing her in my head wearing her Olympia uniform. "She is so far out of my league. I would think about asking her out but I don't think I could get the words out of my mouth."

"Mark, Melissa is down to Earth. She's not into a-holes, and I don't think there is any doubt she would go out with you. But if you do ask her out, make sure Bellows doesn't find out. I've read the company employee guide and you're not allowed to marry or date coworkers. I doubt that guy has read the guide but just in case, be careful. He may have issues."

"Ken, I can't even talk to the girl. Asking her out is impossible."

He sat up and put his hand on mine. "Do you want me to tell Melissa that you like her? Or maybe, you *really* like her? Maybe you could put her and your initials in a heart on your golf bag."

"Screw off," I said, laughing.

As both of us laughed, a voice called from the other side of the pool. A slightly overweight and sunburned man in a bathing suit and white t-shirt waved. Kenny called him over and introduced him to me.

"Mark, this is Mike Tailor. Mike, this is the guy I was telling you about."

With a big smile, Mike shook my hand. Sitting in the lounge chair next to Kenny and me, he grabbed a beer from our cooler. "I hear you can play," he said. "Ken told me about your accident. Tough luck. Hopefully, you can be ready for Q-School next year."

"I hope so," I said. "For now, I'm playing in the desert."

"Yeah, I hear you're part of the Ambassador program at Olympia. That's a good idea if you want to keep your game. I almost worked for them when I graduated back in '72. The guy that ran the program is still there I think; Kirk Bellows?"

I nodded my head. "He's still there."

"Careful with him," Mike said. "The guy is connected. Don't cross him."

"Connected?" Kenny asked.

"That's right, the mob."

"Mob?" I asked. "As in the Mafia? Like the Godfather?" I turned to Kenny. "What the hell have I gotten myself into?"

"You have nothing to worry about as far as the mob goes," Mike said laughing. "You just have to be careful with what you do for the casino. Look, I don't know everything, I just know from what I hear from other guys when I'm playing money games, or from a hustler or two that I run into. Bellows, and this goes back to when I met him, has a lot of action going on. Whether it's money games he sets up outside of Olympia, or the horses, or a ton of other crap, he needs his nine-to-five to be clean. If he thinks you're a risk, he'll dump you."

"He scared the crap out of me when I was in his office," I said.

"Just do what he says and he'll let you work on your game. Having someone like you in the program is going to make the casino some good coin. I didn't take his offer because I knew he would never let me stay in the money games I had going on."

"What kind of money games?" Kenny asked. "Were you hustling?"

"Well, I was playing money games when I was at UNLV, so it was hard for me to give them up just to make 10K a year. That's how much he offered me. And I wasn't hustling. Just money games. Sometimes big, mostly small."

"What's the difference between a money game and hustling?" I asked.

"It's like pool," he said. "Hustlers drive their handicap up by sucking on purpose. They want to get more shots than they deserve. Like a sandbagger. Other hustlers pull in a player that thinks he has an advantage, and all of the sudden the huge duck hook they've been hitting all day becomes two-seventy-five, straight down the middle."

"So, in other words, a 'money game' is straight-up golf," I said.

"Not all the time," Mike said. "You get guys that will lose some holes on purpose to get to a bigger bet. You know, like, 'I'm two down so let's go double or nothing'. I've heard of players that will hit into a bunker and see if the other guy wants to go bigger on the hole. Stuff like that. The best of the best are the ones that fall a hole or two down but make it look like they're actually playing good. Then they have to hit big shots to come back and win. That's all part of the big games. Players trying to set up the other guy. Players challenging themselves. Feeding the desire. Me, I just played straight-up matches. Guess that's why I never got into the really big games."

"What's big?" Kenny asked.

"You mean money?" Mike asked.

We both nodded.

"Well, I haven't played money games much lately. The worst injury in the game of golf is getting married. But when I was single and on the Vegas money tour, a normal game would be five hundred dollars on each side. A good round could make you a thousand, maybe two."

"Wow," I said. "That is big."

"That's nothing. The real players, I mean the real big-money guys. They go for fifty G's per round. But whenever you hear numbers like that, the mob ain't far behind."

"Ask him about Newell," Kenny said.

"Yeah, do you know Ben Newell? I played with him today."

"Ben Newell?" Mike said, sitting up. He spun around in the lounge and faced us. "You played with Ben Newell?"

"I guess you know him?" Kenny asked.

"Everyone that plays in the valley for more than ten bucks knows Ben Newell. Does he play for Bellows at Olympia?"

I nodded. "He was the guy that I had to play with today so Bellows will give me the approval to play with guests."

"I would have thought he was dead in a gutter somewhere," Mike said. "Either from a bullet in the back of the head or the world's longest drinking binge."

"He's a money player?" Kenny asked.

"He's a legend," Mike said. "And if he's playing for Bellows, Newell must owe him a boatload of cash, or a huge favor."

"You're right about the drinking. He puked on the first tee," I said. "Why is he a legend?"

"Look, I don't want to bad mouth the guy. Maybe he's trying to straighten up. And I only played with him one time at a scramble for a UNLV fundraiser. But I've heard the stories, and I believe most of them. That guy is stone-cold the best money player Vegas has ever seen. That guy might be the best of all time."

I shook my head. "No effing way. He could barely stand today."

"When I played with him, he was pulling bottles out of the drink cart," Mike said. "His partying is well known. I don't think he hit driver all day and didn't putt-out once. But on eighteen when our team found out we needed a birdie to win, he hit a seven-iron to a foot. It was impressive."

"That's a little different than being the best ever," Kenny said.

Mike finished his beer and grabbed another. "Well, the reason I believe this stuff is because it comes from people I trust. He's about ten years older than I am and he got kicked out of college after his freshman year. But in that one year, he set course records all over the place. My coach kept in touch with him for a while, so when I started in '68, everyone on the team knew the stories."

"Such as?" I asked.

"Such as beating a current PGA champ five and three for 15K. Such as leading a US Open qualifier by four shots after the first round, but walking off the course in the middle of the second round because he and another guy decided to play for 10K. Newell was beating the guy so badly that the guy ratted him out. Newell walked off the course to keep his amateur status but ended up getting arrested when he found out which car the guy owned and he smashed all the windows. Stuff like that."

"He's big-money?" Kenny asked.

"I know that he played a guy for 20K a side, 30K for the round," Mike said. "The story goes that Newell lost the front with bogeys on eight and nine. Then he went down four after losing ten and twelve. When the guy he was playing agreed to double the back and the eighteen, Newell birdied out. He won 80K."

I shook my head. "The guy never hit a shot today. All he did was get pissed at me for playing safe."

"Well," Mike said, "he never plays it safe. At least he never used to. I heard a few years ago that he backed someone that lost a bundle that the mob had fronted. That guy ended up dead, and as far as I know, Newell dropped off the grid. He still hangs out at Desert Bridge which is a great place to drink but as far as golf goes, it's a pit. That's why I'm surprised he's with Olympia. But, a guy like him can't stay away from it. He has to play on the edge. And his game is a thing of beauty. When he wants, he can play. My suggestion to you would be to be careful when it comes to Newell or Bellows. Both of those guys can be trouble."

I looked at Kenny. "Great. You're the asshole that got me to come out here and pretty soon the mob will be after me."

CHAPTER 5

The next month was probably the most I was around golf in my life. I quickly forgot Ben Newell and Kirk Bellows and became a true Olympia Hotel and Casino Golf Ambassador. My days were boring if you're not into golf. I practiced every day. The facilities at both Desert Oasis where I played with Newell, and Palm Fairways, which was another course that was part of the Ambassador program, were tremendous. I was able to feel good about my entire game. Better than that, my hip was feeling better to the point that I was able to walk nine holes without much pain.

The rounds with guests were always interesting. My first official Ambassador round was at Palm Fairways with a couple in their seventies. Neither of them was good at golf. They both played from the forward tees but asked that I play from the back. Every time I made contact they would both ooh and ahh as if I was the longest hitter in the world. When we were done, the women shook my hand and thanked me. The man threw his arms around me in a bear hug and said I was the most impressive athlete he had ever seen. Later I found out that they were worth millions and spent the rest of their trip gambling away, telling anyone that would listen that Olympia would always be their favorite place on Earth. Melissa told me Bellows was extremely happy with me.

Some of the rounds were fun, some boring. One couple barely paid any attention to me. Another constantly asked me for tips on how they could improve. I played with a former LPGA professional and her teenage son and daughter. During the entire round, the three of them trash-talked each other to the point that I thought a fight might start. When we finished though, there were hugs and smiles all around. I played one round with a single gentleman in his nineties, and another with twin ten-year-olds: a boy and a girl that the parents had dropped off at the course while they went back to the casino to gamble.

It was that round with the twins that I finally got up the nerve to ask out Melissa. Since the kids were not old enough to drive a cart, she and I each shared a cart with one of the kids. Each hole was like playtime as we attempted to move the kids forward toward the green. The girl was a decent player for her age, but the boy was terrible. For me, being with Melissa was worth the time spent pushing them ahead.

Finally, when we were on the sixteenth green, Melissa asked me if I had been to any of the "gang" parties. The "gang" she mentioned was the group of people that she and Kenny sometimes hung out with that were all young and worked at Olympia. When I said no, she mentioned during the upcoming weekend they were getting together. Like a smooth ladies' man, I asked her to go with me.

She smiled, and asked, "Is this a date or are we just sharing a ride?"

The girl, standing a few feet away, looked over at us and giggled. When I looked at her, she said, "Yeah, which is it?"

I felt the pressure of them both looking at me, but through my dry throat I said, "It's a date."

Melissa nodded. "Okay then. Yes, I'll go with you. And it's about time you asked me out."

I felt like a million bucks for the rest of that day. When Kenny found out I had popped the "date" question, he made some calls and turned the party into more than a few drinks at a local bar.

Once in a while the gang would rent out a room and arrange food and drink. He set it up and the night became a fun chance to meet people and to be with Melissa. By the end of the night, we had spent plenty of time talking and getting to know each other. She was easy to talk to, had a great sense of humor, and was by far the most beautiful girl I had ever been on a date with.

My night was not all fun. One of the people at the party was from the Human Resources department. She shared some good and bad news. The good news was my name crossed her desk on a form for new employees. I was going to be offered full-time employment status. The bad news was that I had to be at the office Tuesday to meet with my boss, Kirk Bellows, to get the offer. The second she mentioned his name, my throat clenched and the smell of cigarette smoke caused me to gasp for breath.

Melissa was standing next to me and witnessed my reaction. "Now you know how I feel when I have to see him, which is any day he's in the office."

"How do you deal with him?" I asked.

"He's not that bad, it's the smell of that hallway. I hate it. Forget that for now. Are you going to accept the offer?"

I looked at her as she smiled and waited for an answer. How could I possibly say no? I smiled back at her and nodded. "It's a good job," I said. "And the people aren't bad. I guess I can put up with Bellows once in a while. And having to see you..."

"Great," she said, and she kissed me on the cheek. My knees buckled.

On the day after Labor Day, I was in the office at 8:00 AM sharp, walking down the hallway. I had stopped at Melissa's desk to grab the storage closet key. My reward for making it through a meeting with Bellows would be restocking my golf supplies.

As I got closer to Bellow's office, the smell started. Looking down the hallway, I could see smoke coming out of his open door.

I stopped so that I could take my last clean breath of air and looked to my right at the supply closet. "When I get to go in there, that means I'm done with him," I said out loud.

I started to walk to his office feeling like a prisoner going to the gallows.

"Fuck you!"

I stopped short. You can tell a lot from a 'Fuck you' and this one was said in real anger. It was Bellow's voice. I looked around to see how he could know I was walking to his office. My desired reaction was to turn and run away but instead, I stood still, trying to sink into the floor.

As I assessed my options, another voice spoke. This one was calmer. "No, Kirk, I believe it is I that should be saying, 'Fuck you'. After all, I'm the one that has to be out there with him. And I'm the one that they want. Not you."

I didn't know who the other person was, but my fear subsided now that I knew I was not the target of Bellow's wrath. I grabbed the keys out of my pocket and quickly entered the supply room. I walked to the corner of the room closest to Bellows' office. Standing in the corner, I was only ten feet from Bellow's office door and close enough that I could hear what was being said.

"...not my fault you don't know how to make friends and made a terrible deal." It was Bellows talking. "I saved your ass by doing that so you owe me. I own your ass until you pay off."

"I was set up and you know it, Kirk," said the other voice. "I don't know why I introduced you to Marino, but it happened. So don't make it sound like you're my savior. You need me to keep quiet about what you have going with him, so you let me do my things, my way. Don't bring in some virgin mark and weigh me down with him."

I heard a chair move and some papers being rustled. "Listen to me, you dumb, drunk loser," Bellows said. His voice was closer and sounded like he was in the room with me. "If you ever threaten me again, I'll cut you out. Immediately! Trust me, you'd be dead from either a bullet or the bottle if I stopped supporting you. Got it? You'll do whatever I say. I'm bringing this kid in because I'm smarter than you, and I own you. If you weren't such a dumb Irish Mick, you'd realize that I'm saving you. If it weren't for me, Marino would have dragged your ass out to Hoover and tossed you over the edge."

"Right, but you don't answer to him."

"I didn't stand up like a righteous idiot and vouch for Miner. You did and now you're in for what, three hundred large?" Bellows said.

There was silence. I heard some movement around Bellows' office.

"Well?" said Bellows.

"Okay, I'll play him on one condition. You make sure he's outside the bullshit. Him and anyone he knows. If I hear his name from anyone's mouth, I'm gone. I can't be responsible."

Bellows laughed and said, "No one is going to be interested in him, other than keeping you clean. Those guys don't work that way. Not for the numbers we're talking about. Trust me, you're not that important and if you were, there are other ways to get to you."

"Don't go there," the other voice said.

"No, no, I'm not," Bellow said. "I'm just making a point that there are other ways, like family, that these guys have if they want to make a point. Hey, you're getting upset. Take a breath. They know about my family, too. Calm down. Okay?"

There were a few seconds of silence. "Fine," the other voice said, "but I bring him in as I see fit. I can't throw him into a ton of shit until I know he can float."

Bellows again laughed. "Good, good. Now we're on the same page. You bring him in however you see fit. He is all yours. I'll give you twelve months."

The other man now laughed. "You'll give me twelve months? You're gonna be a tough guy and call Marino and tell him that's what the schedule is? I'm pretty sure he's the one that wants it back by then."

"Listen," Bellows said. "Don't push it. You can talk back to me because I like you. I trust you. But my trust only goes so far. And if that trust is lost…"

"What? You're going to throw me off the dam? How would that fit in your wallet?"

Again, there was a movement in the office.

"Fine, fine," said the man. "We'll try it. Twelve months."

I heard footsteps coming out of the door and the person started to walk away from me toward the exit door.

"Ben," Bellows yelled from his office. "Don't forget I own your ass. You make this work."

"Fuck you, Kirk," came the reply as the exit door opened and a moment later slammed shut.

When it closed, I took a breath and tried to decide if I should go right to his office or wait a few minutes. I heard Bellows pick up his phone and in his usual angry and frustrated tone, say, "Melissa, where is Travers?"

I just about jumped through the wall when I heard him mention my name. I ran out of the storage closet and took a deep breath to calm myself but instead ended up nearly choking from the smoke that was billowing into the hallway. As I tried to stifle a cough, I stepped into his office.

Bellows was still holding the phone when he looked up and saw me. He crashed the phone back down onto the cradle and said, "Get in here Travers, and shut the door."

I reached back and pushed the door shut. Now closed inside his office, I stepped toward the desk and stood straight. I felt like a Private standing at the desk of a General.

Like he did when I was first in his office, Bellows looked me up and down. Taking a long drag from his cigarette, he nodded to the chair in front of me and told me to sit. As I stepped around the boxes and newspapers lying on the ground, I looked at the open drawer where he kept his ashtray. There were three other cigarettes lit and burning. When he dropped the cigarette that was in his hand into the ashtray, it knocked one of the lit butts off the edge. It fell into the drawer. As I sat down, I ran my exit through my head in case his entire desk went up in flames.

"You're a shy kid, aren't you Travers?" he asked. "That's not gonna cut it for what I need from you. So from now on, stop the quiet act and take the lead."

I promised myself the night before as I lay in bed that I would not nod, hem and haw, stutter, or play the part of the scared newcomer while I was with Bellows. Of course, it was easy to say that and be brave while lying in bed. Now in front of him, I did my best to come across as a confident, experienced professional.

"Um, yea. Okay," I got out from my dry throat.

Bellows sat quietly. He waited for five seconds and sat forward in his chair. I could see the red capillaries filling with blood on the sides of his nose. His forehead seemed to tighten and his ears reddened. I quickly surmised that I was two seconds away from being torn into shreds and made to disappear forever.

"Kirk," I was able to get out of my mouth, "I've learned a lot over this month. Melissa has helped work with me on how to do better with the guests. I made relationships with the people at the courses and even had a few guests set up time with the teaching pros. I've worked on my game and seem to have impressed the guests. And I have enjoyed myself. You have a great team here, and I want to continue to be part of it."

When I stopped talking, Bellows fell backward into his chair. I wished I could have frozen time so that I could pat myself on the back. My spiel was word for word what I practiced the night before.

"So, you do have a voice. That's a big step forward from the last time you were here."

"Thanks, I can..."

He stopped me with a wave of his hand. "I've heard good things about you, kid. Good things from Melissa, who I trust. And good things from the guys I have at the courses."

I wondered to myself what 'guys' he had. I sat back in the chair feeling a little more comfortable than when I entered. But as I sat, he again stared at me. Each second he was quiet made my pulse jump higher and higher. I fought to slow my breathing and consciously controlled the shaking that I felt starting in my shoulders.

"How is your game? I mean, how good are you if you wanted to play in a tournament?"

"Real good," I replied. "I'm hitting the ball solidly, and I've figured out the greens here. They..."

He put up his hands and stopped me. "Too many details, kid. One of my guys told me you could hit the ball. He liked what he saw. I assume that if we offer you a full-time job here at Olympia, you'll take it?"

I nodded, but quickly said, "Yes. I like it here and think I can help you."

For the first time, I saw Kirk Bellows smile. "Kid, I was hoping you'd say that. What I want to do is offer you a job. Not as a Golf

Ambassador, but more. I want you to play money games for the casino. Is that okay with you? Oh, and it means that your salary is thirty thousand. Not twenty-five. Good?"

"Sure," I said. "Just tell me what I need to know about 'money games'.

"Don't worry, someone will fill you in. One other thing and this is important. Real important. Okay?"

I moved to the front of my seat.

"I don't want to scare you, okay?"

I kept quiet figuring he could not scare me any more than he had in the past. I assumed he would give me the same speech I received when I started a month earlier.

Without looking away from me, he reached down and grabbed a cigarette from a box that was in front of him. Again, without taking his eyes off of me, he reached for the lighter and lit up the cigarette. He took a deep draw and let it out. The smoke raced at me like it was being pushed by a storm's wind. I did my best to maintain eye contact.

With a nod, he continued. "I want you to do more than play golf. I want you to shadow Ben Newell. He's the guy you played with for your tryout. As I am sure you could tell, he is a bit of a risk. But that man is a key to the success of the Olympia Golf program, and to my success."

He stopped talking but continued to stare. After fifteen seconds, he said, "You will know where he has to be, and you'll make sure he gets there. You'll play alongside him. You'll drive him. You'll keep him away from the bottle when he should be sober, and you'll make sure that he doesn't screw around. I need him to play golf how, when, and where I tell him. It's your job to make sure he does."

I had no idea what he was talking about. "So, you want me to babysit Ben Newell?"

Bellows laughed and said, "You can call it babysitting if you want. It won't be every day. It won't be all the time. But I have a lot invested in him, and so does the casino. It's your job to, to… To 'babysit' him."

I realized that I had no choice but to agree, so I told him I would. His request was not as scary as he made it out to be.

"Now, here is where I hope to scare the crap out of you. And I am serious about this."

I sat back realizing I thought I was out of the woods too soon.

"Don't blow this. I'm not asking a lot. Melissa tells you where he has to be, and you get him there. He needs to play sober, so you keep him sober. If he gives you any problems, you come to me. Directly. Got it? And if he asks you to do something that you think is wrong, you come to me. Directly. Got it?"

"What would be wrong?" I asked.

"Anything that is not part of this casino. Anything."

"Okay," I replied.

"Disappoint me and I will drag and kick your ass out of Vegas so fast that you'll be picking sand out of your underwear for the rest of your life. Don't screw with me. Got it?"

I got it, and I got myself out of his office as fast as I could. I forgot to stop at the supply closet, making my way as fast as I could down to Melissa's desk. She was waiting with some folders and papers for me. She took my hand and the paperwork and led me to a conference room across the hallway from her cubicle. When we were both inside she closed the door and dropped the materials on the table.

"I don't know what you did, but you certainly got on Kirk's good side quickly."

"Why am I on his good side?" I asked, looking at the papers. "He just told me I'm a babysitter for the drunk I played with on my first day. He did give me a raise though."

Melissa walked around the table and sat down. She arranged the papers and folders and told me to sit. When I pulled out a chair on the opposite side of the table, she said, "Not there. Here, next to me."

Her smile made me forget about the smoke-billowing exhales of Bellows. When I sat next to her, she reached over and put her hand behind my neck. Pulling me closer, she kissed me.

"Wow, what was that for?" I asked as I came up for air and allowed the fireworks in my head to subside.

"I wanted to thank you for a great date, Saturday. I had a lot of fun and it was because I was with you."

I looked around the room to make sure we were alone and no one was able to see us through the glass door.

"You're not embarrassed to be with me are you?" she asked.

"Uh, no. I was kind of hoping a lot of people saw that kiss so they would see me with the best-looking girl in Vegas."

I was rather proud of myself for that comment, but Melissa started to laugh. "Very funny," she said.

"Not meant to be funny," I replied. "That was no joke."

She gave me a second-long serious look. "Well, thank you. But we don't want people in the office to know too much about our relationship."

"So, we have a relationship?" I asked.

"I thought we did, but if Kirk finds out we may both be out of a job. I don't know what he would do. So shut up, and let's review this stuff."

My mind was still on the fact that she thought we had a relationship. As she lined up the documents, I said, "Want to go out tonight?"

She stopped and looked at me. "Tonight? Sure."

"Good, that confirms we have a relationship." I sat back and smiled. This was turning out to be a great meeting.

"Okay, Romeo," she said. "Get your wandering mind back to these papers. This is why I said you got yourself on Kirk's good side."

Opening an envelope, she pulled out a stapled document and a set of car keys.

"You have been assigned a car from the auto-pool. You'll get thirty dollars a week for gas and cleaning. It will be added to your paycheck. Read this form and sign it. It details how you handle car expenses and what the insurance coverage is. If you have any questions, I can get you an answer."

She pulled out a small binder that contained twenty pages of legal-looking documents. "You are now part of the Olympia Guest Engagement and Recreation Program. What that means is you will be playing guests in matches in which the stakes and odds are predetermined. By signing this you agree to just play your best, and you will take none of the winnings or pay any of the losses. That is all handled by the casino. It means you are the same as the card dealers on the casino floor."

I took the binder, quickly read some of the headings, and signed it. "I'll trust you," I told her.

We spent the next thirty minutes reviewing other documents and folders. When we were done, she took the signed forms and gave me the rest.

"Any idea why I have to babysit Ben Newell?" I asked her.

She shrugged. "Kirk keeps a tight lid on what Ben does. I know that he plays the big-money guests and that he and Kirk do a lot of things together. I think it's a good sign that he trusts you to help Ben. I think it's less babysitting and more of being a partner. Tomorrow you and Ben are playing together at Cactus Ridge. You also have a match with him and guests on Wednesday so this will give you a chance to play with him before that. I'll get you the time."

"Cactus Ridge? I didn't know that was part of the resort program."

"It's not for the normal program," she said as we started to walk out of the conference room. "It's for the real, real, real big spenders. Ben pretty much demands he play there most of the time."

As she walked into the hallway, I reached out and stopped her. Pulling her closer to me, I whispered, "Bellows was pretty adamant that I don't, in his words... Well, you can guess what his words were. He wants me to go directly to him if Newell is doing anything wrong. What kinds of things would he do that are wrong?"

She looked down the hallway and thought for a second. Looking up at me, she said, "Let's talk about it tonight. Now that you have a car, pick me up at seven."

That night we went out for dinner. Since I now had a car to drive, I was able to see Las Vegas for what I considered the first time. We ate at a drive-in diner, got milkshakes, and drove up and down The Strip. When we parked up in the hills, I was able to take in the lights of the entire area. As impressed as I was with the view, I was more impressed with Melissa's ability to point out every landmark. We sat holding hands, talking until after midnight. Finally, as I was driving her back to her apartment, I asked her about Ben Newell.

"Mark, I think that guy is the biggest moneymaker for Kirk, but as you've seen firsthand, he's an issue. He drinks and tends to show up looking, well, dumpy. Guests should never see that."

"I don't know," I said. "It seems like it's more than that. I heard some things when I was waiting to go into Bellows' office. He was pissed at Newell. He said something about Newell owing, 'three hundred large,' and that he owned him until it was paid off. And he mentioned someone named Marino."

Melissa pulled her hand back from mine. "Marino?" she asked. "Are you sure?"

"Yup, Marino. Do you know that name?"

"I know of a Marino. He used to be an investor or something in the casino, back when I was working there during my junior year in college. It can't be the same person because that Marino was tied up with some illegal betting scandal at one of the race tracks, and had to sever all ties with any casinos. It was in all the newspapers."

As I drove, I tried to remember Newell's exact words. "Newell told Bellows something about 'bringing him in slowly', and seeing if 'he can float in the shit'. I think he was talking about me."

We were pulling up in front of Melissa's apartment. She lived in the same complex as Kenny and me, but on the far side, a good quarter-mile away.

"Look, Mark," she said as I stopped the car. "All you have to do is what Kirk asks. If he starts asking for too much, you tell him. But before that happens, you have me to help. Both as your 'Olympia Recreation liaison', and as your girlfriend."

Her words blew the image of Kirk Bellows out of my head.

"Girlfriend?" I asked. "Really?"

"Well, we've been on two dates in three days. I've been at the casino, counting summers, for three years, and I've been on a total of, let's see… Two dates. And I've been asked out a few times. So, there must be a reason I said yes to you."

"There is," I said. "It's because you're my girlfriend." The smile on my face was hurting my cheeks.

"You don't hide the fact that you are not an experienced lady's man."

I laughed. "Sorry, I'll do a better job. It's just that I usually don't attract the best-looking girls."

"Well, thanks for the compliment, but what kind of girls do you attract?"

"Actually, none of them. All I did in college was golf, study, and drink beer. Mostly golf. I was always hitting balls. I hit balls before I studied, after I studied, and sometimes while I studied."

"Well, I'm glad you saved yourself for me," she said. She leaned over and kissed me. "I have to get to bed. Make sure that tomorrow you're at the course at 10:00 AM. And don't worry about Ben or Kirk."

CHAPTER 6

I took Melissa's advice. The next morning I showed up at the course to play golf and not worry. I drove up to the gated entrance and gave my name. From that point forward, every employee called me Mr. Travers. From the bag checkers to the girls working the bar, to the locker room attendants, I was treated like I was a member with a million dollars in my wallet. Unlike the other golf courses where my locker was in the worst corner of the clubhouse, at Cactus Ridge my locker was deep-colored wood with felt-lined interiors and drawers.

I took my time, figuring that like my last experience with Ben Newell, he would be late. I walked out into the morning sun at 9:40 and made my way to the range. As I stretched out my legs and hips, I looked at the clock hanging on the starter's shed. I grabbed my wedge and took an easy swing, skulling the ball. I didn't watch where it ended up. I used my wedge to pull another ball out of the pile and again took an easy swing, this time making better contact.

"Let's go," a voice said. Looking behind me, Ben Newell was sitting in a cart behind the driving range tee area. His deep blue eyes were staring bullets through me. Again I looked at the clock. It was 9:45. Looking back over at Newell, he raised his hands, and again said, "Let's go."

"Okay, it looks like you're early," I told him as I put my wedge back in my bag and picked it up. After putting my bag on the back of the cart, I stepped up to the passenger seat and went to sit down. Remembering Newell's penchant for flooring the accelerator, I made sure to get a firm grip on the cart's railing before sitting. Instead of gunning the engine, Newell reached over and extended his hand.

"I'm Ben. Sorry for being such an asshole the last time we met."

I looked at him and was surprised that he was coherent, did not smell, and was smiling. I reached out and shook his hand. "Mark Travers, nice to meet you, Ben."

"Nice to meet you, Mark. Let's play some golf."

By the time we rode up to the first tee, I was convinced that I was with a different person. This Ben was conversational, inquisitive, and polite. I did my best to hide my shock, but when we stepped out onto the tee, I couldn't hold back.

"So you're going to play this time?"

He laughed. "Yeah, I'm not going to puke either."

We walked up onto the tee. "I'll be totally honest with you, Mark. When Kirk asked me to try you out, I told him to stick it. When he asked me to partner with you in some of the money games we play, I again told him to stick it. But I'm okay with it now. As long as you and I are honest with each other, we'll be a good team."

I shrugged and said, "Whatever he wants is okay with me. I just want to play."

"Good attitude," Ben said. "Of course, I know he asked you to do more than play. He must have asked you to keep me in line, correct?"

I didn't say anything and tried to avoid his gaze.

"Mark, again I'll be perfectly honest with you if you'll be honest with me."

I exhaled and nodded. "Yes, he wants me to keep an eye on you."

"That prick," he said. "Listen, you and I don't have a problem now, and we won't as long as we act like a team. There's a lot of stuff going on behind the scenes that you don't have to worry about. It's between me, Bellows, and some others. I know I'm no choirboy so I can't complain that he wants you to shadow me. But if he asks you to do anything else, you tell me first."

"He said the same thing. He wants me to tell him if you do something wrong."

Ben shook his head. "Let's play golf. I need to see what you can do. Forget Bellows. You're up."

I said okay and teed up my ball. The first hole was a thing of beauty, snaking through the desert with the deep green fairway providing a clear contrast to the tans and browns of the desert. As I stepped up the ball, Ben stopped me.

"Wait, this is what I want to see from you today. Play this like you and I are, well... Hold on. How much money do you have in your wallet right now?"

I stepped back from the ball and looked at him.

"I'm serious, what's in your wallet?"

I leaned my driver against my leg and reached behind me, taking my wallet out of my back pocket. Opening up, I pulled out a ten and two one-dollar bills.

"Twelve bucks," I said, holding up the money.

"Okay," Ben said. "We're playing for ten bucks a side with a carryover, ten for the eighteen. Let's go a buck a point. Birdies, Sandys, and Rommels. We'll play a match like we're a couple of weekend duffers. The cheaper the action, the better."

"One sec," I said. "First, I got twelve bucks..."

"Never bitch and moan about the bet. It makes you look like an easy target. Mark, I'm gonna teach you how to be a player in the desert. Got it? And the first thing to do is don't relate a bet to what you have in your wallet. The amount of the bet is not a problem until it is more than you can drag up without clearing your checking account. If you start whining about twelve bucks, it tells me that you have no confidence in your game. Info like that spreads out in the valley, quick."

I tried to understand what he was saying, but I still only had twelve dollars in my wallet. His comment about confidence did ring true to me though. My college coach always said whether you're playing Jack Nobody or Jack Nicklaus, walk up to him on the first tee, look him in the eye, and know that you will beat him.

"Okay, that makes sense," I said. "And I understand what a Nassau is. I assume a 'Sandy' is making par from the bunker? So what is a Rommel?"

"That's making a par from the desert. Your ball goes into the desert and you make par, you've got a Rommel. Make a birdie from a trap or the desert, two points."

"Okay, fine. Ten a side and the eighteen, carry over the front, and a buck for each point." I took a deep breath and let it out. The most money I ever played for was twenty dollars when I was in college. Since we were always competing to make the travel team, or to win a match, or to do well in a tournament, we never played for money. Of course, none of us in college had any money. If we weren't playing on the team, we were practicing or screwing around with stupid games like night or Yahtzee golf.

As if Ben knew what I was thinking about, he said, "You college kids, and playing pros, think you know what pressure is. You don't. A professional with a putt to win a tournament is cashing a check with someone else's money whether he makes it or not. If he doesn't make it on tour, he goes home and gets a job as a club pro that people flock to because he was once a touring pro. No one cares that he's a club pro because he was a failure trying to get and stay on tour. That ain't the case out here. Pressure out here in the desert is playing for food. It's playing for money you don't have. So remember, it's your game that you turn to when you're challenged. Don't think of the bet, think of your game."

The lecture was a little much, but I could not overlook the passion with which he delivered it. I put my wallet back in my pocket and turned back to the ball. After a waggle, I said, "The money's no problem with me. I wanted to make sure you're good for it when I kick your ass."

Newell started to say something but laughed so hard he could barely get the words out. "Brilliant, kid. Brilliant. Go ahead and hit."

I didn't wait for him to stop laughing. I stepped up, took one quick look down the fairway, and put a solid move on the ball. My drive was long and straight.

"Good ball," Ben said.

He teed up his ball and moved back behind to see the layout of the fairway in front of him. Stretching his neck left and right, he then stepped up. I was interested to see how he hit the ball. The comments from Kenny's friend Mike, that Ben was a legend, stuck in my mind. Ben stood over the ball, took a deep breath, exhaled, and started his swing.

Ben was a tall guy, about six foot two. He was in good shape with strong shoulders and thick forearms. I was expecting his swing to be tight, muscular, and fast. Instead, his swing was long, slow, and loose. His move through the ball was athletic and his follow-through high and balanced. His ball shot off the clubface, landing near my ball, but running another twenty yards past me.

As we rode out to our drives, Ben was talkative, asking me about where I was from, about my family, and why I was in Las Vegas. This was not the same person that got pissed at me when I didn't play the shot he expected a month earlier. When I knocked my second shot on the green on the par-5, he made it sound like I was ready for the tour.

This went on for the front nine. He was easy to talk to and I was having fun. At the turn, he went into the clubhouse and came out with two sodas, which we drank while waiting for the fairway to clear on the tenth. He took a deep breath and looked at the scorecard.

"You shot a thirty-four. Not bad for this course, seeing that it's the first time you've seen it. We're even in the match and on points. You feel good about that?"

"To tell you the truth, I wasn't focused on the match at all," I told him.

He threw the card into the compartment next to the steering column of the cart. "I was," he said. "During every question, every comment, during everything I said to you, I was thinking about the match."

I looked at him. He wasn't lecturing me, or any more intense than he had been on the front nine. He was just talking.

"What's your point?" I asked him.

"The point is, that if you're going to be a player, you need to focus. You can laugh, fool around, joke, and do whatever it is you want when you're playing. But if you have so much as a dime on the game, in your head, you keep your focus. You hit a great shot on the seventh. How far did you have? Twelve feet for birdie? Why didn't you put any action on that putt? You had leverage. I was five feet from par."

"What could I have done? We had a bet already set."

He smiled. "No bet is final. If I were you, I would have asked for two, maybe three-to-one on our putts. You could have asked for three points if you made your birdie, and one point if I made my par putt. You could have doubled our bet on the front. Standing on the ninth tee, I'm wondering if you believe enough in yourself to go for it and increase the action. The fact that you didn't, tells me you don't like something. Maybe it's your game, maybe you don't like hitting driver with trouble right and left. Maybe it's the pressure. Whatever it is, I'll remember it and wait for the opportunity to jump you."

I thought for a second and finally said to him, "I guess I could have done either of those things. I didn't think about it."

"Right, because you were too busy having a good time." He smiled. "Mark, don't fret about it. I'm not trying to be an ass, but I am trying to offer you insight. You have the game. If you want to be a player, you need to learn how."

"Who says I want to be a player?" I asked him. "I'm trying to get my game to the point where I can try to play for a living."

The expression on his face told me he was not happy with the question.

"I'll just tell you this once," he said as he stepped out of the cart and walked to the back to grab his driver out of his bag. "You want to play this game at a high level? Then don't buy that bull from Hogan about having to dig it out of the dirt. You can hit balls all day long, but that doesn't mean a thing if you can't pull the club back when there's pressure. Playing money is the best way to learn how to handle yourself."

I stood up and grabbed my driver. Standing next to him, I sensed there was more to him right now than being my mentor. "That makes sense. The problem is, you sound less like you're giving me pointers, and more like you're getting me ready to help you make money."

He patted me on the shoulder. "Excellent. No, really. That is excellent." He walked up a few steps onto the tee. I followed him, waiting for him to continue.

When he teed up his ball, I asked him, "Alright, Ben. What's excellent?"

Without stopping his pre-shot routine, he said, "That you felt I wanted more. Remember, and I'm not kidding. Never, ever forget this. Anytime anyone offers you advice or gives you something while you're in Vegas..." He stopped and looked at me. "I mean anytime. If someone gives you something and you have sand under your feet or it's under the floor or wherever you're standing, they will want something more in return."

He then turned back to his ball and in one motion, started his swing. The instant he made contact, he turned back to me. "Are you standing over sand?" he asked.

I moved my attention away from his drive, which was headed down the center, down to my feet. "Yeah," I said. "I guess I am."

"Then you're right. I need you to listen to what I'm telling you so that you get the point when I can start making money with you."

The next nine holes were some of the most interesting of my career. On every shot, Ben told me about options for bets I could make or bets I might expect to receive. They included driving in or out of the fairway, how far from the hole an approach may be, making a putt, up and down from a bunker, presses, double or nothing, odds, and even challenges with different or random club choices.

When we got to the eighteenth hole, he pulled out the card. "You're three under, one-up on the back nine, and the eighteen. You're also one up on the points. If I wanted your money, I'd press you for both. If I really wanted your money, more than the thirty we have on the match, I'd press you, and then hit one into the desert."

"Why?" I asked.

"It's part of the setup. Here, watch."

Even though I had the honor, I stepped back. The entire day, Ben had hit a tight draw. The eighteenth hole was a long, slightly uphill par-4 with deep bunkers left, and palm trees right. He went through his routine, but instead of a draw, he hit a high slice that started at the palm trees and faded a good twenty-five yards into the desert.

"Where's the draw?" I asked.

"Right where I want it," he said. "Go ahead and hit."

I hit what I thought was my best drive of the day. I carried the bunkers on the left and got at least another twenty yards of run.

"Okay, so you're one up, and in the fairway. I'm lost in the desert. I pressed you so I owe sixty if you win or tie this hole. Do you want to double the odds? How about, say, double again on the press for the entire day, all on this hole. That's one-twenty for you if you tie me here, but I want thirty for me if I win. And since I'm one down, and in the desert, you give me twenty-five points for a birdie, and I'll give you ten points for a par, twenty for a birdie."

My head was about to explode trying to think about everything Ben just said to me. One thing I knew was that he was in the desert, and I was in the fairway. Every bet he threw at me seemed to be in my favor.

"Okay, I would take that. Right?"

He nodded. "You'd be smart to take the action. I have no idea where I am. Let's just assume that you take the bet. C'mon."

We jumped in the cart and drove up to our drives. I was perfect, with a good line to the flag and one hundred and sixty-five yards away.

"So, you feel good?"

"Yeah, I'm in okay shape."

"Not the right attitude, kid," he said. "No wishy-washy stuff like that. You're in great shape. Let's go find mine."

We rode across the fairway to the edge of the desert. Walking through the palm trees, there was a small clearing where the ground was a hardpan. His ball sat in the center of the clearing.

"Well," I said. "You got lucky with the lie." I walked behind his ball to see his line to the green. "Too bad you have no shot." When I lined up his shot, I realized that he was slightly past the line of trees. "Actually, you got extremely lucky. You have a shot."

"Luck? I don't think so," he said.

I looked over at him. "You knew it was open from here?"

"Of course I did. I have a better line to the green from here than from the fairway."

I laughed and said, "Pretty bold move on your part, especially playing away from your draw."

Ben walked over carrying an iron. "I do play a draw a lot but my normal shot is a fade. I just wanted you to think I hit a bad drive."

He didn't even look at this shot. He stepped up and hit a high approach that hung in the air before fading slightly at the top. It landed below the hole, took one small bounce, and ended up five feet from the pin.

Without looking at me, he walked back to the cart. "Can you get inside that?"

I shook my head. I knew that I was played by an expert. The word 'legend' popped back into my head. Walking to my ball, I grabbed my seven-iron from my bag. As I went through my routine I tried my best to clear my head and forget about his ball sitting on the green. My shot was a good one, but adrenaline sent my ball twenty-five feet past the hole.

"Control," Ben said as he pulled up next to me in the cart. "Ya gotta be in control."

I dropped the club into my bag. "You sound like my college coach. He always talked about distance control when the shots started to mean something."

As I sat down, Ben floored the accelerator and I flew back into the seat. "Smart man, that coach of yours," he said as we headed for the green.

My putt was not an easy one. Downhill, left to right, twenty-five feet. In the back of my head, I was not sure if Ben thought the bet he explained on the tee was in play. Given all the different bets he had thrown around on the back nine, I hoped that he was teaching and not betting me.

As I looked down the line, I told myself to make it and see what happens afterward.

I made the putt.

Ben gave me a nod and rolled in his short putt. He walked over and we shook hands. "Nice job," he said. "And a nice round. You have a solid game. Listen to me and we'll do some good things together."

He drove the cart to the parking lot. When I pointed out my car, he laughed. "That's a casino fleet car, isn't it? So Bellows gave you a car to make sure I don't screw up. That guy is..." He didn't finish his thought.

I stepped out of the cart and loaded my bag into the trunk. "Hey, I get a car out of the deal. And gas money. I'm not complaining."

"No, I guess you're not." He pulled out his wallet and pulled out a small stack of bills. He counted off six twenties. Here, I owe you one-fifteen. Now you owe me five. I'll collect it later."

I looked at the money in his hand. "I can't take that," I said. "I didn't think we were betting when you were talking about all the options."

"Take it, I was betting. If I beat you, I would have collected."

I thought for a second that maybe he was testing me and that if I took the money, Bellows would jump out from behind a car and fire me. I dismissed the chance of that happening knowing that would mean Ben was working with Bellows to screw me. That didn't make any sense to me, so I took the money. Before I lowered my hand, I looked at Ben.

"You pull stuff like that all the time? Like driving into the trees on purpose?"

He smiled. "Some of the best shots of my life never hit a fairway or a green. Now, do me a favor, and let's not include Bellows in any of our fun. We have a casino match tomorrow. That's his business. Anything else is not."

I nodded. "Sure, no problem." As he drove away in the cart, I took the money and stuffed it in my pocket. Later that evening I told Kenny I felt like I was receiving charity. Ben spent most of the time doing anything but paying attention to his game.

"The guy is a player," I told Kenny. "I mean, a serious player. I think he'd take his mom's last dollar out of her pocket if he had to make a putt to do it. I don't know why, but he wants me to be part of his game. For some reason, he's pulling me in."

CHAPTER 7

Over the next month, I was a player. At least in my mind, I was a player. I stopped being a Golf Ambassador and started to play guests for money. I was nervous for the first few matches. Instead of showing up, shaking hands, and talking about whether or not the guests were having fun, money matches started with a casino official reading the agreed-upon stakes and the rules that, according to the State Gaming Commission, had to be followed. The most important rule was that the official was the final arbitrator when it came to rulings. While some of the guests that wanted money matches were experienced players, most were not. On a few occasions, I stood around as the guest had a ruling explained to them. Some of them were upset, but most of the time they played on without a problem.

My first match was with Ben playing at Palm Fairways. We were playing best ball, where our team's best score on each hole counted against the best score of the two guests. The casino would come up with ways to make the match competitive by giving the guest or guest team one or more strokes on a hole. Because the casino wanted the guests to have fun, and because the stakes were not usually high, the advantage was to the guest. In my first match, Ben and I were giving each of the guests two strokes per hole, on all eighteen holes. The match was for two hundred and fifty dollars per player.

Of course, none of this mattered to Ben and me. No matter what the stakes were, we played as well as we could. We paid no attention to the status of the match. We putted-out everything and listened to whatever the casino official said. When the match was over, we shook hands and walked off the green without saying anything to the guests. We were nothing more than card dealers.

When I was playing with Ben, I found myself paying less attention to the guests and more attention to Ben. It was clear that he was also watching me closely. The competition between us was at times intense. Sure, we smiled when a guest made a putt, or when they won some money. Inside though, I was always angry if I lost our personal match. I played to beat him and did so on a few occasions. But like my round with him at Cactus Ridge, I always felt like he was holding back. In the time I played with him that first month, I never thought I saw his best. I never thought I was seeing the real Ben Newell.

One day, he asked me for a ride to the course. He lived in a new complex of condominiums a few minutes from The Strip. When I walked up to his door, the stereo inside was playing Frank Zappa so loud, the condo's front window was shaking. I knocked three times before Ben turned off the stereo and opened the door. When he stepped away to grab his wallet, I was able to look inside. The living room was full of stuff, from golf clubs, to empty beer cans, to clothes. One chair was knocked over and the sofa cushions were thrown haphazardly around the room. I walked away so that he would not see me peering inside.

If this was a view into the real Ben Newell, what I saw was a troubled man that had no real place to go home to.

Up to this point, my time in Las Vegas would best be described as innocent. I had a job, received a promotion, played a lot of golf, got healthy, met a great girl, and was having fun. Melissa and I were seeing each other every night. If we weren't going out, we were sitting by the pool. Kenny started calling us Mister and Missus.

Things started to change near the end of my first month as a casino money player. First, Ben had issues with drinking. I got a call one evening from a man telling me, "come and get Newell at Rosy's before someone kills him."

I had no idea what this person was talking about, but when I mentioned the bar to Kenny, he said it was close. Both of us drove over, and we found Ben alone in the parking lot, yelling something I could not understand. When I walked up to him, he smiled and threw up on his shoes, all at the same time. We cleaned him up, threw him in the back seat of my car, and took him home. During the entire ten-minute drive to his condo, he lay with his head wrapped in a towel telling us that he had first-hand knowledge that Jim Morrison from the Doors was still alive.

As we dragged him out of the car, he stood up and said, "Boys, faking your death is the only way to convince those that want you dead, that they've already reached their goal."

After getting him inside and into his bed, Kenny and I sat on the curb next to the car.

"What the hell is that guy talking about?" Kenny asked. "And who can live in that apartment? There's more garbage on the floor in there than in all the rest of Vegas"

I shook my head. "I'm not sure, but if you ever want me dead, tell me so I can read up on Jim Morrison and see how he faked it."

That was not the first time I had to pull Ben out of a bar, or out of bed so that he could make a match. The one thing that he was able to remember when he was drunk was my phone number. He gave it out to a bystander or dialed it himself when he was in trouble. I quietly did my duty to ensure he was safe or got him to where he was supposed to be.

I stopped being quiet the Friday night before Halloween. The group from the casino had a costume party at a local restaurant. Kenny was with his girlfriend so I had our apartment to myself.

But when Melissa and I got back, I found Ben passed out on a chair next to the apartment door. He was covered in vomit and piss. What I hoped would be a night spent with Melissa turned out to be a nightmare.

I could not allow Melissa to get involved, so I drove her back to her place. As much as it hurt to drop her alone, what came next was worse. I could not get Ben to wake up. I yelled, slapped his face, and as a last resort threw a pitcher full of water on his face. Nothing worked. The only reaction I got was a grunt. As I became angrier he slipped deeper and deeper into an alcohol-induced coma.

After contemplating my next move, I decided to leave him outside the apartment. I dragged him off the chair and pulled him underneath the apartment's air conditioner. Pushing him against the wall, I went inside and tried to go to bed but the anger kept me awake. Lying on the couch in the dark apartment, I stared at the ceiling, wondering why I let a drunk ruin my night. The angrier I got, the more I swore to myself that I had to go to Bellows and ask for an end to my 'assignment'.

At 4:00 AM, I heard the door open. I smelled Ben before I saw him. Looking over at the door, his silhouette stumbled into a chair. With a loud deep breath, he went limp and I saw his head start to lull back and forth.

Reaching over my head, I turned the lamp on. When the light hit Ben, he jumped back and tried to cover his face.

"Turn the light, light off, you…"

He stopped and leaned forward. I jumped off the couch. "If you puke on this rug, I'll break your neck, you drunk piece of…"

I stopped when Ben tilted his head and looked at me. "Wow, t..t..tough guy." He took a deep breath. I could smell his exhale from across the room. "I don't have to puke, I already did. Hmm, I need a shower. I pissed myself."

I wanted to kick him out. I wanted to physically pick him up and throw him out the door. Of course, doing that would mean having to touch him, and I wasn't going to do that. Taking a few breaths to calm myself down, I told him, "Go shower, and throw your clothes in one of the bags under the sink."

He nodded and tried to stand up. It took him three tries and finally, he stood and stumbled down the hallway and into the bathroom. I cursed myself for letting my anger subside, but I figured that if I wanted to sleep, I had to help him out. I went into the bedroom and pulled some clothes together for him from my closet. Throwing them in the bathroom, I sat and waited for him.

The longer I sat, the angrier I became. Finally, he walked out and I jumped all over him.

"What the hell is wrong with you?" I asked.

Ben looked at me but did not answer. He walked over and sat in the same chair he was in before. His eyes were more clear and his balance more stable. The shower sobered him up.

"I'm serious, Ben. What is your problem? You ruined my night, and now you're ruining my sleep. Why the hell am I coming home with my girlfriend and finding your drunk ass passed out at my door? Are you kidding me?"

"Listen, Mark," Ben said. "I…"

"No, none of this 'I'm really sorry' drunk crap. What kind of person can't live their own life without having to call someone to scrape them off the ground and carry them home? You're forty years old. What is your problem?"

Ben looked down. He knew I was pissed. Twice he started to say something, but both times he stopped. I kept staring at him, pressuring him with my silence. Finally, he shook his head and said, "You're right. I'm…"

"Don't apologize. I don't need 'I'm sorry'."

"Okay," he said, looking down. "Mark, I am sorry. I know Bellows dragged you into this. I don't know what to say."

I moved forward on the couch. "Why the hell do you drink so much? Are you an alcoholic?"

He nodded. "I don't know, Mark. I know it's a problem. I guess I can't take the pressure from Bellows and Mar... Well, you don't have to worry about that."

"Who," I asked. "You mean Marino?"

He looked at me and was quiet for a few seconds. "How do you know that name?"

"I heard you and Bellows talking about it a few weeks ago. Why would you drink because of a problem with the casino? Who the hell is Marino? I thought you liked playing."

"It's not the casino, it's something else." He took a deep breath and slowly let it out. "Look, Mark. I have no excuses for my drinking. And as for Bellows and Marino, don't worry about that. I'll keep you out of it. That's my promise."

"Out of what?"

"No, I'm not getting into it. And it would sound like excuses."

I looked at him. He was forty years old and looked eighty. Wearing my Kansas 'Audio Visions Tour' concert t-shirt, he looked like an old man pretending to be a teenager. Even his deep blue eyes looked dull.

"You screwed up my night," I said. "I want to make sure you know that."

"Where was I when you got me?" he asked.

"You were passed out on the porch of the apartment. You don't remember?"

"No, I don't. You came home and found me?"

"Me and Melissa. We found you covered in puke and piss. Thanks for that."

He rubbed his face with both hands. "I, well... Crap, I suck." Shaking his head, he looked at the couch. "Tell you what, you take the bedroom and I'll finish the night on the couch. I'll be out of here when you wake up."

I looked at the clock and nodded. "Fine, but please, try to clean up this crap. I can't keep doing it. I'd like to say I look up to you but I don't know who the hell you are. Are you the great golfer and player that people call a legend, or are you a drunk that pulls everyone around you down? Who is the real Ben Newell?"

Ben nodded and shrugged. He looked down at his feet for a few seconds and then quietly said, "Okay. I get it. You won't hear from me for the rest of the weekend. Next week, well, we'll play. I'll be clean. And I'm serious, I'll keep you shielded from the Bellows and Marino stuff."

I ended up in Kenny's bed looking at the ceiling for the rest of the night thinking about Ben, Vegas, the mob, and why I ever listened to Kenny and flew out here in the first place. I hoped my talk with Ben helped. At least he admitted there was a problem. As for what I was being shielded from, I had no idea what he was talking about. When I got up in the morning, Ben was gone. He kept his promise. I was able to enjoy the rest of the weekend without hearing from him.

CHAPTER 8

When the calendar flipped to November, I started the day by buying a round-trip ticket home for Thanksgiving. My mom was ecstatic that I was coming home and I was happy I would be seeing her. Looking back, I should have bought a one-way ticket. My life would have been far simpler if I left Vegas and stayed home. It also would have been far safer.

November 1st was my first full day in a new apartment. Now that I was making decent money, Kenny and I moved into a bigger, two-bedroom apartment. After returning from purchasing my airline tickets, I went back to the new place, and for five minutes appreciated the fact that I had my own space for the first time in nearly three months.

My quiet was interrupted by the phone. It was Ben calling me. All he said was, "Be at Desert Bridge in one hour. Bring at least one hundred." Click. That was it.

I didn't know it at the time, but I was about to be indoctrinated into the world of 'The Bridge'.

I had been planning on a quiet Tuesday fixing up the new place. Now I was dragging myself to a course I had never seen, but heard about from Ben all the time. Ben was a movie fan. He loved to quote classic and new movie lines alike. One day I asked him about Desert Bridge, which he said was the hangout of a lot of money players. He said it was like the spaceport Mos Eisley in the movie Star Wars. Quoting the character Obi-wan Kenobi, Ben said Desert Bridge was a 'wretched hive of scum and villainy'.

I got dressed, dug up money from my small lockbox that was hidden under my mattress, and drove over to the Mos Eisley of Las Vegas golf.

Most courses in the desert had ornate entrances off of the main roads. Some had gates, others had flashy, almost Roman-like entrances. The borders of these courses along the main road were always a combination of green grass, palm trees, colorful vegetation, and desert beauty.

Desert Bridge was the opposite. The entrance was off of a service road a half-mile from The Strip. The signage was made up of what appeared to be the original wood placard held up by three two-by-fours. The first look you had of the course when you turned onto the entrance road was of a putting green with bunkers void of sand. The grass behind the green was brown, dead, and looked like the desert itself. When you got fifty yards onto the entrance road, you came across a palm tree which was propped up by more two-by-fours and a wire tied from the top of the tree to a telephone pole. The entrance road itself was full of potholes. When you reached the parking lot you had to slow down and drive through a gully left by a heavy rain years ago, but it was never filled in and repaved.

For most Vegas courses, the clubhouse was a major selling point. Large, inter-connected bars, restaurants, shops, and locker rooms made the environment feel like class, money, and comfort. It was a place that made you forget the world outside. If it was over one hundred degrees in the sun, the clubhouse was always a cool sixty-five, and you were never more than ten steps from a bar to get a drink.

The clubhouse at Desert Bridge was made up of a small Cape Cod house that had no right to be sitting in Las Vegas. For all I knew, it was built in the east, put on a truck, and moved to the spot it now sat. And if that was true, whoever placed it to the side of the parking area put it down with no thought of being careful. The outside walls were all at odd angles, some pushed out, others falling inward. The roof was three levels of shingles, the last level looking like someone threw the shingles on while standing on the ground. There were loose shingles over the entire roof, with many more lying in piles on the dirt.

The structure was made larger by two thirty-foot trailers that appeared to be built into either side of the house. One had a flat roof where players tossed old golf bags, clubs, lawn chairs, and other garbage. The other was a silver trailer with smokestacks and pipes coming out of the roof.

As I would learn, the trailer on the right, with the flat roof, was the bar. The silver trailer on the left was the kitchen. In the middle, the house was open without any walls. Card tables and a picnic table made up the sitting area.

I pulled into the lot a few minutes before noon. After stepping out of the car, I looked around. The only thing that told me this was a golf course was the golf-related trash on the trailer roof. Looking out at what parts of the course I could see, I was pretty sure I was surrounded only by the desert. I saw brown grass, cactus, scrub, and dirt. There were no golfers on the course that I could see.

Walking closer to the house, I started to hear voices. They grew louder, and when I pulled open the door, I thought I was looking at a party. Stepping in, I saw at least two dozen people, all with drinks, laughing, talking, and singing. To my right was the bar. It was built into the attached trailer. The bar itself was three long, rectangular folding tables pushed together with an old kitchen countertop laying across them. The countertop was a peeling blue laminate that was covered with dark burns from cigarettes. Six scratched and beaten wooden bar chairs sat haphazardly in the area in front of the bar. The chairs were too tall for the bar, so the people sitting in them had their knees pushed up against the edges of the countertop.

I walked through the room looking for Ben or any face that I knew. Seeing no one, I walked up to the bar. A younger man, maybe thirty-five years old, was behind the bar cleaning up a spilled drink. He was laughing at something he heard and after putting down a towel, he picked up a shot glass and downed whatever clear alcohol it held. Exhaling the effects from the shot, he saw me walk up and yelled over, "Well, we have a fresh face at the Bridge!"

He walked over and reached his hand out. "I'm Miller Halverstrom. Call me Milly. What do they call you?"

I shook his hand and said, "Mark Travers, I'm looking for Ben Newell."

"Looking for Benny? Well, he was here. Hold on one second, please."

Milly walked over to a cooler sitting on the ground and opened it. "Well," he said, "I see three cans of Blue Ribbon still sitting here, so that means he hasn't gone far."

I thought back to the empty Pabst Blue Ribbon cans in the golf cart the first time I met Ben. "He likes Blue Ribbons?" I asked.

"I do!" came a loud voice from behind me.

"Well, there he is!" Milly yelled out to the bar. "The man, the myth, and the legend! Ben Newell!"

A mock roar went up through the bar's crowd.

Ben laughed. He grabbed my shoulder and led me over to Milly. "Mark, this is Milly, and he knows everything. If you ever have a question about this or any place, you come to him."

I nodded at Milly. "Okay, I will."

Milly smiled and said, "Of course, having all this knowledge hasn't gotten me too far. But, most of the nightmares have stopped." He pointed at Ben. "Except the ones about this guy. They'll never go away."

Ben gave Milly the finger and said, "Eff you, bartender."

"Thank you for your order. Right away, sir," Milly said. He reached down and grabbed a Blue Ribbon can from the cooler and tossed it over my head to Ben. Ben took a bow to thank Milly, opened the can, took a long drink, and then stepped over to the far wall. He raised his fingers to his mouth and let go with a long, shrill whistle that immediately quieted the room.

"Ladies and gentlemen," Ben said, "I wish to introduce to you a friend of mine. He is an honest person, which I beg you to not hold against him, and he is one hell of a golfer. This is Mark Travers."

Everyone in the room turned, looked at me, and started to clap and whistle. I was not expecting to be the center of all of the room, so I took a breath and forced myself to smile. With a quick nod, I said thank you and looked over at Ben. He was in the process of finishing his beer. When I looked back at the people in the room, they had already moved on. The noise in the room picked back up, and the party continued.

A hand grabbed me by the shoulder and pulled me toward the front door. As I was being led out, Milly yelled my name. When I looked over, he tossed a can of beer at me. I grabbed it and looked back at the door barely in time to safely make my way out.

Now in the parking lot, I turned around. Ben was behind me, fumbling in his pocket for something. Pulling out his keys, he handed them to me. "Here, pull my clubs out. Get yours. I'll go get our cart." He turned and started to walk around the side of the house.

"Ben," I said, but he kept going.

"Ben!" I now yelled and he stopped.

Turning back, he yelled, "What?"

I took a breath. "What am I doing here?"

He stood for a few seconds, seemingly trying to understand what I was asking.

"Why did you tell me to come here?" I slowly asked him, not sure if he was drunk, disoriented, or both.

"Oh," he said. "Yeah, I guess I didn't tell you." He started to laugh and took a step back to me. "You're playing a match."

"A match? With who? Against who?"

"With?" he asked, again looking confused. "You're not playing with anyone. You're playing skins, straight up. You're playing against all of us. You, me, Gonzo, and Clip."

Now I was the confused one. "Who, or what is Gonzo and Clip?"

Ben started to walk back around the house. "They are two of the best money players in the valley. I need to see how you do. Get the bags."

Ben disappeared around the corner, leaving me alone in the parking lot. I walked over to his Eldorado and opened the trunk. His bag was covered under about a dozen cartons of golf balls, three pairs of golf shoes, and maybe twenty empty cans of Pabst Blue Ribbon. I reached through everything and pulled his bag out. As I turned around, a golf cart skidded to a stop next to me.

"Let's go, they're on the tee," Ben said. He sat still barely long enough for me to put his bag on the back of the cart. At my car, he never stopped. I jumped out, grabbed my bag and shoes, and jumped back on as he rolled forward. I was still putting on my golf shoes when we pulled up to the first tee.

As Ben got out of the cart, he turned to me and said, "This is one of the things that you do not tell Bellows about."

"Sure," I said. "Why are we playing skins?"

Ben grabbed his driver out of his bag and started to walk to the tee. Looking over his shoulder as he pulled on his glove he said,

"Because if I let you play these guys in a game where we had side bets, they would gut you and leave you for dead in the desert."

I started to laugh, but then I stopped when I looked at Gonzo and Clip who were standing on the tee. These were not your run-of-the-mill looking golfers. One of them stood well over six-feet tall and appeared to have been living in the weight room. The other was so thin and slight that I didn't think he could hit it further than two hundred yards. As I walked onto the tee, both men were laughing at something Ben said.

"Fine," the big guy said. "As long as once his cherry is popped, I get a piece of him when the blood is cleared."

"You're a sick man, Gonzo," Ben said. He turned and said to me, "Mark, this is Gonzo. And over there is Clip. They both want nothing more than to kick your ass and take your money, but they promise to keep it straight up skins."

Gonzo walked over and shook my hand. I assumed he was fifty years old. He was wearing a sleeveless t-shirt and shorts, and around his neck was a gold chain with the word 'Slayer' written out. Standing next to him, I guess he was at least six-foot-four inches tall, and a good two hundred and eighty pounds. His arms were tattooed with several Navy-related images, and he had a tattoo of a naked woman on his left calf. The woman was lying on her back with her arms crossed over her head, and the words, 'She's your wife? Not any longer' written under her.

"Mark, nice to meet you. Call me Gonzo, I hear you can play. We'll see."

I nodded and walked over to Clip. He was younger than Gonzo, maybe in his forties. He had a thick mustache and looked stronger as I was standing next to him than my first impression. His face reminded me of Sonny Bono. He was also wearing a sleeveless t-shirt and shorts. His shirt had the Grateful Dead's "Steal Your Face" logo on the front. He did not attempt to shake my hand, but he nodded. "College player, huh?"

"Yeah, I played…"

"I don't give a shit, kid," he said, interrupting me. "Let's play. I want to get done quickly so I can make it back to the party."

"One hundred bucks up," Ben said. "The kid will carry it."

All three of them walked over and handed me a one-hundred-dollar bill. It hit me that I was putting one hundred of my money on the line without so much as asking Ben why he had called me. I remembered what he told me though, to never react to the amount of the bet. He also once told me that when you played for money in Vegas, it wasn't golf like I was used to it. He always used the term, 'player'.

> *"A player never talks about golf like you do. When a 'player' says someone can 'play', they don't mean they can hit the ball well, putt, or know how to score. They mean they know how to win money. The best 'players' win money. That may mean they can't break eighty-five or that they can't get the ball off the ground. But if they collect at the end, in the eyes of a 'player', they can 'play'."*

Thinking of those words, I looked at Gonzo and Clip differently. Ben said these guys were 'players'. Clip just said to me that we'll see if you can play. I closed my eyes and told myself to forget golf as I knew it.

"Let's play," I said. "Who's up?"

Ben looked over at me, no doubt surprised I spoke. With a nod, he said, "You are. Skins, straight up. Four hundred to the winner, zilch after that. Ties on eighteen get taken to the desert."

I pulled a ball and tee out of my pocket and walked over to the tee area. I knew what a skins game was. Each player was playing their own ball against the other three. If you had the best score on a hole, you got the skin. If there was a tie, the skin carried over to the next hole where all four players had a chance to win that hole's skin plus the carryovers. As for what 'taken to the desert' was in case no one was able to win the eighteenth hole's skin, I figured it was some sort of playoff that would start with players hitting their ball from the sand and hardpan off of the fairway.

The first tee itself was nothing more than dirt and some brown grass. The tee markers were pieces of wood with faded paint distinguishing the white and blue tees. I assumed we were playing the back, blue tees, so I teed up and stepped back. I hadn't stretched out, so I needed a few practice swings.

"Hit the fucking ball, kid," Gonzo said.

I didn't look back at him. Ben always said a money game is the same as poker. Players look for weaknesses. I didn't look back at Gonzo or the others. I continued to slowly take practice swings and then stepped back behind the ball. Looking down the fairway, I got my first look at the opening hole at Desert Bridge. All I could see was a faint outline of the fairway, and the green four hundred yards out. There were no fairway bunkers, no mounds or rises, just dried-out grass and desert.

I stepped back up to the ball and let loose with a hard swing. Since there was little difference between the desert and the fairway, I wasn't worried about hitting it straight, but it didn't matter. I launched a high, booming draw that when it hit the ground, shot like a crazy ball toward the green.

"Get all of that, college boy?" Clip asked as he stepped up to the tee around me.

"No, not really," I said. "I hit it off the toe."

Clip said something like, "Fuck you," under his breath. When I looked over at Ben he was holding in a laugh.

There is no way to equate the golf swings of either Clip or Gonzo with that of Ben or any other competitive golfer I have played with. I had to keep reminding myself that the goal was not par. The goal of these guys was to win money. Today, their goal was the most skins. Win the most skins and you get all the money. It only took me two holes to learn that one of their strategies was to pull better, more talented golfers like Ben and me down a few notches to narrow the gap. They did this by never shutting up. The only time there was quiet was when you were about to pull the club back. The quiet ended milliseconds after impact. While most golf competitors looked to take advantage of using the best parts of their games, these guys looked to gain an advantage by finding weaknesses between their competitor's ears.

Clip was a nervous talker. His swing was fast and loose, and he never hit the ball higher than thirty feet in the air. Most of his shots rolled further than they flew. Around the green though, he was deadly. On the first hole, he made a thirty-five-foot birdie putt, forcing either Ben or me to make far shorter birdie efforts to carry over the skin. Ben made his.

Gonzo was a swearing, angry, tight, and scary talker. Between holes, he asked me where I went to school, how I liked Las Vegas, and even about my mom. Once we got to the tee, he said things that would make a longshoreman blush. By the time we walked off the second green, my life had been threatened (I assume that the comment 'you hit the green from here I'll stick that club down your throat' would be fatal), and most parts of my body had been ridiculed, including my feet ('with feet like that how the hell can you stand still to putt?').

In a straight-up stroke play round, both Ben and I would beat either Gonzo or Clip by eight to ten shots. But in skins, they only had to win a hole. If it was the right hole, with a large number of carryovers, they could win the money. They both knew that, and it was clear that when they had to, they would combine their formidable vocal talents to bring down the competition.

That was never more evident on the third hole. No skins were won on the first two holes, so there were carryovers to the third, a long par-3 over two hundred yards. The green looked like an island in the desert. There was no rough or fairway, only fringe and putting green. I hit first and my shot landed a foot short of the green and bounced straight left after hitting something on the hardpan ground. Ben went next and hit a beautiful high five-iron to the center of the green. Both Gonzo and Clip left their shots short in the desert. That left Ben in great shape to win three skins.

The moment we started to walk off the tee, Gonzo and Clip started. They were verbally abusing Ben so badly that by the time we pulled up to the green, Ben's entire family had been attacked, his drinking analyzed, and his bowel movements criticized. Perhaps worst of all, his soul was damned to an eternity of performing a sexual act so perverse that I swore I would never try to picture in my head what it would look like.

I am not sure if all that abuse worked, but the three of us that missed the green got the result we wanted. Clip chipped up to two feet away, and Ben missed his long birdie putt. It was another carryover.

Another thing I learned about money golf was that the pace of play was fast. We finished the front nine in seventy minutes. There were no skins won, so with all the carryovers, the first skin won on the back nine would mean winning the four-hundred dollars. As we waited for Gonzo to use the bathroom when we reached the tenth tee, Ben told me that in normal circumstances each player would be making multiple side bets in an attempt to either hedge against a loss, or leverage an advantage, real or perceived.

As Gonzo pulled up with Clip in their cart, I asked Ben how I was doing in my tryout. His answer was simple: "Not too good if you have to ask. There's only one way to know you're doing good, and that's to win."

Clip had a great chance to win on the twelfth hole, a short par-3 with an elevated tee. Since he was the shortest hitter in the group, this hole was one of his best chances. Up to this point, Ben and I canceled out each other with birdies four times. Both of us had been tied by Gonzo or Clip a few times. But neither of those guys had an advantage on a hole until number twelve when Clip hit his tee shot to four feet. I pulled my tee shot hole high and was unlucky as my shot rolled just off the fringe onto the hardpan, twenty-five feet to the left of the hole. Both Ben and Gonzo hit bad shots and were thirty feet above the hole. So Clip was in great shape.

Now it was our turn to ride Clip. I was still a rookie at this, so I kept my mouth shut. I would have liked to remind Clip about a missed putt of similar length, but he had made every putt under fifteen feet so far. Ben's attacks were subtle, mostly around Clip's history and any failures that he witnessed. Gonzo went all out, even to the point that he described Clip's sister's first forays into the world of sex. Clip did his best to keep his attention away from us, and when he marked his putt, he smiled looking at his flat four-footer. Comparing his situation to ours, he pulled out his wallet and asked me to fill it up with the bills I was holding.

I took a look at my situation. I was on hardpan desert, with no grass anywhere near my ball. Fifteen inches in front of my ball the fringe of the green rose eight inches. It was as if I was in a sandless bunker. I needed to chip my ball over the ridge of the fringe, land it about two feet onto the green, and let it roll down an incline to the hole. As I looked at my line, there was at least three feet of break, left to right. My biggest problem with the shot was getting it high enough over the ridge, but short enough that it would not take the downhill of the green and run ten feet past the hole. If I got too cute with the shot, I could leave it on the fringe.

Having figured out my shot, I looked up at Gonzo and Ben. Both had similar thirty-foot putts and would go before me as I was closer. I hoped both of them would make it so that I didn't have to even try my shot. Their putts were the best chance we had of tying Clip.

Gonzo went first and hit his putt way too solid. I knew right away it would run well past the hole, and it did, ending up five feet past. Clip laughed as Gonzo marked his ball. "Money in my pocket, Gonz. Your money."

Gonzo walked to the side of the green and I counted at least ten 'fuck yous' on the way.

Ben was next and my hope was he learned something from Gonzo. He did not have the same line, but he should have seen that the speed was fast. When he hit his putt, I thought it had a chance. The ball was headed for the center of the cup, but six inches away it lost pace and broke over the right edge finishing a few inches past the hole.

"Yes, baby. Nice try but then again so is an old man's last dollar spent on a whore," Clip said as he ran over and knocked Ben's ball back to him.

Gonzo groaned and started to swear at Clip and his 'old man' analogy. I agreed with Gonzo that I didn't understand what Clip was saying either, but my attention quickly went to my shot. I knew what I had to do, and my last decision was the club I would use. Normally, a wedge was the right choice. But as I stood over the ball holding my wedge, I pictured a shot that had trouble keeping its line. I decided to use my nine-iron, play the ball back in my stance, and get some pace on the shot. As long as I got it over the ridge onto the fringe, it didn't matter if I went by the hole. I was planning on hitting the pin and having it fall in. This shot would either be a great one or would end up way past the hole.

I took two practice swings and moved over the ball. Just as I was about to hit the shot, I heard Clip say, "Ka-ching."

I made perfect contact and the ball brushed over the ridge of the fringe. It landed just on the green, and the spin slowed the ball enough so that it caught the line I wanted. I watched as it began to roll down the hill, started to take the left to right break, and then leveled out four feet from the hole. At that point, I knew it was in. So did Gonzo. He started running toward the hole. When it hit the pin and dropped, all four of us yelled. Gonzo, Ben, and I yelled, "Yes!" and high-fived each other. Clip yelled, "Shit!" and dropped his putter.

I felt like I won a tournament. The rush of adrenaline was as strong as any I felt when I won a college tournament, maybe stronger. I looked at Ben and he was smiling. I knew he was feeling the same thing I was. As I pulled my ball out of the cup, I thought to myself, 'This is what it feels like to be a player'.

I started to walk back to the cart, but I stopped while Clip put his ball down and stood over his putt. Pulling the putter back, he hit a solid putt, and the ball headed straight for the center. I started to walk away, but in the last foot, the ball turned left, hit the lip, and did a one-eighty, spinning back at Clip and finishing a few inches outside the cup.

We were all quiet for a moment until Gonzo yelled the loudest, 'You asshole!' that I have ever heard in my life. He repeated it before taking his putter and flinging it in the direction of the cart. Clip stood there, looking at his ball, saying nothing. When I looked at Ben, he had what I can best describe as a satisfied grin.

I could not believe Clip's ball stayed out of the hole. I laughed at the reaction of the others, and then took two steps toward the carts. That's when it hit me: I won the hole. I won the skin. I won the carryovers. Unbelievably, I just won the match.

After a few minutes of swearing and abuse, most of it leveled at Clip, we jumped in the carts and headed back to the clubhouse. Once inside, it was as if the match never happened. Clip and Gonzo melted into the crowd, while Ben and I had a beer at the bar. Pabst Blue Ribbon. The only mention of the match was when Milly asked some questions. I liked Milly right away. With all the partying and noise, he seemed to me to be the only voice of reason in the room. He pulled me aside and said that taking down the threesome of Newell, Gonzo and Clip was monumental. When I mentioned that maybe they cut me a break because I was a 'rookie', Milly stepped back and said, "Ben may have eased up a little to test you, but the other two? No way. On the course, those guys won't ease up for a nun's last penny." I laughed and so did he.

After I finished my beer, I told Ben I was leaving. It was not my plan to get drunk in the middle of the afternoon on a Tuesday. He nodded and followed me outside.

"So, money man, how'd that feel?" he asked me.

"Great," I said. I thought for a second, and said, "Really great. I guess when that chip went in I had my first taste of what it's like to be a player."

Ben shook his head. "Partly. The feeling from making the chip shot, that's what it feels like to be a golfer. Winning the bank, that's part of what it feels like to be a player."

"What's the other part?" I asked him.

"The other part is the feeling you get when you lose bank. Trust me, that feeling lasts much longer than any good you feel when you win."

I thought about what he said, nodded, and headed for the car.

"Hey," Ben said. "You remember what I told you about remembering a shot?"

"Yeah, something about confidence," I replied, turning back to him. "The brain bank."

He shook his head. "Something about confidence?" he asked rhetorically. Shaking his head, he said, "Unreal. You don't realize how a shot like that needs to be stored in your memory. I call it the brain bank because memories like that have value. Trust me, there'll come a time when you'll need to remember that shot you just hit."

I smiled and said, "Ben, I'll remember it. And I'll remember this round. Thanks for asking me to play."

I only took two more steps when the door to the clubhouse opened and everyone inside ran out after me.

"Get that stork back in here," someone yelled.

A woman's voice was cursing at someone, damning their soul to eternal hell for letting me leave.

I looked at Ben and he shrugged. "Just go with it," he said. "Trust me, it won't hurt."

I was surrounded by everyone. They moved tighter around me until I started to feel claustrophobic. Then they all stopped moving and became quiet. The only noise I heard was a burp, and the retching sound of someone vomiting around the corner of the clubhouse. Finally, the circle of people parted, and Milly walked up to me.

"Mark," Milly said. "You almost committed the one sin that is unforgivable here in the city that sits at the gates of hell. And because of that, you must be judged. Grab him."

A few of the guys lightly grabbed me by the elbows and guided me back into the clubhouse. I was led to a chair in front of the bar. After I sat, the rest of the group moved in around me.

"Ladies and gentlemen," Milly said as he walked around to the back of the bar, "sitting in front of you is the man that just kicked the asses of three esteemed members of the Bridge."

"Fuck you," came a voice from the back, which I knew right away was Clip.

"And," Milly continued, "this man attempted to leave the premises without sharing in his winnings. That, as we all know, is the most heinous of crimes at The Bridge, and in the Valley. What penalty shall we impose?"

As if in unison, the entire room shouted, "Two rounds!"

"So be it!" Milly said. "Two rounds it is!"

With that, everyone walked around me to the bar. I received several slaps on the back, and many of the people shook my hand. It was obvious that at The Bridge, the most valuable currency was a free drink. I withstood the onslaught of appreciation until I was finally able to find some space in the corner next to the bar. I reached into my pocket, took out my winnings, and pushed the bills toward Milly.

"Woah, Mark. This is The Bridge, not what I would call a five-star place. Here."

He reached over into the register and pulled out a fifty-dollar bill. Taking one of the hundred dollar bills from my money, he said, "That should cover two rounds. Here, I take it you like beer." He opened a bottle of Coors and slid it over to me.

"Thanks," I said, looking around the room. "Interesting group of people."

Milly laughed. "That they are, and a great group. Best people in the valley, not even close. You get them on the course and sometimes it almost ends up in fists. Well, it does end up in fists. Get them back here though, and it's all forgotten. If they respect you, they'll do anything for you."

A roar went up in the far corner of the room, and a group started to move my way.

"Well, well," Milly said. "It looks like they respect you."

Gonzo led the group, and when he stood in front of me, he waved his hand, telling me to stand up. After I stood, he silently stared. I felt like I was in front of Bellows. After ten seconds, he started to laugh.

"Yup," Gonzo said, turning to the group. "He does look like it. I'm good with it."

I looked over at Milly. "What are they talking about?"

Ben walked out of the crowd, pushed me back into my chair, and then he sat down next to me. "Your nickname. They gave you one. It's a sign of respect from player to player."

"Nickname?" I asked. I leaned over closer to Ben. "What is this, a fraternity?"

"Hey," Ben said, "not too many people that play want their real name out there. A nickname is, well, kind of like a pen name. Most of the guys or gals in this room I've known for years. I couldn't tell you the real names of half of them. I thought Gonzo's real name was Gonzales. It isn't. It's Sherwood. I have no idea where Gonzo came from."

The man behind Ben waiting for a drink said, "It's because when he was in the Navy, he screwed a girl in the Philippines named Gonzales. After that, he called every girl he was with in the Philippines, Gonzales. The guys started to call him Gonzo and it stuck."

"There, it's because of his overseas sexual history," Ben said with a laugh.

The guy behind Ben stepped up to me and we shook hands. "I'm Squat, nice to meet you, Vlad. Thanks for pissing off Clip. When he's pissed off, he drinks more. He's more fun when he drinks more."

"You're welcome," I said. After he walked away, I said to Ben, "Why Vlad? What does that even mean?"

Ben nodded and smiled. "Clip came up with it. He said you walk like you have a pole up your ass. Like you're impaled."

I looked at him and shook my head. "Meaning...?"

"C'mon, kid," Milly said. "Don't you know your history? Vlad the Impaler. He was a real son of a bitch in, like, the fifteen hundreds. He liked to impale people, so he became Vlad, the Impaler. Now, that's you."

I started laughing at the name. My friends at home said when I played basketball I would move faster if I could get the pole out of my ass. I had to agree with Clip.

"And where did Clip get his nickname from?" I asked.

"No idea," Milly said. "He walked in here a couple of years ago, challenged everyone to a game, and said his name was Clip. Maybe that's his actual name."

I took a long drink from my beer and said to Ben and Milly, "You guys don't have nicknames, how come?"

"Like Ben told you," Milly said, "it's a sign of respect amongst players. I can't hit a ball fifty yards. I hate to play the game. That's why I'm always here, and never out there. 'Milly' is as close to a nickname that I'll ever get."

I looked at Ben. "How 'bout you?"

"Oh, I have a nickname. It's just that no one here has the guts to use it. They know if I hear it, I'll take it out on them on the course and leave every pocket and wallet they own empty."

Milly laughed and said, "That's why I call him Benny but no one else does. I don't play. It ain't the nickname someone came up with, but it's close."

"Benny?" I asked. "That's no nickname."

I saw that Ben was, for some reason, not comfortable with my question. I reached over and took his empty beer can from the bar top. Stepping down, I reached into the cooler on the ground and pulled out a can of Pabst Blue Ribbon. "Here, it's on the house."

The three of us laughed and it was clear that Ben was relieved to have the subject changed. Looking around the room, I asked, "What do all these people do for a living? Like, Gonzo and Clip.

What are they? Retired military?"

Milly replied, "Gonzo is. He's been playing The Bridge since I got here five years ago. As for Clip?"

"He works for the feds. I think he's a court stenographer or something like that. No one knows and no one asks," Ben said. "I always assumed he won the lottery somewhere and now he plays. I was here that first day he showed up. He just walked in, ordered a beer, and challenged a group of us to play. He threw two hundred on the bar and said, 'Let's go'."

I stayed for another hour. By the time I left, everyone was calling me Vlad. I met a lot of people, and other than Ben and Milly, all the names were nicknames. I met Slinky, Hooks, OB, Booker, and so many others that I stopped trying to remember who was who. They all knew me though; I was Vlad, the rookie that beat down Ben, Gonzo, and Clip. That night, after explaining everything to Melissa and Kenny in the new apartment, they also started calling me Vlad. Coming from them it seemed weird, but coming from everyone at the Bridge, it was perfectly natural.

CHAPTER 9

I continued to play money matches with Ben for the casino and to work on my game. In the afternoon I would head over to the Bridge and hang out in the clubhouse. There were always people there drinking, playing cards, and having a good time. Since I was younger than everyone, I never felt completely comfortable sitting amongst the group, so I would sit next to the bar and talk to Milly. He was like a color commentator, telling me stories about the Bridge and the people. I would stay there until Melissa or Kenny got out of work, and I would head back to the apartment.

Ben seemed to have himself under control. I mentioned to Melissa that I thought Ben felt bad about the times I had to pull him out of a bar and get him home. I know he felt terrible about ruining our Halloween party night. His guilt seemed to be motivating him to clean up. He was arriving at the course on time, and when I was with him at the Bridge, he mostly drank soda. He set up a few more matches for me to play at the Bridge, and although I lost some money, I was learning the 'game of the desert'.

One night I was sitting with Kenny watching TV when the phone rang. It was Ben asking me to come over. My first thought was he needed help, but when I arrived at his apartment, he was sitting on a chair on the sandy ground behind his patio drinking coffee. I knew something was bothering him, and he wanted to get his mind on something else. But my surprise that he was not drunk on the floor was enough to make me laugh.

"What's funny?" he asked.

I shook my head and told him the expectations of what I was going to find were much different.

He understood. We spent the next two hours talking about his time in college and how his life grew and changed in the valley. He asked me about my past and how I saw my life moving forward. I was shocked when he told me I should take Melissa's hand and never let go. The way he said it was surprising. It was a side of Ben I had not seen before. I thought for a moment I was starting to see the real Ben Newell. But when I asked him about his personal life, he started to say something and stopped.

"What?" I asked. "Did I go somewhere I shouldn't have?"

Ben looked down, sighed, and then kicked some sand up from the ground. "No, Mark. I just don't want to mix that with this."

I nodded and let him drive the conversation. It was not the last time we talked like this. Over the next few months, we spoke many times about things other than golf. I started to look at the sober Ben as someone I could learn from. The fact that he was older than me but willing to share his ideas, thoughts, and concerns with me became an important part of my time in the desert.

I took my trip home to see my mother and celebrate Thanksgiving. Melissa drove me to the airport and I was surprised about my reaction to not seeing her for four days. I was sad. When I turned and walked away from her at the airport's curb, I had the idea of turning around and staying. I kept going though because I knew my mom was planning the biggest feast in family history. Her reaction to a call telling her I could not make it outweighed any sadness I felt missing Melissa.

Besides, if I told Melissa I saw staying she would probably have grabbed me by the ear and forced me into the airplane.

That weekend, I spent the entire time home eating, convincing my mom and visiting family that I was not living at the card tables, and answering all of her questions about Melissa. Her expectations were sky-high and I could see she was already planning a wedding.

On the day after Thanksgiving, I drove over to see Mr. Wittich. The sky was dark and gloomy, and the temperature was in the low forties. That did not stop him from walking me out to the practice tee. Giving me a 5-iron, he kicked over a bucket of balls and stood on the back of the tee. He nodded his head and said, "Let me see."

I pulled off my coat and started to hit balls. The feel of his icy glare and presence behind me got my heart racing. I smiled to myself thinking that the pressure I felt from his intimidating silence was much worse than all of the disgusting personal attacks Clip, Gonzo, or any of the other players at the Bridge could inflict on me.

When I was warmed up, I started to hit the ball in earnest and after hitting five straight solid balls, Mr. Wittich grunted and started to walk back to the Pro Shop. After cleaning up the balls strewn on the ground, I followed him.

Back inside I leaned on the display case as he pulled up his chair and sat.

"Your hips are moving through the ball better than the last time I saw you," he said.

I let out a breath and was able to relax. "Thanks, I'm not feeling tightness anymore."

"Your ball flight is lower by about ten feet. How many rounds a week are you playing?"

"Four or five." I knew where he was going so I answered all of his questions before he needed to ask them. "I hit each club on the range beforehand. After the round, I try to warm down with each club. There's usually a one-club wind so I've been playing the ball back a few inches to keep my flight down. The courses are pretty soft around the greens so the ball sticks. That's except for one course where I play a decent amount. There I keep the ball lower and let it run on."

He listened to what I was saying and kept nodding. I knew him well enough to know he was taking all of this info in and analyzing details I was not aware of. Finally, he nodded. That was the approval I was hoping for.

"Are you playing for money?" he asked.

I was not prepared for that question. When I hesitated, he knew the answer.

"What's the goal of the matches?" he asked.

"Um, well..." I stammered.

He stood up and leaned over to me. Putting his hand on my arm, he said, "Mark, you remember what you went out there for. Playing for money will never make you rich, no matter how much you win. So, what's your goal?"

I took a deep breath. "I'm not playing to get rich. I'm playing for the experience. Most of my rounds are with the casino, so I'm not allowed to gamble. The place I play with some friends is where the money games are. I appreciate the concern, I do. I'm not going overboard."

He stood back and smiled. "I know, Mark. I know. But you can get sucked in. If you're healthy, then play for the experience. Set limits. Remember what you're there for. What's the name of the course you play these games at?"

"Desert Bridge," I said. "I've had some good games there."

"Okay," he said. "Maybe I'll make a few calls. Now you get home and see your friends."

He turned away and walked back into the storage room.

I smiled. Every conversation with Mr. Wittich ended this way. On his terms. I turned and walked toward the door but stopped. I knew there was more.

"Oh," he said from the other room, "remember that your hands should finish high, even if you're playing the ball down. Don't be hitting knockdowns all the time. The ball can be back, but the hands should finish high."

I laughed a little and said I would remember.

On Sunday, the tears and crying I dealt with when my mom dropped me at the airport were bearable because I could not wait to see Melissa. The happiness I felt when I saw her as I walked off the plane made me realize that my mom may be right. This relationship was getting serious. I wasn't sure if she felt the same thing, but on the short drive back from the airport she asked me if I was going home over the Christmas holiday.

"If my mom has her way, yeah," I answered, "I'm going to have to. If not, she's coming out here." I started to laugh thinking of my mom meeting the misfits at The Bridge.

My laughter stopped immediately when Melissa said, "Well, I think I want to meet her. Let's buy the tickets this week."

I stared at her for a few seconds. Feeling my gaze, she looked at me and said, "And I think you should meet my parents. My dad is asking about you all the time."

When I told Kenny, he ran around the apartment yelling that love was in the air, and that we needed to start planning the wedding.

"Is it going to be a Vegas wedding?" he asked.

I looked at him like a lawyer whose client just admitted he was guilty in public. "Are you kidding me? Don't ever say that. If my mom found out I was getting married in one of those crappy Vegas chapels she would never talk to me again."

"I think Melissa's dad would kill you too. I met him. He's a big guy, you know."

I nodded and took a breath to calm myself. "I heard. Meeting them is going to suck, no two ways about it."

Later that week, Melissa and I celebrated our three-month anniversary. At dinner, we made plans to meet our parents. No mention was made of marriage or a Vegas wedding although I knew the next time we were both with Kenny, the topic would come up. I did bring up one matter with Melissa and was able to get her to agree. That week, Milly talked me into bringing Melissa to the Bridge to meet everyone. I wanted her to see that I was not making up stories and descriptions of the members there. She was starting to think that these were not real people but cartoon characters.

When we pulled into the lot, the music, yelling, and singing from the clubhouse carried through the desert. As we walked to the door, Melissa stopped. "Are you sure this is okay?"

"What? That you're here?" I asked.

She nodded. "I feel like I'm walking into a beehive."

I pulled her along. "Don't worry, they're not even gonna notice that you're here."

She nervously nodded and we walked up to the door. I walked in first, and a cry of "Vlad!" went up. I looked back and told Melissa it was okay. She took a breath and walked in.

As soon as she stepped in, everything went silent. The music went off, and each person in the room stopped singing and talking. They all turned and stared at Melissa, whose face went white with fear.

For the next five seconds, no one moved or made a noise. Then Milly jumped to the front of the bar and said, "Ladies and gentlemen, proving that Vlad's better half is indeed one of the prettiest girls in the Valley, may I introduce to you, Melissa!"

With his introduction, the entire room exploded with applause and screams of welcome. Poor Melissa took a breath, and after seeing that she was the subject of an innocent joke, she smiled. As we walked over to the bar, everyone said hello to her. By the time we had our first drink, she was thought of as a regular at the Bridge.

CHAPTER 10

December was a fairly quiet one at Olympia. For the first two weeks, I played only two times for the casino and both times as an Ambassador. It seems that December is a slow month for money matches. The rest of the time I was playing matches at The Bridge against anyone that wanted to put down their drinks and pick up a club. Some days I played for a few bucks against players that could not break a hundred. On other days I went up against Ben or Clip for a few hundred. I even got Kenny to play there in a few matches. Each match was played with high tension, unimaginable insults to each of my family members both alive and dead and some of the most fun golf I had ever played.

After each match, I would sit with Milly or Ben and talk about the world while I waited for Melissa to get off work. Milly was more than open about the problems he had in life with gambling, drinking, and trying to live a good life in a city that worked so hard to exploit each of his vices. He would joke that one day he was going to write a book about The Bridge.

"I think you'll have to tone it down or no one will believe it," I said.

He laughed. "To tell you the truth, I'm not that good a writer. I don't know if anyone is. How do you put into words how great these people are, but still capture the raw insanity we see every day? These people would do anything for each other."

I looked around the room. "Well, I think you just named your book."

"What?" he asked.

With a smile, I said, "'Raw Insanity'. It's perfect."

Milly started to laugh. "I like that. It's a start."

Two weeks before Christmas, golf at the casino shut down. With no matches to play, Ben suggested we head over to Cactus Ridge to play together. We played there each day that week. I started to feel like I was a millionaire with the treatment we received. Ben was somewhat of a celebrity there. People would stop him to say hello. The staff loved and fawned over him as if he was the owner. When I asked why he was so popular, he shrugged and mentioned something about years of big tips and a few late nights drinking.

The week was memorable for me because of the time I spent with him. Our conversations were more than about golf. Like my time spent sitting with him behind his apartment, he shared stories about his life growing up. He was also very curious about me, life back East, and the things I experienced growing up. I still felt he was not sharing everything, but I hung on to his every word. Like his golf, it seemed Ben was never willing to give you everything. He was always holding back. But what he gave me was good enough.

As for golf, Ben worked with me that week on my shot preparation. Like with Coach Tipton in college, Ben worked on my mind. I cannot recall him saying anything about my swing. It was all about my thought process. Before this week, I would see the shot I wanted to hit, and then step up and hit it. He took me through how he approached each shot.

It was the first day we were playing that week. It was late in the afternoon and the course was empty. The only sound was Christmas music coming from a party on the clubhouse patio behind us. We were playing for twenty dollars a side, but by now

I was well-versed in how to leverage my situation by making side bets. It seemed every hole we were throwing out two or three additional wagers. On the tenth hole, he had a long iron into the green. I focused on his face as he looked at the shot, took a loose practice swing, and then stepped up.

"Hold on," I said. "You keep talking about prep. Go through that routine again, but talk it out so I know exactly what you're thinking."

He nodded and stepped back behind the ball.

"First, I review the situation," he said. "New nine, so I can be aggressive. You're a few bucks up on me but there are a lot of holes left so I can try and hit a hero shot." He looked up at the fairway and the green in front of him. "Two-fifteen to the front. Another fifteen to the hole. Bunker right and the ground falls off into the desert, so I cannot short this ball. My miss is left. And that mound on the front right means I need to fly this at least two-twenty to land and stay tight to the hole."

He started to take a few loose swings. "Second, the lie. This lie is good and slightly down grain. I need to play this ball an inch forward to get the height because I need to hit this with my three-iron to get that clearance. That means a fade which fits perfectly for this shot. Third, conditions. The wind is nothing, and with the temperature what it is, I have enough club. I know my miss is left, but I also know I need to avoid coming over the top. I did that on the sixth hole and if I do that again, I end up in the left bunker and lose my leverage. And last, tempo. I want to put a charge into this one, so I can give it a nice full swing. Oh, and I also know I need to hit this shot quickly."

"Because you don't want the breeze to come up?" I asked.

"Nope, because over there at the party they are on the last few verses of 'Here Comes Santa Claus' and I don't want to be pulling the club back when the song ends and they start clapping and cheering."

I looked over at the patio and the hundred or so people that were drinking and dancing. "Yea, I can see that. So, go ahead and hit. Ten bucks you end up more than twenty-five feet."

Ben laughed. "You won the first nine and you're pushing your advantage. Nice."

He then stepped up and without hesitation hit a high fade that cleared the mound on the front of the green and kicked left before rolling at the hole and stopping what looked like ten feet away. He smiled and rubbed his fingers together. "I just halved your winnings. But I like the bet. You were right to make it."

The entire week was a learning experience for me. By the time we finished our round Friday, I approached each shot the way he taught me: situation, lie, conditions, club, line, good and bad misses, tempo, deep breath, and hit the ball. I took that with me for the rest of my career.

The week before Christmas, I did meet Melissa's parents. Her mom made us a phenomenal dinner. Her dad was indeed a big guy and a little intimidating. I was nervous as I sat alone with him on their back porch after dinner with a view of the Vegas lights in the distance. After small talk about golf, politics, and jobs, he asked me about my intentions with Melissa. I fumbled through my answer to the point that he laughed and told me to relax. I tried, but then he sat up and leaned over to me. His laugh stopped and he got serious.

"Just don't forget why you're nervous answering me," he said. "It's because you know how special she is to me." He pointed in the direction of the city. "I have a lot of friends in that town over there. Remember, I'm Melissa's number one protector and I won't hand over that role easily. I'll never fully step aside, and neither will they."

Suddenly, her dad looked a lot bigger than I already thought he was. My heart stopped and I felt the food in my stomach start to look for a way back out. With a dry throat, I croaked out that

I understood. After another moment of him staring at me, and sweat falling off my forehead, he started to laugh.

"That was a pretty good line, wasn't it?" he said.

I was still trying to breathe when he reached over and slapped my forearm. "I'm kidding you. That's a line from an old movie. I've always wanted to use it on the man that my daughter fell for."

I eventually laughed with him, but no doubt he scared the crap out of me. When I later told Melissa what he said to me, I expected her to show some support. Instead, she mentioned that he uses that line on all of the men she brings home.

Two days before Christmas, Melissa and I flew back east. She and my mom got along great. Melissa was able to enjoy her first Christmas with snow, and I was able to introduce her to some of my friends from home. When we walked around the neighborhood on Christmas night looking at the holiday lights and decorations she told me she liked snow, but could never live with it.

"When we settle down, I think Texas is perfect," she said. "You get to play golf, I get to open my own business, and we get three seasons instead of four."

"You've done a lot of thinking," I said. "I'm still trying to figure out if your dad was serious or not about me protecting you. I keep wondering what kinds of friends he has in Vegas."

She laughed and grabbed my arm. "I'm just like my dad in two ways. I'm always thinking ahead and you'll never know if I'm joking or serious."

"Great," I said. "Thanks for the support. Next, you'll tell me he really does have a lot of friends in Vegas."

"Well," she said, "he is a pretty popular guy."

Typical Melissa. Her sense of humor was always something I

loved about her.

The only time I left Melissa alone that week was when I drove over to Water Edge to see Mr. Wittich. I found him in the back of the Pro Shop boxing up golf sweaters. He threw one at me and told me it was my Christmas present. I then handed over my present to him. It was a scorecard from one of my rounds with Ben at Cactus Ridge. I knew this present would be more special than any other I could give him.

He looked at the front of the scorecard. "Cactus Ridge, huh?" he asked, putting on his glasses. "What's the rating?"

"Around seventy-three," I responded. "It's a good layout."

Looking inside, he analyzed my round the same way he always did; like a CPA. He taught me long ago that you recorded more than your score when playing. Besides how many strokes, I learned to write down the info on each corner of the area on the card for a hole that would help recap how it was played. An X or O in the top left corner signified a fairway hit or missed. A square around that mark means a green-in-regulation. The number of putts goes in the top right corner. The bottom left is the club hit to a green and after a slash, the approximate distance from the hole the shot ended up. And in the bottom right, a check indicated if the hole was played the way you wanted. It was a complex system that became second nature after a short while.

Mr. Wittich looked over the round and then up at me. "Sixteen checks? You played that well?"

I smiled and said that was not the most important thing. "I walked the entire eighteen."

He looked up at me. "And?"

"No pain, just a little tightness the next day."

Not once did he look at the score. His reasoning for marking the card was that the score was immaterial in the long run. Ball striking, consistency, and putting were what mattered. That and the ability to perform at any time. In that regard, Mr. Wittich and Ben were very similar.

"So, who is Ben Newell?" he asked, looking up from the card.

I hesitated for a second and then realized it was an innocent question. I had written Ben's name on the card before we started to play that day. "He's one of the guys that I play with a lot. Both at my job and in my spare time."

"Is he a good player?" he asked me.

My first reaction was to take his mention of 'player' and use it the way Ben and the rest of the desert golfers used it. "Well, he is more than good," I said. "He's excellent. I'm learning a lot from him."

"Such as?"

I knew I would not get off easy so I went into detail about the pre-shot routine Ben talked to me about. As I went into details, Mr. Wittich started to nod. When I finished, he said, "I like that, use it all the time."

He then turned around and walked over to a shelf full of clothes and started to rearrange them. Over his shoulder, he said, "So, I understand that Ben Newell is a big-money player at Desert Bridge, correct?"

I took a quick breath and stared at his back. That information was not written on the scorecard.

After another moment of silence, he turned to me. The look on his face said everything I needed to know about what I was about to hear. When Mr. Wittich was serious and about to give one of his lectures, his face turned to stone. I saw that look now and stood back waiting for him to continue. One thing I realized long ago in my relationship with him; his lectures may be stern but his words were fair and true.

"When you stopped in over Thanksgiving, I believe I mentioned I would make a call or two. I did that, I heard some potentially dangerous information from two of my friends that live in Las Vegas. Would you like me to share that information?"

Talk about a rhetorical question. I kept my mouth shut and waited.

His eyes bore through mine. He then nodded. "Mark, I have no problem with what you are doing out there. I know you have that head of yours screwed on right to the end of the threads. But you need to follow one rule. And one rule only. Do you hear me?"

I nodded and fought to find any moisture in my mouth and throat.

"Never play for more than you have. And I don't mean what's in your bank account. I mean never play with money you need to eat, live on, and hold for a rainy day. You remember that when you set the stakes."

I was expecting him to say I should never play for money again. Or maybe to leave The Bridge and never go back. Instead, he seemed to speak from experience.

"Don't play for money. Play for the experience," he said. "Don't let your feelings about the result be driven by ego. You do that and you become a mark for experienced gamblers. You're out there to gain experience, not to make money or show you're a better or tougher person than the opponent. If you only play for money you can afford to lose, you'll never be in a position to lose sight of the real goal."

I took his words seriously. The way Mr. Wittich looked you in the eye when he was talking forced you to take everything he said seriously. But I needed to know one thing. After he gave me a silent few seconds of staring, I nodded. "Thanks, I get it. And I always remember why I'm there, and so do the people I'm playing with. But, sir, you seem to know what you're talking about here."

He took a few steps and stood right next to me. With a smile, he said, "Is there a question coming?"

He may be a former Marine and a hardass, but he was also a friend. I knew I could ask him anything.

"Yea," I said. "Were you ever a money player?"

Again he smiled. Stepping away from me, he said, "Mark, I spent more than a few days on the course with some money on the line. In fact, after the war, I still had three years to go. I made the mistake of taking some money off of an Army Colonel who felt the loss to a Marine more on his ego than his wallet. I had him and every other golfer on that base wanting to take me to the cleaners. They very rarely did."

That was the most personal info Mr. Wittich ever shared with me. I tried to get from him how he found out about Desert Bridge but he would not budge. As I walked out of the Pro Shop, he laughed and over his shoulder, said, "By the way, Vlad fits you."

I kept walking knowing it was no use trying to find out how he knew about that. One thing was certain, Mr. Wittich had a wide reach when it came to finding out information about the world of golf.

From that point forward I had this evil, somewhat twisted idea that I would be able to put together the dream foursome of me, Mr. Wittich, Gonzo, and Clip. It would be a skins match, and on the first hole, all of us except Mr. Wittich would be in the desert with our approaches. How would my Marine swing coach react to the onslaught from the two Bridge veterans? It would be quite an interesting thing to watch.

In January, Ben and I had a few monumental matches against each other. I wanted to see his best golf, but I don't think I ever did. He would beat me, and I would beat him. But I never could shake the feeling that he was mentoring me, not playing me. I also had to rescue him from Rosy's a few times. He was never over-the-top drunk, but well on his way.

On the first Saturday night in February, I was sitting in the apartment complex's open bar by the pool with Melissa, Kenny, and his girlfriend, Kara. I was enjoying my first winter in the desert where the temperature during the day got into the low seventies, while back home there was a foot of snow on the ground. Kara was an accountant from The Olympia who had a great smile, a better laugh, and a lot of insight into my boss, Kirk Bellows. We shared a few bottles of wine and talked about the golf program. They were all interested in my stories about the different guests, and they loved to hear stories about the people at the Bridge. Melissa and Kenny were able to back up my Bridge stories to Kara, so she could not accuse me of making things up. Kenny had fallen in love with all the nicknames, saying that most, like Gonzo and Clip, were perfect Las Vegas gambler names.

When I mentioned that Ben did not want me to share news of my matches at the Bridge with Bellows, Kara started in on what she knew about the Director of Olympia Guest Sporting and Fitness.

"You know," she said, "Kirk Bellows brings in as much money to the casino as some of the most popular games on the casino floor."

"That makes sense," Melissa said, "since he gets the revenue from the high rollers into his budget."

"No," said Kara, "I mean from the horse and dog tracks. He's got blind control of the casino's activities there and the revenue comes in as one number. But I saw the details once. And my boss said that no one in the casino is allowed to touch him. He does what he wants."

Melissa looked surprised. "I never hear him talk about that area."

"Well," Kara said, "it's millions. And the legal fees, which include the work with the Gaming Commission, are high. My boss keeps all that information under lock and key, but he trusts me to help him with the monthly and quarterly reports."

Kenny and I both laughed. "Seeing that you're telling us about it, I'm not sure he should have trusted you," I said.

"I'm not sharing the numbers with you," she said, laughing. "It's just that you and Melissa work for the biggest profit producer in the resort. He has so many CAs that my boss says it's as if Bellows Incorporated exists."

"What's a 'CA'?" Kenny asked.

"Commission Agreement," she explained. "When a casino has a financial relationship with an external organization, the Gaming Commission has to approve it. Bellows has CAs with all the tracks, golf courses, and a bunch of others that are sealed."

"Sounds like he is a connected guy," Kenny said.

"Careful with that word 'connected'," Kara said.

We all looked at her, waiting for more. She looked back at us, nervously smiled, and took a sip of wine.

"C'mon," I said. "You can't say something like that and not explain it."

"No, I'm getting drunk, and I don't want to be talking about stuff like investigations. Especially organized crime stuff."

"Shit," Kenny said, "you just told us more." He reached over and grabbed one of the open wine bottles. Pouring wine into her cup, he started to smile. "Drink up. The more you drink, the more you tell. And the more I get later."

She reached over and playfully slapped Kenny on the shoulder. While the two of them laughed, both Melissa and I waited for her to continue.

After she and Kenny calmed down, I reached over and grabbed Kara's hand. "Is he involved with the mob?"

Kara got serious and closed her eyes. "Look, I don't know the details. I don't. But the casino has a lot of people that are supposed to be making sure that everything we do is legal."

Melissa sat forward. "And Bellows is part of that," she said. "I control his calendar. I see all of the Commission meetings and training with Legal that he does."

Kara held up her hand. "I'm not blaming him, Melissa. It's just that there have been times that he has to meet with legal authorities about potential conflicts and stuff that involves the federal..." She paused and took a drink. "As I said, I don't know the details. I just see the expenses and the explanations."

"Have you ever heard of the name, Marino?" I asked.

Kara looked at me. "How do you know that name?"

"I heard Bellows and Ben Newell talking about him. Who is Marino?"

"He's somebody that those two should not be talking about. He was involved in organized crime hearings like, ten years ago. He had some interest in the casino but had to sell it. I think he might be dead now, but you're not supposed to talk about people like that."

"I don't think he's dead," I said. "From what I heard, he's alive."

"Can we drop this mob stuff?" Kenny said. "Enough about the casino."

We all agreed that we would not speak about anything relating to the casino for the rest of the night. In the back of my mind though, I was still wondering to myself just what I had gotten myself into out here in the desert.

CHAPTER 11

The money matches at the casino started to pick back up toward the end of February. By March things were back to normal, and when the calendar hit May, we were playing in the heat of the desert. The thermometer finally hit the 100-degree mark the second week of May.

I was healthy and feeling no pain in my hip at all. I was also feeling great about my game. I got a phone call from Mr. Wittich in April to tell me he signed me up to play in a PGA Assistant qualifier. It was one of his reminders about what my focus should be. The qualifier was nothing special but needed if a golfer wanted to start the process of becoming a member of the PGA organization. For me, it meant walking thirty-six holes in a day. By the back nine of the second round, I started to feel tightness in my hip. By the time I putted-out to end the day, my lower back was on fire. I bogied the last three holes, but I finished and even ended up with a top-ten score.

I told Melissa and Kenny in May that I think I was near ready to get back to trying to make the game a career. We looked at the calendar and circled September. That would give me time to move back east, practice, and start the process of becoming a professional. I made the mistake of mentioning how that would mean I would have survived one year in the desert.

I spoke too soon.

Two days later, I played a casino match against who I can best describe as a prototypical high-roller. The man had brand new everything from clothes to equipment. He was a nice person, but could not stop talking about himself and his successes in business and love. The agent from the casino told me beforehand that the casino wanted this guy to win, but that he would probably shoot well over one hundred and ten. Since that would mean I would have to give him nearly three shots a hole, and that could prove to be embarrassing for him, I had to play badly. I would be giving only two strokes a hole which meant I had to shoot somewhere around eighty-five. The challenge was doing this while somehow staying within the rules as defined by the gaming commission that I was playing as well as I could.

To prove his point that it would be beneficial to the casino for me to lose, the agent shared that our match was for $5000, the largest casino money match I played. This man regularly ran up a gambling debt and liquor bills of $25,000 in a night. The thousands we wanted him to win on the course was considered a down payment on what would be a big bill later in the night.

I stood on the tee wondering how I would do this without making it obvious I was blowing the match. Ben, who was playing in a match behind me, told me on the first tee as we were waiting to start, to aim for the bad places. I wasn't sure what he was talking about until I got out on the course. By the third hole, I was hitting some of the best shots in weeks, and all landed in either a bunker, a stream, or right on line with the flagstick, but short of the green. I had my guest telling me that I was the unluckiest player he had seen in years.

On the seventeenth hole, our match was tied. On the short par-4, I used my driver in an attempt to drive the green. At least that is what I wanted him to think. I aimed at a small mound short and left of the green. If I could hit the side of the mound, my drive would kick hard left and, hopefully, run out of bounds. It may have been the best drive I hit during my time in Vegas. The ball did just what I wanted, and as I watched it roll into someone's backyard, and out of bounds, I felt as if I had just hit it stiff to the hole.

That night, I got a call in my apartment from none other than Kirk Bellows to tell me what a great job I had done. He informed me that the guest was on the casino floor, telling everyone that would listen about his great golfing victory. While praising the 'mature, great young golfer' that he had beaten, he opened a $35,000 line of credit. Bellows told me he was going to pay for airplane tickets for anywhere I wanted to go because I deserved it and the casino owed me.

I sat back in one of the apartment's La-Z-Boy recliners that Kenny and I bought for ourselves, and said out loud, "What a great night."

I could not have been more wrong.

Later, around 10:00 PM, I hung up the phone after what was becoming my weekly Sunday night call from my mom. I stopped trying to figure out why she was up so late telling me all the things she had going on and finding out the details of my life, especially Melissa. I laughed to myself, turned the television off, and headed into my bedroom. I had a 9:00 AM match in the morning and wanted to get some sleep.

As I sat on my bed, the phone rang. I thought it was my mom. Picking up, I said, "Mom, you know these calls cost money, right?"

"I ain't your Mom, asshole. It's Rudy," said a gruff voice.

"Okay," I said. "Who are you?"

"I'm Rudy, asshole."

"Okay, Rudy," I said. "Are you from the Bridge?"

"The strip place?" he asked. "You mean the Golden Gate Bridge Club? That place closed ten years ago."

I shook my head. "What are you talking about? Who are you?"

"I'm Rudy, from Rosy's. Come and get Newell."

The phone call ended with a click and I threw the phone back down on the cradle. For the past few months, Ben had been doing well with his drinking. The last thing I wanted to do was start having to deal with drunk Ben again.

When I pulled up in front of the bar, only a few cars were in the lot. I parked under the torn and dilapidated awning over the entrance. Stepping inside, there were a handful of people sitting around the room. I walked up to the bar and asked for Rudy.

"That's me, bud," the bartender said. "You the guy whose mom keeps calling too much."

I smiled and nodded.

"He already left," Rudy said. "After I called you, three guys picked him up."

"Three guys?"

"Yeah, he seemed to know them. He wasn't super drunk like some of the other times we called you, but we thought he might be heading that way. I thought if I called you early, he wouldn't get so shit-faced that he'd puke on my floor. But his buddies took him."

I walked back out to my car feeling I had dodged a bullet and would get some sleep. I got back into the car and started to drive to the exit. As I was cutting across the lot, I saw something on the ground. I stopped and looked out the window. It was a wallet. When I stepped outside and picked it up, I saw it was Ben's.

"I knew it was too good to be true," I said as I sat back in my car. "I am in no mood to see him."

I drove over to Ben's. It was now after 11:00 PM and I was pissed that my plan for a long night's sleep was gone. I talked myself out of being mad at Ben, mostly because I didn't want to make a scene in front of his friends. For all I knew he was picked up by some of The Bridge people. As I pulled into his condo complex, I thought that maybe he was still drinking every night, but was calling The Bridge instead of me for rides home.

I parked on the side of his condo building and jumped out of the car with the idea that I would leave his wallet in his mailbox. This way I could get it to him without the confrontation. When I walked around the back of his condo to the wall of mailboxes, I found the slot too narrow.

I then thought maybe I would leave it on the table that was on the small patio off the side of his place. I quietly walked around the back corner of the condo. The last thing I wanted was for one of Ben's neighbors to think someone was trying to break into their place. As I turned the corner I came to Ben's sliding side doors. There were privacy walls on either side of the cement patio. I walked up to the wall nearest to me and stopped to listen to make sure there was no one on the patio.

"You're not doing yourself any favors, Ben. I want to try and help you."

The voice was coming from inside Ben's condo, not the patio. As I peered around the corner, I could see into his place. The double glass patio door was partly open with the sliding screen door closed. Sitting near a dining table was Ben, surrounded by several boxes haphazardly lying on the ground, and what appeared to be folded laundry lying on the tabletop.

Three men stood over him. One of the men was leaning on the table. He was in a suit and tie. The other two were standing on either side of Ben. Both of the men were huge and wearing the same style of black turtleneck shirts and black pants.

I took a look around me to see if I could be seen by any of the neighbors. I was in a safe spot from being discovered, concealed by some bushes, and in the dark. Looking back into Ben's condo, I felt sure they would not see me since I was in the dark looking into a well-lit room.

There was a reason I was being so careful about not being seen by the three men inside. It was the look on Ben's face. He was scared.

The man leaning on the table reached out and brushed something off of Ben's shoulder. "We're not asking for much, Ben. Mr. Marino is not asking for much. At least I don't think he is, do you?"

Ben lowered his head. "Spano, I don't know what you want from me."

Spano, the man in front of Ben, used his hand to lift Ben's head. "It's not what I want, Ben, it's what Mr. Marino wants. And he needs you on this. You know how much he's done to help you, and how much he supports you. Well, this is something you need to do to pay him back."

"And if I lose?" Ben asked.

Spano smiled. "You won't lose. C'mon, you love this stuff. There's nothing more exciting for a gambling man like you than to play for more than the money."

"I don't know," Ben said.

Spano leaned back. He looked up at the man to his left. "Hey, Anthony, did you hear me ask Ben a question?"

"No, sir, I did not," said Anthony.

Spano looked up at the other man. "How about you, James? Did you hear me ask Ben a question?"

"No, boss, there was no question," James said.

Ben exhaled loudly. "Can we stop playing games?"

Spano reached out and started to pat Ben on the head. He then leaned in and grabbed a handful of hair, and forcibly pulled upwards. Staring into Ben's eyes, he shook his head back and forth. "Games? Do you think I'm playing games? You think you can pull that shit on me by staring with those deep baby blue eyes of yours?"

Ben tried to move back from Spano's grasp but Spano yanked upwards. "Don't you pull away from me. Do you think I want to be here? I'm not asking, cause Mr. Marino is not asking. He is telling. You will get your ass to Phoenix, and you will win. If you don't, then don't worry about coming back."

The two men stared intently at each other for five seconds. Finally, Spano pushed Ben's head away.

"Jeez, Spano," Ben said, "I thought you said you wanted to try and help me."

"Oh, don't worry about that. I already did help."

Ben reached up and patted down his hair which was pulled straight up from Spano's grip. He shook his head. "And what did you do for me?"

"James, do me a favor and get me a beer from Ben's refrigerator. And get one for yourself and Anthony."

"Sure, boss," James said. He walked back into the kitchen.

Spano waited, staring at Ben the entire time he waited for James. The silence was uncomfortable. I kept myself behind the patio's wall and looked at Ben. He seemed to have relaxed. I didn't see the same fear in his eyes that I sensed when I first saw him surrounded by the three men. Ben stared back at Spano, wiping his eyes which were tearing up from having his hair pulled so violently. When James returned, he handed a glass of beer to Spano, and then to Anthony. The three men then took their time, drinking their beer.

After finishing his beer and placing the glass on the table behind him, Spano said, "Do you know that you're still alive because you made Mr. Marino a lot of money? And you still do. But he's running out of patience with you. With your drinking and gambling, you're a risk. Do you know Mr. Marino likes me? Isn't that true, Anthony?"

"Yes, sir," Anthony said. "He likes you a lot."

"He does," Spano said. "And do you know what I tell Mr. Marino after I see you, Ben? I tell him what a disrespectful little shit you usually are. Like this time. Who the hell are you to speak to me like that? You have the balls to ask what I did for you? Do you know what I did for you, asshole? I saved your worthless life."

Ben was looking up at Spano. "What the hell did you tell Marino?"

"Mr. Marino," James said.

Ben looked at James and then back to Spano. "What did you tell, *Mr.* Marino?"

Spano laughed. "I gave Mr. Marino a way to control you. Just like I gave him a way to control Miner."

Ben looked confused. "What the hell does Miner have to do with this?"

"Ben," Spano said, "You don't have a clue. Mr. Marino Senior was owed a lot of money by your old mentor. And like you, Miner was making money for the family in other ways. We needed to keep him working hard. You see, you golfers can only make money if you have all your fingers. We can't break them to keep you in line. But Miner was an old emotional pussy. He liked you the minute he met you. And that gave us the leverage over him we needed. Even when he was over in Europe and not playing golf."

"You mean..," Ben started to say.

"Yeah, we told Miner we'd kill you if he ever screwed around or stopped doing what we wanted. And Mr. Marino liked that idea. He liked that Miner was playing for more than just the threat of me, and maybe my boys here, breaking his head open. The only thing that saved your ass is you became a better earner than that dumbshit."

"A lot of good it did. So how does that relate to me now?" Ben asked.

"C'mon, Ben, why the hell do you think we paired you with that new kid from back East? You are one dumb fricking Mick, aren't you."

"I don't..," Ben said. He tried to stand up but Anthony reached over and pushed him hard back into his seat.

"Listen," Spano said, getting up and taking a few steps away from the table, "I gotta get out of here. I got a date with the foxiest-looking dancer from over at The Strip that you've ever seen. Let me put this as plainly as I can so even your alcohol-damaged brain can understand. If you don't stop pulling crap and telling Mr. Marino that you won't do what he asks, I'll be paying a visit to your friend. What's his name, James? Is it Rick?"

"His name is Mark, sir. And he lives over at the Tall Cactus Apartments," James said.

My heart stopped when I heard my name and the fact that these guys knew where I lived.

"Right, his name is Mark," Spano said. "And doesn't his pretty little girl live there too? She's the one that works for Bellows."

When I heard them mention Melissa, I thought all the blood ran out of my head. I had to lean into the porch wall to hold myself up. My legs went to jelly.

"You wouldn't touch that kid or his girl," Ben said.

Spano started to laugh. "You're right, I wouldn't."

Ben shook his head. He started to say something but stopped. He muttered, "None of you. None of you will touch him."

"Is that a threat?" Spano said, still laughing. He looked at James who also moved away from the table. "James, would you or any of our guys touch that boy?"

"No, sir," said James. "We won't touch him."

Ben stood up. "Good." He took a step away from the chair. "That kid isn't any part of any of this."

"Go ahead and finish what you were saying," Spano said to James.

"Yes, boss," James said. "We wouldn't touch him, we'd shoot him in the back of the head. He's young, so we'd make it quick. But my hands would never touch him."

Ben turned and looked at James. He stood there with his mouth open.

"So, you see," Spano said, "that's how I saved your worthless life. I convinced Mr. Marino that you'd keep playing and winning cause you don't want to see your kid get hurt. So, instead of breaking your dumb skull open, Mr. Marino agreed we'd have the kid."

Ben started to say something but Spano put his hand up. "Let's go, I'm done talking."

Anthony took a few steps toward Spano. He stopped in front of Ben and with a quick thrust of his right hand, he punched Ben in the stomach. Ben folded over and fell to the floor, coughing.

The three men walked away from the table and out of my sight. I heard the front door open. "Good night," Spano said. "Ben, don't let us down in Phoenix."

I stepped back into the darkness and crouched behind a small bush waiting to be sure the three men were gone. After three minutes, I walked onto Ben's porch and up to the sliding doors. Ben was sitting at his dining table, bent over with his hands on his head. Looking around, I didn't see anyone else but Ben. I started to slowly open the door, but when it stuck, I forced it open.

Ben jumped out of his chair and spun to face me at the door. It took him a second, but when he saw it was me, he took a slow, deep breath.

"What's wrong, you think I'm one of them?" I said.

"One of who?" Ben asked. "I'm alone."

"Alone?" I asked. "I hope so because if those guys are still here it sounds like they want to kill me. I believe they said, I think it was James who said it, they wouldn't touch me, just shoot me in the back of the head."

Whatever color was in Ben's face drained out. "Where were you? Why are you here at all?"

I took his wallet out of my pocket and flipped it in his direction. "You left this in the parking lot at Rosy's. My new friend, Rudy, called. I guess I can call him a friend because he didn't threaten to kill me. He called me to get your drunk ass out of the bar, but it seems that Spano, James, and Anthony got to you first."

"Jeez, kid…"

"Don't 'kid' me, Ben," I interrupted him. "What the hell are those guys talking about? Who..? Who are they, and why, again, did I hear the name, Marino? The guy is a mobster, right?"

He was quiet so I stepped in front of him. He looked up at me and shook his head.

"That's all you can do is shake your head? A mobster is threatening to kill me, and he knows about Melissa? I feel like I should be packing and getting my ass out of Vegas. Should I? Should I be taking Melissa?"

Ben stood up and when I looked into his eyes I saw fear. This was not the fear I saw when I first saw him through the patio doors as he was surrounded by three thugs. I was looking at a more empathetic fear. He was afraid for me. His deep blue eyes looked into mine, but then he looked down and started to breathe quickly. Whether it was from his drinking or the fact that he just took a punch in the gut, he was starting to fade from me.

"Ben," I asked, putting my hands on his shoulder, "am I in danger?" I shook him hard, and he seemed to come back to reality. "Ben, should I be leaving?"

"No, no, kid, no. Nothing's gonna happen to you." He wiped his eyes and walked over to the sink in his kitchen. Filling a cup with water, he drank it all down in a couple of gulps.

"Ben, these guys just threatened me."

"Kid, I mean Mark, don't listen to that crap. They're trying to scare me. They want me to do something, and I don't want to do it. It has nothing to do with you."

"So how do they know where I live?" I asked. "And how do they know about Melissa?"

Ben nodded and lowered his head. After he took a few deep breaths, he looked up at me. "I'm not sure, but I have a good idea. Bellows."

That made no sense to me. "Why would Bellows be telling those guys about me and Melissa?"

Ben shrugged. "Listen, they're not good guys. If you think you should leave, then, by all means, get out of the Valley and don't ever look back. But, they're just blowing smoke and trying to get me to do something that I don't like. But, I'm gonna do it. I was always gonna do it. So they'll be happy and they'll…" He stopped talking and took a few deep breaths. Looking me in the eye he said, "I swear, you're safe. And so is Melissa. You're both safe."

There was something I saw when I first met him that day when he puked his guts up that I never thought about. I was only twenty-something, and I had little to no experience in judging the honesty of a person. But to me, even when he was struggling with his drinking, Ben was an honest guy. He was an honest guy that had a lot of problems. In the back of my head, even when he was drunk or in the middle of a group at the Bridge, or telling me my life was not in danger, I thought he was a good guy.

"Ben, I like you, you're a great player, and someone I could look up to. But I can't be pulling your ass out of bars, and now watching you get your ass kicked by guys that want to kill me."

"They don't want to kill you. I'm sorry they brought you into this. And I'm sorry that Bellows made you babysit me. I know what I am. But I want you to stay. You're a good guy, and you're a hell of a player. I told you when we met, if you want to make a living in this game, you need to be a player. Whether it's here in the Valley, or on Tour, being a player here in the desert will help you."

I looked at Ben and then down at the ground. I took a few breaths thinking of what had happened over the past thirty minutes. Shaking my head, I said, "No more calls in the middle of the night."

He knew I was serious.

Ben stuck his hand out to me. "Mark, you're a friend. One of my best friends. I won't ever forget that. No more calls in the middle of the night. I swear it."

I stepped up to him and shook his hand. Walking over to the dining table I sat down on one of the chairs. "What does this guy, Marino, want you to do?"

Ben also sat down. "He wants me to go down to Phoenix and play a match."

I was confused. "Why is that an issue? You always want to play."

"This is a little different. He wants me to bring back a big bank. I mean, a really big bank."

"So what? Seems like that's right up your alley."

"Yeah, it is. I just had to play a little game with him when he asked." He sat back and looked at me. "You want to come? I could use the company, and I'll fill you in on everything. Seeing that Bellows and his friends are throwing your name around, I think you deserve to know what is going on. Plus, he'll love the fact that I'm taking you with me in case I go on a bender."

I looked at him for a few seconds. "Are you planning on going on a bender?" I asked.

"No," he said, "I'm serious. No more of that. I was only making an argument."

"Okay," I nodded. "When?"

"We're leaving at ten in the morning, the day after tomorrow. We'll fly down and stay at a great place in Scottsdale. The match is first thing Wednesday. And if you go, you tell absolutely no one, including Melissa. Okay?"

"Sure, no problem," I said.

"Good. I'm glad to have the company on this one. We'll be back here by Wednesday night."

"Unless you lose," I said.

Ben shook his head. "What do you mean?"

"Your mob buddies told you not to come back if you lose."

He smiled and said, "Yeah, well, have you ever known me to lose?"

"Yes," I nodded, "I've beaten you."

Now he started to laugh. "Kid, you can play. And you've beaten me when I wanted to win. But you've never beaten me when I have to win. No one has."

CHAPTER 12

Two days later, Ben and I were sitting on the patio overlooking the Scottsdale Desert Golf Resort. Everything was first class from the food to the tables to the service. This trip was the first time that I experienced anything first class. It was something I could get used to. We sat in first class on the flight down and had breakfast that was better than most meals I could ever remember eating. We were picked up by a limo at the airport and ferried to this resort which can best be described as an oasis in the desert. Now we were drinking cognac while sitting in lounge chairs overlooking the beautiful Desert course of the resort.

"This job does have its perks," Ben said.

"Bellows is paying for all of this?" I asked.

"Technically, no," he said, sipping his drink. I thought to myself that I had never seen Ben sip anything before. "This match is not for the casino. That's why we need to keep it quiet."

"But, Bellows knows about it. He knows I'm here with you, right?"

Ben sat for a moment. I could see that he was running something through his head. "Quite a sunset, huh?" he asked.

I shifted on my lounge chair and faced him. "I don't care about the sunset. Bellows knows, right?"

Ben sat up. After another moment, he looked at me and nodded. "Yeah, kid, he knows. He knows. And it's only fair that you know."

Ben hailed the server. "You want another one of those?" he asked me.

I shook my head, no.

When the server walked over to us, Ben ordered two glasses of water and a six-pack of Pabst Blue Ribbon. My first reaction was that a place like this would never have the world's cheapest beer, even if it was Ben's favorite. The server, though, nodded and walked away.

"Listen, I need to do something later, and I can't do it without a few beers. I never said I wasn't going to have a beer or two, just that I wouldn't call you to peel me off the floor."

"Ben, I don't care if you drink a few beers. I'm not your judge."

"Good," he said, leaning back. He was quiet for a few seconds. "Mark, Bellows is nothing more than a lowlife bully. I think you know that. You, on the other hand, are top-notch. You deserve to know."

The server came over and set two glasses of water on the small table between our chairs. He placed a paper bag down on the ground. "Your beer, sir."

Ben nodded to him. When he walked away, he picked up the water and drank the entire glass.

"Thirsty?" I asked with a laugh.

"Kerry Miner," Ben said.

"Who?"

"Mark, promise me that when I leave the Valley, you'll get out of Vegas and go home. If you find out I'm gone, or if I disappear, you get out. Take Melissa with you. Ask her to get married and leave."

"What the hell are you talking about, Ben? Where are you going?"

He was starting to breathe heavier. Now that it was starting to get dark, the air was cooling. After a temperature of ninety-five degrees when we arrived, it was now a comfortable seventy-five with a slight breeze. But I could see the sweat on Ben's face.

"Kerry Miner. He was, well... He was my mentor. When I got out of school, I met Kerry. It was 1968. He was a legend. He knew everyone and could make friends anywhere. He was the type of guy that could screw the widow at her husband's funeral. As for golf, he was the best player, well, maybe ever. He was in his forties and had a swing that looked like he was still in college. He was the best I ever saw. I heard the story that when he was twenty or so he challenged Hogan to a match out in LA. Hogan was playing a practice round at Riviera. Hogan's Alley. Kerry made it into the tournament and asked the great man to play for fifty bucks on the Tuesday before the tournament. The story was Hogan beat him on the eighteenth hole with a long putt. The truth was Kerry beat him on the fifteenth hole. Because he respected Hogan so much, he never told anyone how badly he beat the man.

"I met Kerry in Vegas, at The Bridge. You think the place is a dump now, it was worse then. He took me in. I lived with him, played with him a lot, and learned everything I know about being a player from him. From Kerry Miner. The Legend. He always said that you need to do two things if you want to be successful in life. The first was to live with passion. The second was to always maintain control."

Ben reached down to the paper bag and opened it. Pulling out a can of Blue Ribbon, he started to open it but held off. "I guess the greatest lesson he taught me was to never believe what you see or hear from others. If you want to know the truth, you have to experience it for yourself. You have to live it."

He lifted the beer can to his cheek and held it there as if he were hugging it. He closed his eyes and for a moment, I thought he was going to break down and cry. I felt his emotion.

After a few moments of silence, he lowered the beer can and looked at me. With a serious and honest face, he said, "Mark, I know I trust you more than you trust me. But if you share this info with the wrong people, I'm dead."

When he said that to me, my stomach dropped and my heart jumped up to my mouth. There was no doubt in my mind that Ben was completely serious and truthful.

"Never," I said. "I would never share anything you tell me not to."

Ben smiled and opened up his beer. "I remember saying the same thing to him." Under his breath, I thought I heard him say something about life being a vicious circle. Shrugging, he said to me, "You want one?"

I nodded and he reached into the bag and handed me a beer. As I opened it, he continued.

"Kerry and I played all the time. The matches we had against each other were the toughest and best golf I've ever played. Together, we got into bigger and bigger games. Most of the casinos were calling us, and Kerry had pretty much every booker in the Valley asking about our schedules. We started to go up against some of the big wallets that flew into the desert. They started to fly in just to play us. Big-money players, international, PGA players, we even played against a former President out in Palm Springs. But as much as Kerry spoke about control, he lost it in 1971. He got wrapped up with the wrong people. That's when he met Mr. Marino. Aldo Marino Senior was as dirty a mob guy that was in Vegas. Marino asked Kerry to do some business with him, mostly to play golf for him. The upfront money was too good for Kerry to say no. I already knew Marino's son, Aldo Junior. We lived in the same dorm for a semester until he got kicked out of school. One of the biggest pricks on the face of the Earth. I hate that asshole.

"In '73, Kerry lost a lot of money at the track. That's when he lost control. He screwed up that first mistake by asking Marino to cover him."

Ben sat shaking his head, looking down at his beer. Again, I thought he was going to break down. He tried to continue a few times but had to stop and slow his breathing. Finally, after a deep, slow breath, he looked back up at me.

"God damn, I told him to find another way. He didn't listen to me. Hell, I was so young. I guess he thought, 'why should I listen to the kid?' Once Marino got his fangs into him, he never let go. I started seeing him less and less because Marino had him doing a match here, or having him carry money for him there. Kerry became a runner for Marino. I couldn't do anything about it. Finally, one day I was at a bar with some friends, and Kirk Bellows walked in. I knew Kirk from a bartending job we both had years before. Another world-class prick. It just so happens that Marino Junior was in the bar that night. When he sees that I know Bellows, he asks for an introduction. Turns out Bellows was working for the Gaming Commission as an inspector. Marino knew exactly what to say and those two have been partners ever since."

"So, Bellows is not on the up and up?" I asked.

Ben laughed. "Up and up? No. Not even close. Those two guys started a partnership at the track where Bellows was one of the Gaming Commission guys. He was able to feed Marino with info. It was a small-time operation, but it made them money. That's when Kerry stepped in. His debt was getting bigger and bigger. He told Marino Senior that he could get Bellows a job at the Olympia. Kerry was sleeping with the head of hiring there and knew that Bellow's background with the Gaming Commission would sell everyone that he was the guy. Marino agreed. If Bellows got into the Olympia and the two scumbags started to make real money, Marino Senior would forgive Kerry's debt.

"In other words, Marino wouldn't kill him."

"Kill him? Really?" I asked. "How much money did he owe him?"

Ben took a deep breath and let it out. "Probably three hundred large."

I fell back into my chair. "Wow, that's a lot of money. Did Bellows make enough to pay it back for Kerry? I mean, how much money do Bellows and the Marino guy make?"

"A lot. A really high number. No one but those guys knows, but if I had to guess they're clearing about five hundred G's a year each for themselves."

Now I sat forward in my chair. "What? How the hell can they do that? Do they walk out with cash in their pockets? Where do they put it all?"

Ben looked at his watch. "They don't carry it out. It doesn't work like that. But when you consider they have their hands on the track, the casino floor, the counting rooms, the book that is taken. There's a lot of money there. It all goes to Marino and his organization. My guess is after that it ends up in a foreign account."

"The old Swiss bank account?" I said. "I thought that was bull."

"Oh no, trust me. It isn't. Listen, I need to take care of something. I'll see you in the morning. We have to talk before this match. This is no casino guest stuff. This is the real deal. Let's meet for breakfast at seven."

"Sure, but what happened to Miner? I still don't get why these guys are threatening you. Does Miner still owe them even after all these years?"

Ben reached over and grabbed the paper bag with his beer. He stood and turned toward the steps running off of the patio. "Kid, they threatened me because I told them I'm finished playing for them. I've had enough of their bullshit. What you saw happen in my apartment is exactly what I expected to happen. It's what I wanted to happen. But that is nowhere near the front of my mind right now. Golf is. And I have one hell of a tough match in the morning. I'll fill you in on all the other stuff later. For now, enjoy your evening. Sign anything you eat or drink to your room. I'll see you at 7:00 AM."

With that, he walked away leaving me with my beer and just as many questions as when we sat down.

The next morning I sat at a table in one of the resort's restaurants. Ben walked in, grabbed a big plate of food from the buffet, and sat down right next to me, avoiding the other four chairs around the large, round table.

As he shoveled food into his mouth, he started to talk. "Welcome to the real world of big bank, kid. Now listen, the guy I'm playing is a strong player, and he doesn't lose much. It will be me, him, you driving my cart, whoever he has driving him. There will be a guy or two in a cart trailing along behind us."

I tried to get a question in as he continued to eat, but he held up his hand. After he swallowed his mouthful, he continued. "Now, this is important. Unless I ask you a question, you don't say a word on the course. Not one. The last thing I need is this asshole thinking you're giving me info or help. Don't make any faces, don't shrug, don't laugh, don't do anything. This is me and him. So, nothing comes out of your mouth unless I ask."

I nodded wondering exactly what I was about to witness. "Can I ask you something now?"

Ben stuffed more food into his mouth and nodded.

"Who is this guy?"

Ben swallowed, took a long drink of water, and said, "His name is Miguel Monroe. He's from Spain but he's French with an English last name. Don't let his accent fool you, he speaks perfect English. He won a lot over in Europe at the Amateur level. I know he won on Tour over there and would have been a strong pro, but there was more money for him as a player. So, now he's one of the biggest players out there. He's also a great card player. He loves action. I've played him a few times, the last time two years ago."

"Did you beat him?"

Ben shook his head and took a drink of juice. "No, I've never beaten him."

I couldn't hide my surprise. It made no sense to me that the legend sitting across from me would run up against someone that he was unable to beat. "He's that good?" I asked.

"No," Ben said. "He's not long, but steady. Very good ball striker. Solid with the putter. But, he's a hothead. You wouldn't know it from looking at him, but under his calm demeanor, he can get pissed. He has trouble shying away from a confrontation. What he lacks most is an aggressive playing style. He's the kind of player that thinks he can take an early one-up lead and hold it until the end. He reminds me of you on the first day I met you."

"How so?"

"He'll play it safe when he has the advantage. He's got no killer instinct."

I smiled. "Hey, I'm better, right? I've learned."

Ben also smiled. "Yeah, you're better. But I know Monroe hasn't changed."

I had to ask the question. "So why did this guy beat you?"

Ben replied, "Because we weren't playing for enough money. Today though, we are. And I have to find a way to light that guy's fuse."

"How much are you playing for?"

Ben put his fork down and leaned back. "Well, that's the issue. Marino thinks that the money is why I told him I wasn't going to do it."

"Why?" I asked.

"Because we're playing for an open-ended two hundred and fifty G's. Straight match play. But Marino wants me to pull at least another one hundred and fifty over that from the match."

I knew 'open-ended' meant that each player would be able to raise the bet and negotiate with their opponent on odds or amount. Still, that was a big spread from the base amount of two hundred and fifty. I looked at Ben for a few seconds. "I don't get it. Even if you roll this guy, that's only two-fifty. How do you get him to bet the other hundred-fifty?"

Ben smiled and said, "I have an idea, but I'm gonna have to play really well to pull it off. That's another reason I don't want you to say a word. I'm gonna have to get inside his head and play off the fact that he thinks he owns me."

"So you're telling me you lost to him in the past for just this moment?"

Ben didn't say anything, he just gave me a look and a shrug.

"Fine, I'll keep my mouth shut," I said. "One thing I don't get. Whose money is on the line here? Yours?"

"Yes and no," Ben said. "I don't have that much to hang out there. It's all Marino and the guy that's backing Monroe. But if I win it'll help with some old debt."

"So, these guys are banking you and this other guy, for something that they have little to no control over. Sounds like they need to get their asses off the couch and try to win something on their own."

Ben nodded. "Kid, I agree with you. But it's like betting the ponies. Me and this guy are nothing but a couple of mudders. One thing I've learned when dealing with Marino and guys like him, it's less about money, and more about ego, and who can get the best of who. Marino wants Monroe's guy bad. Sure, he'll gladly take his money. But even more than his money, he wants this guy to owe him. It's real macho stuff. The fact that you're owed is more important than the amount."

"So will they be there to watch?" I asked.

"No," Ben responded. "They wouldn't take the risk. The guy they'll have there will update them."

I shrugged, not sure exactly what Ben was talking about. He looked at his watch, stood up, and started to walk out. "Remember, not a word."

I nodded and sat back in my chair. I had been playing and watching golf my entire life. Sitting there, I knew that the great memories I had such as watching Nicklaus and Watson's 'duel in the sun' on TV were about to be pushed back in the pecking order of the great golf events I had seen. I knew as I stood up that Newell vs. Monroe would be at the top.

An hour later, I was sitting in a cart next to the first tee at the resort's championship course. It was a beautiful morning with crisp, cool air and a blue sky. I expected to find other players on the course but saw no one. Whoever set up this match, must have a lot of pull at the resort. Ben and his opponent would have the course to themselves.

Ben walked up to the cart and threw his putter into his bag. He had spent twenty minutes on the putting green, and thirty minutes before that on the range. Taking a towel and wiping his face, he walked over to me. "Okay," he said, "here we go."

I looked around him and saw a cart driving up. Pulling up behind us, the person in the passenger seat jumped out and walked around to the back of his cart. Stepping back into my line of sight, he nodded at Ben. "Mr. Newell," he said with a thick accent, "it has been a while. I hope your game is better than when we last met?"

Ben was taking something out of his bag. He quickly turned

around and, ignoring the question, said, "Mr. Monroe." He immediately turned back to his bag.

As for me, my heart rate was sky-high. I thought I was about to see a gunfight. Monroe was older and shorter than I expected. He reminded me of Gary Player. He was wearing black pants and a white shirt which he filled out with strong arms and shoulders. As he grabbed his driver from his bag, he never looked at or acknowledged me.

I was so struck by the look and attitude of Ben's opponent, that I completely overlooked the driver of Monroe's cart. My counterpart was a woman that looked like she could have been a model. She was blonde, obviously fit, and acknowledged my presence with a glance that shot through me like a cold dagger. I thought that if this match turned into a fight, she would kick my ass, break my neck, and spit on my dead body. I looked away from her and avoided her gaze for the rest of the match.

Both players walked up to the tee. From out of nowhere, and I mean nowhere, an older gentleman walked in between the two carts and up to the tee. He was overweight and wearing shorts that were way too tight. With no effort to hide it, I could see he was carrying a gun in an ankle holster underneath one of his pure white tube socks that were pulled up to his knees.

"You guys listen to what I say about this match. I represent both sides on how this happens. Got it?" he said after he reached the tee box.

Neither player said anything. They just nodded.

"You got anything to say about the stakes, you call me up. You have any issues with the game, you work it out. If you need me, you wave. My decision is final."

Again, neither player said anything. The man looked at both of them for a few seconds, then turned and walked back off the tee. He walked right by me without looking up. He was breathing so heavily that I thought he might have to stop and rest. But he walked by me and down a small hill. A cart was waiting for him and he slumped into it. I took a quick look at the driver and thought he could be the man's son. He was huge, with no neck and perfectly slicked-back hair. Both of them were the perfect stereotype for the mob. In my head, I nicknamed them, 'the mob guys' for the rest of the day. The older one was 'Pops', and the younger one was, 'Junior'.

I sat back and watched Ben toss a tee in the air. Even the big-money matches started like two guys would start a Sunday match for a few bucks.

The tee landed pointing at Monroe. He stepped past Ben without as much as a glance and up to the tee marker on the right side. Teeing his ball up just a few inches from the blue marker, he stepped back and took a few long practice swings. He then stood behind the ball and closed his eyes. Taking four deep breaths, he rolled his head back and forth. He then held up his club in front of his eyes and lined up his shot down the fairway. After another deep breath, he stepped back to the ball. With a quick twitch of his right leg, he pulled back into a long and slow backswing. At the top, he paused for what seemed like a full second before driving through with his legs and hips. His shoulder turn was impressive, and the club swept through the ball with an ease that told me he would not be missing many fairways. His drive was a low fade that hugged the left side of the fairway before running out into the middle. I was impressed.

As Ben moved up to the tee, I took a look down the fairway at the hole. I was so caught up with the show happening on the tee, I never looked at the course. The resort's Desert Championship Course was your typical desert layout with deep green fairways framed by a few yards of green rough, and then the browns and tans of the desert. There were cactus and brush along the entire length of the hole with a tree here or there, and dozens of boulders that added to the stark beauty, but presented problems for any wayward shot that missed the grass.

The first hole was a dogleg to the left. It was a good poke to try to cut the corner. Monroe's drive was a safe one, ending up in the fairway ten yards past the dogleg. I wondered if Ben would play aggressively and take on the cactus that stood at the corner of the dogleg. He played faster than Monroe, teeing his ball up and taking just a quick look down the fairway. Playing much faster than I was used to seeing him, he hit a nice high draw that ended up carrying Monroe's drive by ten yards. He ended up almost through the fairway, stopping a yard from the rough.

When Ben sat back in the cart, I made sure to not even look at him. As we started to drive down the cart path I noticed I was putting a death grip on the steering wheel.

"Relax," Ben said. "Take a breath."

He was right, I was holding my breath. I realized I was feeling as much, if not more pressure than at any time when I was playing. I released all my built-up tension with a deep breath and forced myself to unfurl my fingers from the steering wheel. As we pulled up to Ben's ball, I was wondering if I would be able to make it through the entire match.

Ben had a little more than a hundred and fifty yards to the flag. He stood next to the cart as Monroe, who had at least another fifteen yards than Ben, went through the same, slow pre-shot routine as his drive. His shot was solid, playing over the left side of the green before fading to the middle. It stopped twenty feet short of the pin.

As soon as Monroe's ball stopped on the green, Ben pulled his nine-iron. He played quickly, hitting a high draw that ended up hole high, fifteen feet left of the hole. When we arrived on the green, I waited until both players were on the green before I stepped out of the cart. I was not sure if I should wait at the cart, or if I was allowed to walk up and get a better view. I looked over at Monroe's driver. I figured I would do what she did, and when she stepped out of her cart and took a few steps closer to the green, I did the same. The mob guys were sitting in their cart fifty yards down the fairway. Junior was sitting with his legs out of the cart and appeared to be sunning himself.

Monroe was away, his putt was an uphill twenty-footer. If you thought he was slow when hitting the ball, he was twice as slow on the greens. He circled the putt twice, stood over the ball and made four practice swings, went back and crouched behind the ball, and then circled it once more. All the time, Ben stood off the side of the green looking down at his feet. When Monroe finally hit his putt, he missed it on the edge of the low side. Ben gave a quick nod conceding Monroe's par and stepped up to his putt.

While Monroe took nearly two minutes to hit his putt, Ben took just fifteen seconds. I was standing right behind him and saw that he was lined up six inches left of the hole. I thought to myself that this was a putt that he could make in his sleep. What a great chance to jump out to a lead, and put the pressure on Monroe. I thought of a quote from Mr. Wittich who said, 'You want to win a match, try and win every hole. And to do that, you have to win the first one."

Ben made what looked like a good stroke and the ball rolled smoothly to the hole. As I waited for the break that Ben played, the ball stayed straight. It moved a couple of inches down to the hole in the last foot but rolled a foot past.

"Mother..." Ben said as he swung his putter in the air. "How the hell did that stay high?"

Monroe started to walk off the green. "Good," he said.

I wasn't surprised Ben misread the putt. I was surprised that he showed anger. That was new to me. Monroe was in his cart and driving to the second tee by the time Ben dropped his putter into his bag. After seeing his reaction on the green, I expected him to say something to me, but he was his usual calm self. I wanted badly to ask him whether it was misread as I thought, or a bad stroke. I kept my mouth shut though, respecting his wishes.

The second hole was a long par-5 that bent slightly to the left. After his now annoying pre-shot routine, Monroe hit the same drive he hit on the first hole. He ended up in a good position in the center of the fairway.

Ben played as fast as ever. I watched his swing, and as soon as he made contact, I noticed something strange. Instead of his normal high finish, his hands ended lower. My initial reaction was wondering why he was hitting a fade on a hole that begged for a big hit with his draw. I watched as his drive went high and right, and it barely hung on in the higher rough. Whereas on the first hole he outdrove Monroe by thirty yards, his drive here was twenty-five yards shorter than his opponent.

As he bent over to pick up his tee, Ben let out a muffled 'shit' and angrily threw the tee into the small trash can. "Stop thinking so much," he said mostly to himself. I don't think he realized that I could hear him, and if I heard him that meant Monroe heard him also. Ben looked like he was trying to control himself, but so far he was not doing a good job.

When we got to his drive, Ben calmly looked at his lie. Taking a quick look at where Monroe would be hitting from, he pulled out an iron. His lie was pretty good, but after seeing the practice swings he was making, I had to check again. He took two big, hard swings. After the second, he took a deep breath and slowly let it out. His actions were loud enough that Monroe turned to look at him. If Ben wanted everyone's attention, he got it.

As he started his swing, I looked at the ball and again I told myself that his lie was good. He was two hundred and fifty yards from the hole, and with the fairway so wide, he could have easily reached the green with his three-wood. Instead, he hacked at the ball and drove a low, running draw down the fairway. He ended up in a good position, one hundred yards from the pin. His swing and ball flight made it look like he had dug out from a deep lie.

Monroe did pull out his three-wood and hit a straight, high approach that landed just short of the green and ran onto the front fringe. He was in great shape and forced Ben to make a birdie from his position in the fairway.

When Ben ended up fifteen feet past the hole with his approach, I shook my head. After giving away the first hole, and playing a second shot from the rough on this hole with the wrong club, Ben needed a big break to halve this hole.

After Monroe lagged up his third putt to two feet, Ben conceded his birdie putt. He then proceeded to miss his birdie putt to tie the hole, missing on the left as he did on the first.

He was one down and again he unsuccessfully tried to conceal his anger.

Ben finally made a putt on the fifth hole. The two players traded pars on the third and fourth. The fifth hole was a dogleg that ran left around a large waste area of sand, rocks, and cactus. I learned that the pattern of this course was tight fairways in the landing area and well-guarded greens. The fifth was tight for anyone trying to go over the corner which was not a problem for Monroe. He hit everything short of trouble, seemingly not fearful of having a longer iron into the green. On five, he showed why.

After leaving his tee shot well right of the problem, Monroe nearly holed his approach from one hundred and seventy yards out. That put the pressure on Ben, whose drive was over the corner, thirty-five yards closer. His approach ended ten feet above the hole. His putt was not easy and since he missed each of his putts today to the left, this downhill twister was a tough putt. I watched as he dropped the putt straight in the center. I felt that even though he tied the hole, this had to be a big confidence boost and would get his putter going.

On the seventh hole though, Ben again missed right. On the par-5, he hit the same high and right drive he hit on the second.

Walking off the tee it looked to me that Monroe said something to him, which drew a curt response from Ben. There was another exchange after Ben missed his eight-footer to tie Monroe's birdie. I wanted so badly to ask Ben about his alignment or to get his hands higher on his swing to prevent missing his driver to the right. But I kept my mouth shut, and even scolded myself for thinking I knew more than he did about his own game.

The match stayed Monroe two-up until the thirteenth. On a beautiful par-3 over water to an island green, Monroe hit a solid tee shot to fifteen feet. After another comment from Monroe, I saw a different Ben. This was the first time in the match that Ben went through what I considered his normal pre-shot routine. He moved more slowly than he had so far in the match. Although he was still much faster than Monroe, he stood a good thirty seconds behind the ball looking at the green. When he stood over the ball, he had the aggressive resolve that I was used to. His swing was his normal move through the ball, and the resulting high draw ended up two feet from the hole. When Monroe missed his putt, his two-hole lead was down to one.

They both parred the fourteenth with two putts. Ben had a chance from twenty feet but came up short. On fifteen, Ben came up with a great save to keep the spread at one hole. After again missing right off the tee, he ended up in the green-side bunker with his approach while Monroe was safely in the middle of the green, thirty feet from the hole. Ben's shot from the bunker was average at best, ending up ten feet from the hole. After Monroe lagged to within two feet, Ben drilled his par putt into the center.

I waited in the cart next to the sixteenth tee as Ben and Monroe walked off the fifteenth green. I looked down at my hands and realized I was choking the wheel so tight my knuckles were turning white and my knees were shaking. This was the most pressure-filled golf I ever witnessed. If I was playing I'm not sure I would be able to make a tap-in.

Up to this point, I was aware that the two of them had gone

back and forth with comments to each during the match about missed putts or wayward shots. Although the bantering was tame when compared to what I was now used to from playing at The Bridge, with so much money on the line I understood why Ben was showing his emotions.

As Monroe walked past me and up to his cart sitting next to the sixteenth tee, he said loudly over his shoulder, "Maybe you should stop being weak and start to back up your play with some action? Don't you think, Mr. Newell?"

As Ben dropped his putter in the bag and pulled out his driver, he was clear with his response. "Eff off, *Mr.* Monroe. You play your game, and I'll play mine."

Both players stepped up to the tee. "We are playing for what, two-fifty? The way things are going, the man you play for will be a very unhappy one, no? I wish to be there when you have to tell him, 'Oh, I was unable to beat Monroe. I was too weak. Please forgive me.'"

Ben shook his head as he teed up his ball. "You're one up, and I just birdied. I think I'm feeling pretty good about my position." He took a step back and looked down the fairway. The hole was a straight, par-4 that had a few trees down both sides, and a few bunkers down the right.

Monroe walked out in front of the tee and stood three feet in front of Ben's ball. "Perhaps you want to run that number to a higher total? Is your mind able to take the pressure? I only ask so that you have a chance to win more. I know your man has wanted you to bring to him a bigger win."

Ben stood tall behind his ball. He said nothing and slowly swung his left arm back and forth while holding his driver.

"I am surprised," said Monroe. "I have always heard that Ben Newell was such a big player for the money. Yes, I offer you the chance to play higher. I can call the man in the cart over there right now and tell him we go for fifty more. But the great Newell does nothing."

Ben lowered his head and took a deep breath.

Monroe laughed. "Your reaction tells it all. I see you are not up to it. And, Mr. Newell, I can understand. You do not have your game today. Then again, you did not have your game the other times we have gone against each other. So we will keep our wager where it is, and you do not have to tell your man that you lose more."

Monroe stepped back and with a loud exhale, said, "Go ahead, Mr. Newell. Go ahead and tee off. We will play this out with the current wager remaining."

Ben kept his head down. I thought that Monroe was being overly confident seeing that he was only one up. I then remembered what Ben told me: Monroe was the type of player that believed he could take an early one-up lead and hold it throughout the match. Ben also told me that Marino wanted him to win more than the original two hundred and fifty thousand dollars. Here Monroe was offering to raise the stakes and Ben refused. Maybe the swing and putting problems he was having were hurting his confidence.

After another deep breath, Ben took a quick look at Monroe and stepped up to his ball. I could see that he was concentrating and working something through his head. When he did finally hit the ball, again he hit his ball right and short. His shot landed just in the rough and kicked slightly right, ending up under one of the palm trees running down the hole's right side.

"Shit!" Ben said, almost at the level of a yell. He slammed his driver down on the ground and walked back to the cart. Keeping his head down, he missed Monroe again hitting one down the middle. This tee shot was shorter than his others and it was obvious he wanted to press his advantage by staying in the fairway. Still, he was twenty yards past Ben. As he got to his cart, he said to his woman driver, "Well my dear, it seems my opponent is not looking to increase our wager. We will only be able to afford one new set of diamond earrings for you from our winnings."

Ben practically jumped into the cart and angrily said to me, "Go. Hurry it up."

I hit the pedal and we sped to his drive. I remained in the driver's seat as we got to his ball. He stepped out, looking at Monroe as his cart passed us, and stopped next to his drive. The best way to explain Monroe's attitude was cockiness. He slowly stood up next to his cart and looked at his ball, and then back at Ben. Walking over to the driver's side of the cart, he smiled at his driver and said something to her. They both shared a quick laugh, and Monroe walked to the back of his cart and pulled a club.

After looking over his shot, and spending a lot of time looking at the shot Monroe had, Ben turned his back to Monroe and said under his breath to me, "Don't say anything, just cough if it's true. Did he pull his seven-iron? I can't tell if it's his seven or eight. Cough if it's his seven."

I slowly looked over at Monroe. By now I knew the layout of his bag which, like the way he played, was in perfect order. Each club had a separate hole where he consistently made sure his irons were arranged in order. I noticed it on the first tee. Looking at your opponent's bag was something that Ben, Gonzo, Clip, and The Bridge gang taught me. Always know how your opponent lays out his clubs in his bag so that you can tell what club he or she is hitting. They also taught me to never pull your club until your opponent has hit, a rule that Monroe failed to follow. He was standing at his cart with a club in his hand. I noticed that from where Ben was, he could not see around Monroe whereas I could.

Monroe was holding his eight-iron so I made no sound.

"Okay," Ben whispered.

I wasn't sure what that meant to Ben's strategy. After all, Monroe could be baiting Ben by pulling a different club than he intended to use. Looking again at Monroe, I doubted that. He was studying his yardage book and again sharing a laugh with his cart driver.

Ben had little to no shot at the green. The palm trees blocked his direct line. His only option was to play a low, running fade and try to get the ball to land short and roll up to the putting surface. He took out his three-iron and did just what I thought. His shot started at the left of the green, landed thirty yards short, and ran up to within fifteen feet of the hole. It was not a good shot, it was a great shot. He dropped his club into his bag and stood next to me, watching Monroe.

Looking over at Monroe, I thought I could see just a hint of disappointment at the shot Ben hit. In his mind, he was planning for a par to win the hole. Now Ben was in a position to make a birdie. He did not change clubs and hit his eight-iron to the front of the green, outside of Ben's shot.

Ben sat down and as I started to pull away, I thought I heard him whisper, "I got him."

His confidence helped me take a deep breath and relax. From where I sat, Ben being one-down to this machine of a player, and hoping to out putt him when he had not made a tough putt all day, was not a position that made me think Ben 'had him'. As I drove the cart I told myself that Ben must know something I don't.

Whatever confidence I found in Ben was lost when Monroe made his birdie putt. Monroe smiled and made a fist, his first show of emotion after a shot all day. I looked at Ben expecting to see his shoulders drop, but I saw the opposite. He had an ever-so-slight smile, and he quickly pulled his ball out of his pocket and placed it on the green.

If I didn't know any better, I would have thought that Ben wanted Monroe to make it. From my position standing near the back of the green, his deep blue eyes were lasers staring down the line of the putt. When he stood over the ball, he wasted no time in draining it.

One down, two to play.

The seventeenth hole was a signature par-3. Playing two hundred and thirty-two yards from the back tees, the green looked from the tee to be a sliver hidden behind two deep front bunkers. The pin was tucked on the right side, seemingly just a few feet over the lip of the bunker. Ben needed a birdie to ensure that the match would go to the eighteenth. If Monroe also birdied, the match would go to the last hole with Ben one-down. A win on the hole by Ben meant the match would be tied.

I sat forward in the cart's driver seat as Ben stepped behind his ball with his two-iron to look at the shot. Twice he slowly worked his hands away from his body simulating an outside-in swing that would produce a fade. As he stepped up to the ball, I saw him take a deep breath to calm himself. Once over the ball, he wasted no more time.

The shot I witnessed Ben hit was without a doubt the best golf shot, to that point in my life, witnessed in person. The ball started at the middle of the green and seemed to hang at its apex. As it started to descend, the ball started to move to the right.

"Move," Ben said, barely loud enough for me to hear. The ball listened. As it came down, it kept moving further and further to the right. Finally, it landed slightly right of the hole and took a kick left. With the lip of the bunker blocking our view, I guessed the ball must have ended up within ten feet of the hole.

Ben leaned over and picked up his tee. As he walked to the back of the tee, I could tell he was happy. He looked at me for just a half-second and ever so slightly smiled.

Monroe let out a long breath and said, "I will need to know how far that is from the hole." He was doing his best to hide his disappointment at Ben's shot.

"Then go check," Ben said. "I'll wait."

Monroe didn't look at Ben. He turned and walked over to his cart. Jumping in, he and his driver took off. We waited while they drove down the cart path and watched as they turned around and headed back after they reached the green.

Monroe said nothing as he walked back to the tee. Taking longer than usual, he went through his pre-shot routine and twice stepped back away from the ball. As he struggled to clear his head for the shot he needed to hit, I began to wonder if Ben's shot was closer than I originally thought.

When Monroe did get around to hitting his shot, the results were not anything different than the rest of his round. He used his five wood to hit a low, straight shot that ended up running to the back of the green. As he walked past me to his cart, I could see the frustration on his face. He was in danger of going to the eighteenth all-even. Given the length of his birdie putt, he would need Ben to miss a short putt to keep his lead.

Except, there was no short putt for Ben to make. As we pulled up to the green, I had to hold in my reaction when I saw his ball less than a foot from the hole. Monroe conceded the birdie and then spent the next three minutes trying to decide the line on his forty-five-footer. When his putt ended up three feet short, we headed to the last hole with the match tied.

Ben sat next to me taking deep breaths and slowly exhaling. I wanted so badly to ask him what he was thinking, what his game plan was, and what he could do to get the wager up to the amount Marino demanded. But I kept my focus forward as we drove on the cement cart path, weaving through cactus, desert brush, and rocks. Like Ben, I also worked to control my breathing. I felt Ben was in a great position with momentum on his side.

As we pulled up to the tee though, my stomach dropped. The eighteenth hole was unlike any other hole played so far. As I looked down the fairway I thought we were on a different course. The hole was a tight, straight par-4 that was lined with some Aleppo pine trees on the right and four deep bunkers and water on the left. It was not the type of hole that suited Ben, who had been struggling to hit fairways all day.

Waiting for us on the tee was Pops. He stood at the top of three steps leading to the tee box with his arms crossed, seemingly daring someone to get by him. Both Ben and Monroe walked up to the steps and stood on the cart path, looking up at him.

"Gentleman," Pops said, talking between his heavy breathing, "your match is tied. I need to tell you that the men supporting this match do not want to see it end this way. I will be waiting for what you two decide."

He walked down the steps and over to his cart where Junior was waiting.

"Well, Mr. Newell, you must be feeling quite the amount of tension right now," Monroe said as soon as Pops started to walk away. "You cannot like…"

"Shut the hell up," Ben said, walking up to the tee. "You want to raise the stakes, I'm all for it. I'm making a three on this hole. If you think you can match it, great."

Monroe followed Ben up to the tee and said, "So we raise the amount, say fifty, and maybe you will shake so much that you screw yourself. Right?"

Ben turned to Monroe. "Fine. Let's make it three hundred. That works for me. But you're still gonna have to make a birdie if you want a push."

Monroe started to laugh mockingly and stepped to the back of the tee. "Sir," he said loudly to Pops, "we have raised the stakes to three hundred. Should we be tied after this hole, we will move the match on until the solution is achieved."

Pops gave a wave, the cigarette in his hand sending ashes and smoke into the air.

"You cannot like this hole. Not the way you have been driving the ball," Monroe said. "I understand that they are in the process of removing those trees on the right side. Too bad they have not done it. You must feel like they are a magnet for your upcoming drive."

Ben teed up his ball and ignored Monroe. I looked down the fairway at the trees he was talking about. Starting at two hundred yards from the tee there was a single line of Aleppo pines fifteen yards off the fairway. The trees continued for a hundred yards ending with a dense grouping. I could see a fence some thirty yards right of the trees in front of a maintenance building. The trees must have been the course designer's idea to conceal the building.

Ben stood behind his ball and closed his eyes. I could see the struggle in his mind. He had been leaving his drives out to the right all round. The natural tendency to prevent that was to rush your hands through the swing, but that raised the possibility of hitting the ball left into the water. As he stood up to the ball I felt like I should grab his three wood and run it over to him. Hitting a driver in this situation was a bad idea.

I kept myself quiet and seated though. As Ben pulled the driver back I closed my eyes and said to myself, "get your hands through."

I could tell when he made contact he did it again. The ball started high down the right side heading for the trees. It kept moving right, and as it cleared the trees, Ben let go a loud, "Fuck," and slammed his driver into the ground. I kept my focus on the ball hoping that it would not clear the fence to the right of the trees, but I saw it bounce and run deep into the rough. Although the ball was not out of bounds, Ben was in deep trouble.

"A birdie, huh?" Monroe said.

I looked back at the tee and Ben was crouching like a catcher. He looked up at Monroe who was starting to tee his ball up. "Yeah, asshole, I'm still making a birdie.," Ben said.

"Okay, I do love your hopeful attitude, but why don't you get yourself off the tee so I can put this ball into the fairway? After that, we can talk about your birdie."

Ben took his time and moved to the back of the tee. I was feeling terrible for him. I could see the slump in his shoulders and the almost unbelieving look on his face that he had hit such a bad drive at such a big moment of the match. I am sure if I could look in a mirror I would have the same look on my face.

As I looked at Ben, Monroe stepped up and hit his usual solid drive down the middle. He was careful to keep his ball in play so he sacrificed some distance. As Ben slumped into the cart, I heard Monroe tell his blonde driver, "When I bury this loser, you'll be getting those earrings that you begged for."

I didn't know what to do as I was driving Ben to his ball. I knew he was pissed by the way he kept tapping his feet. When I reached the pine trees, I slowed to look for an opening for me to drive the cart through so we could get to where his drive had landed. The trees were thick and so close enough to each other that the cart would not be able to make it to the other side. I stopped and was about to tell him we have to get out and walk underneath them when he pointed.

"Hurry up," he said. "Turn there."

I said nothing but was surprised. Ben didn't sound mad, but excited. I moved the cart forward and sure enough, there was an opening. When I drove through the trees, I heard another cart right behind us. I quickly looked over my shoulder and saw that

Monroe was following us. He wanted to see exactly what kind of situation Ben was in.

Behind the treeline, the area opened up. There were twenty yards of rough between the trees and the fence. Most of the grass was about six inches deep. On a desert layout like this, it was the deepest rough on the course. As we moved forward, the rough started to shorten and I saw Ben's ball. I realized that this area of rough was used for turf replacement around the course, so the grass was thick and short. His ball was sitting up with a good lie.

I stopped the cart behind the ball and realized that no matter how good the lie was, Ben had no shot. The thick trees that ran down the fairway led to a forest-like section that was thirty yards in front of his ball. My first reaction was that he would have to play underneath them to advance himself toward the green, but the trees grew so low, I don't think he could hit it hard and low enough to get anywhere near the putting surface. To make matters worse, a stream ran from the water on the left side of the hole across the fairway thirty yards short of the green. I shook my head. The only thing Ben could try to do was play sideways and hope to get it through the trees back onto the fairway.

Ben jumped out of the cart and looked at what he had. He crouched and looked back into the fairway to see where Monroe's drive was. He then walked behind the cart and started to rifle through his clubs, looking for the one he would use.

"So, Mr. Newell, things are not looking good, are they," Monroe said as he walked up to Ben's ball. "I believe the term is, 'you are in jail'. Is that not right?"

"Monroe, get your ass over to your ball and hit. You're away," Ben said. He pulled out his three-iron and walked over to his ball. He took a practice swing, aiming back at the fairway. "I'll wait until you hit and get out of the way so I can get back into play."

"Back in play? I think you are way out of play, my friend."

"You're not my friend, you condescending asshole. I told you I'm going to make birdie. So go hit your shot and see if you can halve the hole."

"Ben, this is not a par-5, you do know that, correct?"

Ben didn't reply.

After a moment of silence in which Monroe seemed to be deep in thought, he said, "I do like you Ben, but I don't like you enough to give you a break. I know you would do the same if you were in my position." He laughed and continued. "But, you are not in my position. I do hope your Mr. Marino is not too mad at you for losing so much of his money. He should have known from the other times that we played that you are not in my class of the game."

Ben kept his head down looking at his ball while Monroe was speaking, but he finally appeared to have had enough. "Shut the hell up. Do you think I'm gonna let you beat me? Fuck you. I'm not."

Monroe smiled and said, "What, are you going to get this ball back out into the fairway and then get it up and down from there for a par? I don't think you can get through those trees and be anywhere near the fairway."

"Are you deaf, asshole?," Ben said, his head still down. "I told you, I'm making birdie."

Again, Monroe laughed and he started to walk back to his cart. "Okay, okay my friend. You live with that hope and you take that hope and see what you can buy with it. I will go hit my shot on the green and then you can start to hack your way out of this situation you are in."

Ben walked after him and said, "What, you want to raise the bank on this? Let's double the total."

Monroe stopped and turned around. "Mr. Newell, I want you to stop and think about what you just said. I will pretend I did not hear it."

"Stop your righteous bullshit. You heard me. Six hundred large."

Monroe tilted his head and nodded. He turned toward the fairway and whistled. A moment later Pops and Junior rode through the opening in the trees and up to where we were gathered. Pops got out and walked over to Monroe. The two talked quietly for a few seconds, and then Pops took a few steps away and removed a small notepad out of his pocket. He studied something that was written and came back to the group.

"Five hundred," he said, and then walked back to his cart.

Ben shook his head. "Alright Monroe, we'll leave the match at five hundred, but you and I go fifty personal."

Monroe looked at his cart driver and smiled. Looking back at Ben he said, "Now you show me why there are people all over the world that love to tell stories about you. And I believe I will be able to tell one now also. My story will be about how I took every remaining bit of money from you and left you a penniless drunk. I will tell them they can find you crawling down the Vegas strip. Five hundred and another fifty personal it is."

He turned and hopped back in his cart. He and his driver headed back to the fairway, leaving me wondering what the hell I had just witnessed. I looked again to see if there was some type of shot I missed. The more I looked the more I knew I hadn't missed anything. I got out of the cart and looked closer at Ben's lie.

I nearly opened my mouth to say it could be worse. His ball was five feet from a group of deep divots made by someone most likely hitting balls back toward the tee or to the open desert area to the side of the tee. That's the only reason I could think of for someone to have been hitting balls from this area.

It would not have mattered if he had ended up in the divots. He still had no shot.

While I looked at his predicament, I noticed Pops and Junior were still sitting in the cart behind us. I guess they wanted to make sure Ben didn't pick up the ball and throw it. Junior got out of the cart and took a few steps toward me so that he could get a better look at the shot Ben had. He looked at me and under his breath asked, "What's he gonna do?"

I don't know if I was more shocked that Junior said something to me, or that he seemed to care about the match. I shrugged and shook my head. I had no idea what Ben was going to do.

I saw that Monroe was getting ready to hit. I walked back to the cart and Ben was pulling another club out of his bag. When he walked by me, he showed me the club and winked. It was a seven-iron.

"What..?" I started to say, but I remember the rule. I sat back in the cart and heard Monroe make contact. Looking under the trees, I saw his shot land in the middle of the green, thirty feet right of the hole. It was a safe shot, but a smart one given the huge advantage that he had. I now looked back at Ben who was standing behind the ball. As I saw where he was looking, my reaction was clear, concise, and a memory seared into my mind.

I thought to myself, "What the hell is he doing?"

Ben was looking at the farthest tree to the right of the thick group of trees in front of him. It took me a few seconds to figure out what he was going to try and do. After squinting, shaking my head, and taking a deep breath, I realized Ben was going to try an impossible, ridiculous, unheard-of shot. He was going to try and hook it around the trees.

I looked at the shot. The forest of trees was only thirty yards in front of him. He could never get a shot high enough to go over the trees and far enough to reach the green. So he had to aim right. A straight line from Ben's ball to the right of the last tree would mean he was aiming eighty yards to the right of the middle of the green, and maybe ninety yards to the right of the hole. If you could get a ball to hook that much, the line of the shot would take the ball over a maintenance shed, part of the practice putting green, the patio where people were sitting, and two greenside bunkers.

All this from one hundred and eighty-five yards and made more impossible by the fact that Ben had to use a seven-iron because he had to get the ball high enough to clear the fence separating the course from the maintenance area.

Again, I thought to myself, "What the hell is he doing?"

By now, Ben had gone through whatever pre-shot gyrations he needed to do. I looked over at the fairway and saw that Monroe was confused about what he was seeing. Crouched and looking under the trees, he was expecting Ben to be punching a shot back into the fairway. When he saw what Ben was trying to do, he quickly walked over behind my cart.

Ben stood up to the ball, his feet spread further than normal. He took two deep breaths, pulled his hands back with two long waggles, and then took one more breath. His swing was clearly inside the line, long, and fast. The contact he made with the ball sounded like a hammer hitting wood. The clear and sharp 'whack!' seemed to echo off the surrounding trees. His follow-through was violent and caused him to spin away from the ball.

As for the shot, the ball took off high and at the end of the tree line. It barely got over the fence, nearly clipped the tree, and started going left. We all lost sight of it. I jumped out of the cart and ran a few steps forward before falling on my stomach so that I could see under the trees. I focused on the right side of the green and waited. I felt someone kneeling next to me and assumed it was Monroe. When I saw a large, fat leg in my peripheral vision, I knew it was Junior. He had also run over to get a look.

We all waited. It seemed to me that the ball was in the air somewhere around ninety seconds. While I waited, I expected to hear people on the patio screaming from a ball landing in their lunch plates, or maybe someone on the practice green taking a ball on the side of the head. When none of that happened, and because in my mind the time had come and gone to see where Ben ended up, I started to say something. I assumed the shot was gone to never be seen again. I don't know what I started to say, because I never got it out. I still have not been able to respond to what I witnessed.

From my angle, the ball seemed to come down as if someone hit it directly from the side of the green. It landed on the right front of the putting surface, and because it had so much spin and landed on a slope, it took a big bounce and skidded even further left. When it started to roll, it kept moving closer and closer to the hole. I think I may have sounded a muffled cheer, but I was drowned out by Junior, who loudly said, as if he was at a football game, "Holy fucking shit!"

I agreed with him. The ball slowed and rolled up to the hole, stopping eighteen inches away.

I pushed myself up onto my knees, and Junior lifted me onto my feet. I thanked him and took a few quick steps over to Ben. He looked as if nothing happened, and even gave me a quick look that said, "calm down."

I remembered where I was and what was happening. I turned and walked back to the cart. That's when I saw Monroe. He stood in place, his hands folded in front of his mouth, and the best thing I can say was, he was shell-shocked. His face was pure white, and I am positive he was praying under his breath. I turned my eyes away from him and sat in the cart. Trying to figure out what it was I just witnessed, I again looked under the trees at his ball on the green. I wasn't sure how Ben even considered the shot.

Ben walked over and dropped his club in the bag. I looked at him, and although I could tell he was excited, I could also tell that he was trying to control his breathing. He sat in the cart and elbowed me in the side. "Holy shit," he said under his breath. I started to laugh but held it. I hit the accelerator on the cart and turned the wheel all the way to the left so that we could get back onto the fairway.

As we started to move forward, Ben started to pat down his pants pockets. "Hold on, I lost my yardage book when I dropped down to watch the shot," he said.

I stopped the cart and told him I would go get it. Jumping out, I ran back to where his ball had been. I stood behind his divot and again looked at the line his shot took. I wanted to remember every detail. Taking a deep breath, I shook my head.

"Unreal," I said to myself.

I then looked around for his yardage book and saw it to the right of the group of divots near where his ball was. After picking it up, I stopped to look at the divots. Originally I thought maybe someone was hitting balls into the desert but these divots were aligned in the wrong direction. Whoever made them was hitting balls toward the green. And they were pointed to the right.

"Let's move it, Vlad," Ben said. So I took one quick step back to the cart and stopped. The sunlight reflected off of something on the ground next to the maintenance fence. When I took a step that way, my heart started to race faster than it already was. Lined up along the fence, in tall uncut grass, were four empty, crushed, Pabst Blue Ribbon cans.

Up to this time, Ben's shot on seventeen was the best I had ever witnessed. As I walked over to pick up his yardage book, I knew that the approach to eighteen was even better. And now, after seeing those beer cans, I realized that for years I would have a battle going on in my head trying to decide if Ben's drive on eighteen was the best shot of them all.

I looked at Ben and started to ask him if it was true, but I caught myself. The match was still going on, so I held back. Biting my tongue to the point I tasted blood, I started to walk back to the cart. Stepping on something, I looked down and saw a thick money clip on the ground. Picking it up and seeing that the outside bill was a hundred, I guessed there could be over a couple of thousand dollars. Looking around I saw Junior starting to turn his cart and ride back to the fairway. Assuming it was his money and that the clip fell out of his pocket when he crouched to see Ben's shot, I ran over and cut them off.

"Hey, is this yours? It was over in the grass."

Immediately Junior felt his back pocket and said, "Oh no."

Seeing him up close I assumed he was only a few years older than me. I handed over the clip and Junior took it with a smile and a nod. "Was that a great shot or what?" he asked me.

Before I had a chance to respond, Pops reached out, backhanded Junior across the shoulder, and said, "Drive you fucking idiot."

Junior nodded to me again and floored the accelerator. The cart, which was carrying way too much weight with the two men, lurched and spun its back wheels before moving forward. I waited for them to cross in front of me and ran back to our cart.

"Making friends?" Ben asked. "Be careful with the young one."

"Who, Junior?" I asked.

Ben laughed. "I wouldn't call him Junior to his face. He wouldn't lose a second of sleep after putting a bullet through your head."

I stared at him while I handed him his yardage book thinking that maybe I saved my life by returning Junior his money. I also fought the urge to ask about the drive. As we drove through the gap back to the fairway, Ben simply said, "We're not done yet."

I could not get the cart to move fast enough as we drove to the green. Monroe was already there and standing by his cart. I wanted to be next to him when he had to shake Ben's hand and concede defeat, but I was experienced enough in the game to know that until your opponent misses his shot, no matter how difficult, the match was not over.

As we pulled up, Ben looked at me and said, "Remember, no talking. Even if he asks you something. Just nod and stay quiet."

His words reminded me that I am just the driver. I nodded and stayed in the cart while Ben grabbed his putter and started to walk to the green. When he reached the putting surface, I stepped out of the cart and took a look at the situation. Ben marked his ball, but he was within two feet of the hole. On any other hole, Monroe would have already conceded the putt. But that never happened on the eighteenth hole.

Monroe's ball was sitting thirty feet from the cup. As Ben said, Monroe liked to play it safe when he thought he had an advantage. His assumption that Ben had no chance to hit the green in two led him to play for the center of the green. His ball was slightly above the hole and would be coming down a small ridge that would add at least a foot of break. I am sure that if the shoe was on the other foot, and it was Ben that had a thirty-footer to tie the match, Monroe would be talking to Ben reminding him how difficult the putt was. Ben did none of that. He stood on the fringe, trying to be patient while Monroe attempted to figure out the break of his putt.

I looked over at Monroe's cart and his driver. She was sitting in her cart with her head down. As I looked at her, she raised her eyes and looked at me. For some reason, her stare was not as penetrating and intimidating as it was when I first saw her. Her eyes were red and I thought that maybe she was crying. I could have looked away, but I returned her stare. Finally, she looked down. That was my one victory that day.

I took a few more steps to get closer to the green. As Monroe stepped up to his ball and got ready to hit his putt, I looked at Ben. He was crouched on the opposite side of the hole from his ball mark, reading the line of his putt. I know in his mind he expected Monroe to make it. In Ben's mind, his less than two-footer would be for a tie.

As Monroe pulled the putter back, I took a breath and held it. He made contact and the ball took off, riding the top of the small ridge. As it lost speed it fell off the ridge and started to break toward the hole. From my angle, I wasn't able to judge if he had the ball on the right line. So I looked at the hole and waited. When the ball was within two feet, I thought it had a chance. But the pace was too much. It flew by the hole and ran four feet past.

I silently screamed and as I stood still, in my head I was jumping up and down. Monroe took three steps toward the hole, and then he stopped. Bending over, he stomped his foot and loudly said "Putain de pute!" which I assumed was something bad in French. He then turned away from the hole, made a fist, grunted a few times, and turned back around.

Ben had not moved. He remained crouched on the side of the green. When Monroe turned back around, Ben looked at him, and with a calm, measured tone said, "You're still away, Mr. Monroe."

It was a slap of monumental proportions.

Monroe took a deep breath and walked around the hole to his ball. He looked over at Ben's ball mark, and I thought for a moment he was going to concede. But he didn't, and he started to go through his routine for his par putt. After a minute, he knocked in the putt, retrieved the ball from the hole, and walked over to the side of the green.

Ben wasted no time. He placed his ball on the green, removed his ball marker, stepped up, and knocked in the putt. I wanted to clap, but I kept my silence and walked back to the cart. Looking over my shoulder, I saw Monroe walk up to Ben and shake his hand.

"You should have listened to me," Ben said calmly. "I told you I was going to make birdie."

Monroe said nothing and did not react in any way. He was shell-shocked.

Ben walked to the back of the green to where Pops was standing. He looked at me and waved me over. I drove the cart to him. He said something to Pops about wanting to collect as soon as possible and then walked to the cart.

"Still no talking," he said. "Let's get out of here."

CHAPTER 13

We were at the airport before Ben would say anything about the match. Even then, all I got from him was his opinion that Monroe was a righteous prick.

"No kidding," I said.

"Hey," Ben said, leaning close enough to me that I could hear his whispers over the sounds of the people milling about near the gate as we waited to board, "we'll talk back at The Bridge. It's the only place where I feel safe talking."

I nodded and tried to be patient as we flew back to Vegas. I assumed that Ben was hesitant to discuss his participation in what was an illegal gambling game of golf. I left it at that and waited until he was comfortable.

It was 9:00 PM when we finally made it to The Bridge. As usual, the room was packed. Ben walked straight up to Milly and sat in front of him. Milly didn't need any directions. He reached into the cooler on the ground at the end of the bar and handed Ben a can of Pabst Blue Ribbon. He grabbed another and tossed it over Ben's head to me.

I took my usual place in a chair at the end of the bar and waited for Ben to unwind. It looked to me as if all the tension and nerves that he held in and masked during the match were now coming out. He held the beer can up to his cheek and closed his eyes. After letting out the longest exhale I can ever remember seeing, he chugged the beer and reached his hand out. Like a finely tuned machine, Milly had the next one ready.

Milly walked over to me and whispered, "I take it he won?"

I nodded. "You knew about this match?"

Milly leaned in again. "I can tell when he's been under pressure. And I can tell he's happy."

I looked at Ben. To me, he looked like he had just stepped in front of a train and had it go between his legs. 'Happy' was the last word I would use to describe him.

"I think I would use the word 'relieved'," I said to Milly.

"Will you two hags shut up," said Ben. He chugged the second beer and stood up. Turning to the room, he whistled. Immediately, the room went quiet.

"Ladies and gentlemen," Ben said, raising his arms. "Oh, and Clip."

"Fuck you, Benny," Clip's voice sounded from somewhere amongst the masses.

Ben stood with his arms up and slowly looked around the room. He seemed to be making eye contact with each person. After taking in the large group, he nodded and smiled.

"Go ahead, say it!" someone shouted from the far corner.

"Do it, Benny. C'mon," said another.

Ben turned his head and looked at Milly. "You ready?" he asked.

Milly looked at me and winked. He walked over to the center of the bar, stretched his arms out in front of himself, and cracked his knuckles. After slowly turning his head to the left and then to the right to stretch his neck, he took a deep breath. As he slowly went through this routine, the energy in the room continued to climb. Finally, looking at Ben, Milly smiled and said, "Yes, sir, I am."

Ben nodded and slowly turned back to the room. After another few seconds of silence, he yelled, "On me!"

The entire room exploded and rushed to the bar. Ben stood with his arms up as everyone patted him on the shoulders and back as they started to yell orders to Milly.

I looked at Ben as he watched everyone and I had a hard time holding in my emotions. I was watching Ben react the way I wanted him to when he made the last putt of the match. Finally, I saw him celebrating. I thought for a moment that I might be seeing the real Ben Newell. I reached over and grabbed one of the many bottles of beer Milly put on the bar and took a long drink. I was finally able to celebrate too.

Later, after things calmed down, Ben and I sat at the bar with Milly. Ben looked at me, and after a deep breath said, "Okay, Vlad, you look like you're about to bust. Ask away."

"Finally," I said, putting my beer bottle on the bar top. "Those were your beer cans in the tall grass on eighteen, weren't they?"

Ben nodded. "After I left you on the patio last night, I walked out in the dark onto eighteen and looked for something. It only took me a minute to see it. It was pretty clear how I was gonna play it. I hit that approach shot twenty-five times until I finally got it to hook enough. The first one I hit ended up landing on the patio in the middle of a party. I had a couple of beers waiting for the crowd of people to calm down."

Milly started to laugh. "So you set this guy up with the old 'hook the drive into the woods' play?"

Ben laughed. "It wasn't a hook. It was a high slice, which was easier for me. And Mill, this guy was such a prick. I wanted to rip his head off. And to top it off, he shows up with his girlfriend and tells me he's gonna buy her earrings with the bank. I hope she left his pompous ass at the airport."

I needed to know more. "So, hold on for a minute. You put the entire match on two shots. Both are impossible. But you bet..." I stopped and looked at Milly.

"Vlad, I know all about the money. And this was a big one," Milly said.

I nodded and looked back at Ben. "Okay, so you bet half a million dollars on two shots. The first was a slice over trees to a space as small as this room. The second was a seventy-yard hook over the clubhouse with a seven-iron. Is that what I witnessed?"

Ben shrugged, but I wasn't having any of it. I grabbed his shoulder and shook him, causing him to spill his beer.

"What the hell, Mark, easy does it," Ben said, holding his now dripping beer can away from himself.

I stood up. "Ben, I've been through a lot over the last six months out here. Most of that time I've either been dragging you around or trying to impress you. You owe me. Don't tell me that you don't know, or care. You know you do."

Ben could see that I was serious. He nodded and said, "What do you want?"

"The truth." I quickly replied.

Ben took another sip and pulled his chair closer to mine. He pointed at the chair telling me to sit. Milly reached down and grabbed two more beers and put them on the bar in front of us. He then walked down the other end of the bar, leaving the two of us alone.

"Okay, what do you want to know?" he asked.

I took a breath and opened my beer. After taking a swig, I looked at him. "Was that your play? On eighteen?"

Ben exhaled. "I set the whole match up for that, yeah. And it worked. Listen, sometimes it doesn't, but Monroe has one glaring weakness, and that's his consistent blandness. I knew he wouldn't be aggressive with a lead down the stretch. He never is."

"So you kept it close so that you could beat him on seventeen and eighteen?"

"That was the plan. I missed a lot of putts and hit into a lot of crap, but I hit the ball all day right where I wanted."

"Wow," I said, shaking my head. "What would you have done if he made one of those long putts, or if you hit a tree, or pulled a bad lie, or..."

Ben reached out and grabbed my arm. "Hey, Mark. If you lose, you lose. That's the way it goes. That's what makes a real player. You don't want to lose, but if you do, well... You move on."

Again, I shook my head and exhaled. "But, you hit that drive on eighteen to a..." I replayed the shot again in my head. "How the hell did you do that?"

"Mark, in my defense, I planned all of that. I hit, what, five or six sliced drives all day. Each one was getting me to the point I could feel that drive on eighteen. And the approach, if that was the first time I tried that shot... Well, it wasn't. It's not like I was going out there against him blind."

"So, you didn't do a withdrawal from the brain bank?" I asked him with a smile.

"Still a prick at times, huh, Vlad?" he said. "I pulled the tee shot on seventeen right out of the bank. I don't hit that shot without having hit one like it back..."

"Fine, alright," I cut him off. "I don't want to debate the brain bank. I want an honest answer to one simple question."

"Okay," he said, looking me right in the eyes. "What?"

"Ben, how good are you? I mean, how talented a player are you? I don't think you've ever, I mean in all the times we've played, you've never tried to play your best. So, how good are you? Show me the real Ben Newell. I want to see him."

Ben smiled and looked down. "Kid..." he started but stopped. After a moment, he said, "I don't know how good I am. I don't know how you measure 'good'. Golf to me was never about just hitting the ball and making putts. It was always about the competition. It's about positioning yourself and your opponent where you want them, and then hitting the shots to see it through."

"So tell me, if you played that guy today and didn't pull any of the stuff you did. I mean, if you played him straight up, what's the result?"

Ben turned his head and shrugged. "Well, Monroe was a bad choice by his guy to play in this type of match. He's a great golfer, but not a great player. That's pretty clear since I rolled him good."

I shook my head. "I don't care about any of that. What I mean is, if you both played straight up. Who would win?"

Ben looked pained as he thought about my question. He blinked a few times and took a drink.

"Why is it so hard to answer that question?" I asked him.

"I don't know, I guess I don't like talking about myself. I don't think of the game like that."

I leaned into Ben and said, "Well, for a second, think that way. Who wins? Go ahead, put the bullshit aside and answer me. I promise I won't share what you say with anyone. If the real Ben Newell played Monroe, not the player but the real Ben."

He nodded and sat up in his chair. "Okay. Straight up?"

"Straight up. I want to know how good Ben Newell is."

He smiled. "If I played that prick straight up, on that course, that match is over by the fourteenth hole. Maybe earlier."

I saw Ben's shoulders relax when he told me. He sat back in his chair and took a sip of his beer. It was the first time I saw him take a sip of his favorite Pabst Blue Ribbon and enjoy it. It was as if he didn't have to drink it but wanted to drink it. I realized that even though Ben did not exhibit an ego, like all of us, he had one.

"All the yelling and slamming of your clubs during the match?" I asked.

"All show," he said with a smile. "I wanted him to think he was inside my head. On one of the tees, I thought I may have bent the shaft so I stopped hitting the club into the ground so hard."

I looked over at a wooden sign on the wall, hanging over the bar. On it was a badly painted '64' in red. Whoever hung it did not wait for the paint to dry. Each number had drips of paint running down the wood. On top of the sign, cardboard letters were taped on that said, 'Course Record'. Under the number was a picture of a man that played at The Bridge five years ago, but since passed away. His name was Elliot Yardley, but to everyone, he was 'Scratch'.

I pointed to the sign. "You knew Scratch, I've heard you say he was a great player."

"He was," Ben said, taking another relaxed drink from his beer.

"That sixty-four, on this crappy course, that's a pretty good score, isn't it?"

"Yeah, it is," Ben said, looking over at the sign.

"What's your best score here? And Ben, I'm not talking about what you tell people. I know you go out and play alone a lot. The truth. What's your best score?"

Ben shrugged.

"I won't tell anyone. And I won't scream for your picture to be up there. But what is it?"

Ben smiled and looked over his shoulder to make sure no one

could hear him. He leaned over to me and said, "Sixty. I've done it twice. Missed a ten-footer on eighteen the last time for fifty-nine."

"Woah," I said. "You know, you…"

"Stop it," Ben interrupted. "Don't even go there. I am not made for the professional game. Not mentally or physically."

"How'd you know that's what I was going to say?" I asked.

"Because that's what I'm always asked when the topic comes up." He looked down for a moment and shook his head. "Those guys on tour, playing at a high level for seventy-two holes, week after week? That's not me." He turned around and pointed to everyone in the room. "I need this. I need these people. I need the action. The day I walk away from them is the day I stop playing."

"You think you could ever walk away from the game like that? Like snapping your fingers?"

Ben nodded. "Absolutely. This game is, well… It grabs you in different ways. People like you, you can enjoy the game on every level. Whether you have a putt to win, or you're just hitting the ball on the range, you love it. I knew that the first time I saw you play. It's why you have a chance to be a pro. You can let it go for a while and come back to it recharged with the same passion because you would miss it. Me, when I let it go, I'll never come back. I learned that when I started playing with Kerry. I don't know what it is…." He took another sip from his can and looked me in the eye. "Actually, I do know what it is. It's the challenge. The risk. I get off on what you can do with the game, not the game itself. I get off on what I did today. Shit, I almost put myself in front of a madman's gun. If I lost, I don't doubt that Marino would be pissed and might say enough. But you know what? I'd do it again tomorrow if I could."

Ben was getting serious in the tone of his voice and his demeanor. "Sounds like you're talking about a drug or a gambling problem. But what do I know?" I said.

"You're talking about an addiction," he said. "And you're right. It is an addiction. But not a gambling addiction. For me, it's all internal. I see a spot where I want to hit the ball, and I challenge myself to do it. That happens on every shot. Every time. That's why I need this place. I can come here and there are always twenty people that will go out onto the course and feed me what I need. In some of the rounds I've played here, I may have gone under sixty, but I rarely keep score. When I play alone, I don't think about totals, I think about the perfect shot. And if I get to do that with a little action, all the better."

I asked, "Do you ever have fun just playing the game?"

Ben thought for a few seconds and shook his head. "Truthfully? No. I don't think I've ever had fun playing the game. To me, that action is fun. The challenge of trying to hit the ball to a spot is fun. But the actual game and everything around it. No. Never. That's not what golf is for me. It never has been."

I stared back at him, appreciating his honesty, but shocked at his words. "Ben, I don't know if this is the wrong thing to say, but I'm sorry."

"Sorry," he said, leaning back from me. "Why?"

Now it was my turn to shrug.

"Really?" he said to me. "You whine about me not being honest, and…"

I put up my hands and stopped him. "You're right, but it's tough for me to lecture you on why I find the game fun."

Ben scoffed. "Hey, you've done your fair share of lecturing at me. Go ahead, I can take it."

He made me laugh and I nodded. "Sure, okay." I thought for a moment. "Look, I agree that competition is fun. And the adrenaline from the action is awesome. But there's so much more than that. It's hitting the ball and watching it do what you want. It's feeling it leave the face. It's being with your friends and the camaraderie that happens. It's being on a beautiful course, in the sun, and taking the time to enjoy your surroundings. Even on a crappy pasture like this place, I love it. It's following the game and watching great players. It's the history of the game and the great names, knowing I can play the same courses they played. It's the emotion that comes from loving this game knowing that I share the same emotions as someone like, say, Bobby Jones. I have the same passion as he did. I could sit with him and we would be able to share that."

Ben shook his head. "I guess I envy you, kid. Golf has never been that for me. The enjoyment I get never lasts longer than the shot I just hit. Once it lands and stops rolling, it's time for the next challenge. To be perfectly honest, I'm getting tired of it all. With all the crap from Marino, dealing with Bellows and Spano, my back is getting pushed up against a wall."

"How so?" I asked.

Ben looked over his shoulder, and then back at me. "Kid, things are going to change soon. What happened today is going to make certain people very happy. But it'll also mean they're going to want more. That's the way things work with assholes like Bellows and Marino. They'll always want more. And guess what, I'm sick of giving it to them. There are stronger things at play for me, and their bullshit is stronger than my addiction. You and I, we keep doing what we've been doing. I'll tee it up for the good 'ole Olympia guests and make them happy. But soon, I'm gone."

"Okay," I said. "Why don't you just leave now? What's the big deal?"

"It's not that easy, I need to take care of some things, and while that's happening, I need to keep Marino thinking that although I'm difficult, I'm still on his side."

"What are you buying time for?" I asked.

He looked at me. I could see he wanted to tell me, but as he started to open his mouth, he stopped. "Not now. I owe you about this, just not now."

"Always the mystery man, right?" I asked. "And what happens to me when you leave? Bellows is gonna be all over me because I let you go."

"No, that won't happen. Bellows will be..." He stopped, and I could see that he was holding back. He leaned close to me and said, "We'll talk, I promise. I'm trying to deal with these guys, but they can be difficult. There's a lot of money involved and they'll go pretty far to get it. But right now, I'm almost at the point where I can exit on my terms. And I'll take care of you."

At that moment, it hit me that Ben was not just a player on the course. He was a player all the time. Thinking back to the conversation he had with Bellows that I overheard, I assumed Ben was taking orders. I made the same assumption with his conversation with Spano and his two goons. Considering all of that, along with the way he set up Monroe, it occurred to me that Ben was in charge the entire time.

Was I another mark that Ben was setting up and using?

"I get it now," I said. "To you, I'm just like Marino, Monroe, and all the other people that you use. You're like the great manipulator playing me to get what you want. Setting the game in your favor. And I fell for it hook, line, and sinker. I even bet it was all bullshit with Spano, wasn't it?"

Ben looked at me and I could tell he wanted to leave. Before he could move away I grabbed his arm.

"Tell me," I said. "You said Spano was at your place because you told Marino you didn't want to play that match on his terms. That wasn't the real reason, was it?"

When I got no answer, I tightened my grip on his arm. "Was it?" I said louder.

Finally, he shook his head. "No, kid, it wasn't. I need him to think I'm fighting him on this. On all of this."

I let go of his arm. "So you're playing him like you played Monroe. And seeing that Spano knows who I am, and who Melissa is, you're playing me too. For what? When you look at me, do you see a shot that you want to hit perfectly? Is that it?"

Ben shook his head several times. "No, Mark. That's not it at all. I need to keep Marino at the right distance so that…"

"So that you can feed that competitive ego of yours?" I interrupted. "Seems to me that you're teeing up the ball on everything you do. Look, Ben, in any other circumstances that would be fine by me. But not when mob guys with guns are involved and I'm collateral damage. Remember, I'm not something that can get in the way and be pushed to the side. I'm something that can get killed. And not only me but Melissa too."

My voice was rising, and Ben looked around to make sure no one was looking at us. Most of the people were carrying on as usual and not paying any attention to us. I did see Milly over Ben's shoulder, looking our way.

"Mark," he calmly said, "take a breath. The alcohol is loosening your tongue."

I was too angry to 'take a breath', so I ignored him. The idea that Melissa and I were caught in a web that Ben had spun lit something inside me. "I would think that you could find some other way to feed that perverted and selfish competitive experience you want. I never got an answer about why you drink so much. You got nothing else in your life. It sounds like you have nothing to forget. So is it to help yourself feel better about being so selfish?"

Ben lowered his head. I knew when I said it that it would hurt him, and it did. He was correct that it was the beers I put away in the short time at the bar, but I didn't back down. I wanted to hear what he had to say. I stared him down, silently demanding an answer.

Shaking his head, he shook his arm loose from my grip, pushed his beer can away, and stood up. "Not now, kid. Not now," he said. "And keep this Marino talk between us, okay?"

I also stood up. "That's it?" I asked. "You're gonna run away?"

"For now, that's it," he said. "Later this week, let's meet for a beer at Rosy's. That place is safe too. I'll tell you everything. For now..." He looked around the room again and stepped right next to me. He took a thick folded-up envelope and stuck it in the pocket of my pants. "Don't open that here, wait until you get home."

I looked at him for a moment and then shook my head. "What is it, Ben? Are you buying your way out of this?"

He grabbed my shoulder. "Not here, Mark, okay? You don't want it, give it back to me later." He quickly took a few steps away from me and turned toward the door. He gave a nod at Milly, and a few people called his name. When someone tried to push him back to the bar, he spun away and walked out into the night.

I fell back into the chair and realized my face was dripping with sweat and I was out of breath. I looked down and shook my head.

"What the hell did I just do?" I said out loud to myself.

"What the hell did you do to Benny?" Milly asked, walking back over to me.

"Don't know," I said. "I got pissed at him. I'm pissed at myself, but... I don't know, am I wrong about this, Milly? Is he using me?"

"Vlad, don't think of him that way," he said, leaning on the bar across from me. "Since I've known Ben, he's been one tough nut to crack. But I will say, he's a good guy that's in a bad position. He's in a tough way, but he will always have your back. I see the way he respects you. In this valley, there are not many like him. And that's why guys like him don't last long. Ben's not much longer for the desert."

"Guys like him?" I asked. "You know the story, right? Ben told me that you know everything, so I'm assuming you know what's going on. I believed him when he said I have nothing to worry about. Now I'm not so sure."

Milly thought for a few seconds. Someone came up to the bar for a drink, and Milly waved at him telling him to grab a beer for himself. "I'm on break, so keep it on the honor system," he said over his shoulder.

"Sure, Milly," the guy said as he grabbed a beer and walked away.

Milly looked at me and said, "Vlad, if Ben tells you he's looking out for you, that means he's looking out for you. But you have to do what he says. He can't control everything. These Vegas guys are bad news. But their focus is on Ben, not you."

"You know all that for sure?" I asked.

"I guess I can't ever say one hundred percent, yes, but there's no reason they should focus on you," he said. "If that ever changes and I catch wind of it, I'll let you know."

I gave Milly a quick smile and said thanks. "Maybe I owe him an apology."

"It never hurts to mend fences before they start to need mending," he said.

I took a few sips from my beer. "Milly, you heard him say he's leaving. If he leaves the valley, where will he go? You know what drives him. He needs this place. Forget where he would go. Why would he go?"

Milly thought for a moment and said, "People that have things to live for don't last in the desert. People like him are built for bigger and better. They go to where they're meant to be. But this place grabs you. The shackles come out of the sand and when they lock on, they don't let go. You have to fight to get free and make sure it's safe to do so."

"I'm confused. Where would Ben go that has more meaning than here? I always assumed that he was always here, and always will be because this is where he can get what he wants. A game, big-money, the adrenaline. Isn't that where he wants to be?"

Milly leaned over to me. "No, that may be the Ben you know and the one most people see. It's the Ben that I used to know. But he's fighting it. He's fighting the same battle others have fought when they realized they need to get out of the desert. When they realize this place isn't what they're living for anymore. That's one of the reasons he drank so much. Because it occurred to him his place isn't here. It's killing him to be away from what he wants to live for."

"So what is Ben living for? Where does he want to go?" I asked.

Milly smiled. "Home," he simply said.

I wasn't sure what Milly said, nor why he said it.

"Home? Isn't this place home? Isn't the valley his home?" I asked.

"No," Milly said. "Vlad, Ben has a family."

I dropped back into the chair and nearly fell over backward. I tried to say something, but my voice was gone.

Milly laughed. "It's not like it's a secret, so he wouldn't get pissed if he heard me telling you. Ben got married about five years ago."

"I had no idea," I said. "Where?"

"Where is his wife? She lives with their son," Milly said, pushing back from the bar and grabbing a beer for himself.

"What?" I said. I sat with my mouth open staring at Milly. "Did you say, 'his son'?"

"Yeah," Milly said, laughing as he grabbed me another beer.

I thought back about all the times that Ben seemed hesitant to talk about things. This must have been the reason. He never mentioned or even hinted that he had a family.

I took a deep, slow breath and let it out. "Okay, please tell me: How is this possible? Where do they live?"

Milly opened his beer and took a long drink. "They live in California. Down by San Diego. She used to live here, but Ben thought things were getting too sketchy for her."

"Sketchy?" I asked.

"With all the stuff he has going on with Marino and the casino, and with what happened with Kerry Miner, he got her out of here. His son was born a couple of years ago. He goes home probably every other week for a few days."

"Wow, I never thought about what he does when I'm not seeing him here or playing with him," I said. "I kind of asked but never pushed. To tell you the truth I'm usually glad I don't have to drag his ass out of a bar. I wish I knew when he wasn't in town. I wouldn't always be waiting for the phone to ring."

"The guy has a lot on his mind when he's in the valley. So it's good for him to get out of here," Milly said. "But with the crap he's going through, it's no wonder he isn't drinking more."

I looked at Milly and then around the room. I leaned closer to him. "Tell me, do you know about this guy Marino, and Bellows, and all of the history?"

Milly smirked and looked down. After a second of thought, he nodded. "Ben's a little older than I am. I was pretty young when I walked into this room but he was already a player. Kerry Miner and Ben were well known. I heard all about them when I was working over at the Trop. They were both known as stone cold. So when I started working here and got to know him, I was able to put a face to the legend. And what I found was that the legend was bullshit. Ben turned out to be a good guy, who ended up being a friend that laid everything on the line for his mentor."

"You mean for Kerry Miner?" I asked.

"Yeah, for Miner. Ben would sit right where you are now and talk to me all the time. He trusted me. That's all Ben wants in a friend. Trust. And that's why he likes you. He trusts you. He sees himself in you. And I think that's starting to scare him."

I nearly finished my beer and said, "Tell me about Miner. What did Ben do for him?"

Milly stood up and shook his head. "I think I'll let Ben tell you about that." Milly finished his beer, took the bottle, and tossed it onto the garbage can. He started to walk to the other end of the bar, cleaning empty bottles and napkins off of the bar top. Stopping, he turned back to me and said, "Vlad, I've lived in the valley my whole life, and I know the impact this place has on people. It was tough on Ben when his wife left, but it was the right thing to do. And when she left, it was like his protective force field also left. All of the Vegas demons could now attack unimpeded. Three years later, well... He's got to leave. He has to or..."

Milly stopped and struggled to find the right words.

"You think this place is bad enough for him that he'll end up hurt? I mean, seriously hurt?" I asked.

Milly walked back and stood directly across the bar from me. "He won't get hurt. If he doesn't leave, Marino or one of those guys will kill him."

"Kill him?" I said, too loudly.

Milly looked around to see if anyone heard me. Leaning over to me he said softly, "Vlad, trust me when I tell you this because I see the same things in you that I see in Benny. You're both super talented. Talent in the valley is a magnet, usually for the wrong type of attention. When I see talented people that think this town is the answer, they usually end up used, broken, and a lot of times, dead. When I see talented people like you guys push too hard and too long, they end up dead. Both of you guys are too talented and smart to stay. So you do your time here, get what you wanted when you came here, and then get the hell out. Miner never learned that. If Ben isn't careful, he'll find trouble. You, I'm not worried."

I stared at Milly for a good five seconds trying to understand his message. "Milly, I'm not sure what you're saying, but..."

"I'm not saying anything, Vlad. You're a smart kid and you have talent on and off the course. Be smart and remember what you came to this city to do. Once you've got what you wanted, leave. Plain and simple. Leave."

I sat there thinking about his words and how wrong I was with my assumptions about Ben. After another beer, I headed back to the apartment. I felt as if I was gone for a month, not one day. I found a note from Kenny that he was staying with Kara for the night and breathed a sigh of relief. As I left the day before, I told him I was going with Ben to a big match and that I would fill him in when I got back. Right now, the last thing I wanted to do was answer all of his questions. When I hit the blinking light on the answering machine, Melissa's voice asking me to call her when I got back was soothing, but I didn't have the energy to call her. When my Mom's voice came on asking me if I was alright, I reached over and hit the Stop button.

My brain was clouded with travel, beer, and the pounding idea that I screwed Ben. As I fell back onto the recliner, I closed my eyes and thought about Milly's words. The more I thought about the way I treated Ben, the more clear it became I was wrong. I shouldn't have talked to him like I did. What was more disappointing was that in the months I knew him, I never asked him about his life.

"How selfish can I be?" I said out loud.

I found myself starting to doze off. Opening my eyes, I tried to decide if I had the energy to clean myself up and make it to my bed. The recliner was too comfortable though, and I was too tired. I rolled over on my side, and that's when I felt the envelope in my pocket. I forgot it was there. I raised my hips and fished it out. Tearing it open, a wad of money fell out on top of me. I gathered up the bills and counted them. There were thirty one-hundred-dollar bills. Three-thousand dollars in total.

I sat up and counted the money again. When I confirmed the amount, I looked in the torn envelope and found a note written on a small piece of paper:

'Mark, I wouldn't have won without you. I mean that. I owe you more than this.

Your friend, B'

Shaking my head, I fell back and passed out.

CHAPTER 14

I spent the next week trying to figure out how to approach and apologize to Ben. Luckily for me, our schedules kept us on different courses and I did not see him. I finally decided that I wasn't smart enough to figure this out and I needed to share everything with Melissa. She and I were together now for six months and besides being my girlfriend, she was the smartest person and best listener I knew. Not only did she deserve to know everything, but she was also my best chance of getting good advice.

The two of us went out Friday night for dinner. When I turned serious and started the conversation by saying, "We need to talk….", she jokingly thought I was breaking up with her.

"Breaking up? No, completely the opposite," I said.

"So you're asking me to marry you?" she asked.

"Wh… What?"

With a sly smile, she said, "Well, the opposite of breaking up is getting engaged. Right?"

I sat there with my mouth open. More than speechless, I was dumbfounded.

"Um, well, ah," I stammered.

She started to laugh. "You are so bad at hiding your true feelings. I love you and I won't put you on the spot. What is it that you want to tell me?"

I nervously laughed and shook my head. "Um, I love you too, and, well, marriage. That would be pretty much the plan, but I haven't, well, I haven't gotten..."

She reached over and put her hand up to cover my mouth. "Good, that's all I wanted to know. If it's in the plans, I'll be very happy."

"Wow," I said, letting out a long exhale and the tension along with it. "You caught me off guard."

"I know, it was part of my plan," she said, still laughing. "What do you want to tell me?"

I took one more deep breath and told her I was going to start at the beginning. I filled her in on the conversation I overheard between Ben and Bellows, the world of Vegas golf, and how Ben was my mentor. Her smile was gone when I told her about Spano and what I overheard the night I was on Ben's porch. By the time I told her what I learned about Bellows and Marino, that Ben won a match for more than half a million dollars, and about the way I treated Ben at the Bridge, Melissa was sitting back shaking her head with a shocked look on her face.

"I never knew that about Bellows," she said. "I mean, he's an asshole, we all know that. But to partner with the mob? And for this Spano guy to threaten you and me?"

"Ben says we have nothing to worry about, but I don't know. Does the name Kerry Miner ring a bell for you?" I asked.

She shook her head. "I've never heard that name, no."

"He was Ben's mentor, and something happened to him. I get the feeling that he got caught up in Vegas and just left town. And now Ben feels like he has to make up for something that Miner did."

"Why don't you just ask Ben?" Melissa said. "Mark, I know that certain people in the casino are involved with the fringe element of organized crime. For those of us in the office, it's an interesting footnote that we joke about. But there's so much Federal and State oversight that for people like Kara, it's their full-time job. Even Ken spends most of his time dealing with compliance."

"I know," I said, "but I also know what I've seen and heard."

She bit her lip and shook her head. "That asshole, Bellows. A guy like him is so connected. How could he get away with any of what Ben told you about? I don't know, do you think Ben's being paranoid?"

"Lis, I saw the guy punch him. And the two guys that were following us in Phoenix? These were not good guys. I think all of it is real. What I want to know is; are you in any danger? Am I? And is Ben?"

She nodded and reached out for my hands. Taking them in hers, she leaned over to me. "I agree with what Milly told you. Trust Ben. Reach out to him and talk. And if you don't like what he tells you, or if you think there is any danger, we get out of here. We leave the casino. You and I can move to the next great thing for us."

"You're right," I said. "I don't care about the casino. But I do care about Ben. And thank you for being with me on this. I think I'd understand if you got up and walked out right now."

Melissa did not say anything. She leaned over to me and kissed me. Putting her hand behind my neck she stared into my eyes and nodded. I looked back at her and understood exactly what she was saying.

"Thank you," I whispered. "I'll always be there for you too."

"Talk to him," she said, taking hold of my hands. "Be upfront and honest. Let him know you're nervous and that you want answers."

I nodded. "Okay, I will."

She kissed me again and said with a smile, "I never took you for a gangster."

Her comment broke the tension and we both laughed. When our food was delivered, we silently started to eat.

After a minute, I looked up at Melissa. "So, you sure you would leave with me?"

She smiled and said, "Of course. You know, if you had started this conversation with the question you thought that I thought you were going to ask, I think you now know what my answer would be."

I stared at her for a few seconds with my mouth open. The only thing I could think of saying was, "Really?"

"Yes, really. Mark, do you ever think about our future?"

When I sat back, she put her hand up. "No, don't worry about it. You have too many other things on your mind. But remember that we do have a future. Is that good for now?"

I smiled and nodded. "Yeah, that's good for now. It's good."

I felt much better walking out of the restaurant than I felt walking in. When we got back to the apartment, I picked up the phone and did something for the first time since I arrived in Las Vegas.

I called Ben.

Three days later I drove to Rosy's to meet Ben. When he returned my call, I could tell that he was calling from a long distance. Now knowing about his family, I assumed that he was home with them, but I didn't ask. He told me we could meet at Rosy's on Monday, but his instructions were confusing. He wanted me to drive around the back of the bar and he would jump in my car. When I asked him why we were not simply meeting in the bar, he repeated his instructions and I left it at that.

Pulling in, Rosy's parking lot was empty except for a few cars haphazardly parked around the building. The nearly empty parking lot led me to assume Rosy's didn't do much business on a Monday. Pulling around the back, Ben was waiting for me. He got in and said, "Drive up and down The Strip for a while. Then we'll head over to the Bridge."

When I asked him a question, he told me to wait. So for the next twenty-five minutes, we drove in silence. The entire time he looked around and checked mirrors. When we reached the end of The Strip for the fifth time he had me stop. Jumping out, he ran over to a payphone and made a call. When he got back in the car, all he said was, "The Bridge."

When we parked behind the clubhouse, Milly walked out and knocked on the passenger-side window. "No one's here," he said as Ben rolled the window down. "Just the regulars."

"Thanks, Mill. We'll be in soon," Ben said. "Is he here?"

"Yeah and he says there is no one watching," Milly replied.

Ben nodded and Milly walked away leaving us alone.

"Why the spy bullshit," I said. "Let's go in."

Ben ignored my comment and took a deep breath.

"Ben, who's here?" I asked, pushing to get Ben to talk, but he ignored my question.

"Mark," he said in a wavering voice, "I'm sorry. I'm sorry for getting you involved."

"Whoa, Ben," I said, "getting me involved…"

"Stop," he said, grabbing my arm. "Let me explain all of this. I guess I should say I'm sorry for letting you get involved and not stopping it. There are a lot of things that are happening in the background. I thought that my going along with Bellows and allowing you to babysit me would keep you on the sidelines. I couldn't say no to him about you because he's such an anal and nosy prick he would start asking too many questions. But, well, it's gone too far. And now, even though they're telling me to keep cool, I can't do it any longer. You need to know everything."

I had no idea what Ben was talking about, but his tone was scaring me. "Ben, I wanted to apologize to you for the way I treated you the other night. And now I find out you have a family in California."

"So, Milly has been doing a lot of talking, huh?" Ben said with a smile.

I nodded. "He told me some things I should have already asked you about. I guess I just figured all you did was play in the desert. What's all of this other stuff about? And who's telling you to keep cool? Bellows?"

Ben pulled back and stared at me. "What do you have to apologize for? The language from our talk at the bar? Kid, you've got nothing to be sorry about. I…" He took a deep breath. "Mark, you've done a lot for me and I'll never forget that. Being your friend was the push I needed to make this happen. You gave me the final reason to do it. Knowing you has been…"

His voice trailed off and I could see he was struggling for the right words. After a deep breath, he looked at me and nodded. "Having you as a friend has shown me what I was at your age, and what I can still be now. It's also shown me that you also need to move on. Your future is wide open. And not just golf. There are more important things."

I shook my head and started to say something but he cut me off. Looking at the clubhouse, he spoke low. "Everything is moving faster than I thought it would. That's why we're talking now. It's time to move on and I couldn't just disappear without talking first."

I fell back into the seat of the car. "Ben, you're confusing me."

Ben nodded and held up his hand. "Okay, listen. Just listen."

Ben looked out the car windows, checking all angles. After checking the side mirror, he took a deep breath and let it slowly out. "I know I can trust you, but I need to know that you'll listen."

I nodded and started to talk, but Ben put up his hand to stop me. After he was sure I would stay quiet, he said, "Mark, tomorrow the FBI will be arresting Bellows and a few others in the casino. They're also going after Marino. The son, not the father. For the past year, the FBI has been after me to provide evidence, but so far, well, I've been able to stay out of it. There's someone close to the investigation that's been able to keep me out of it. For now, I'm okay. We're okay."

I sat silently for a few seconds trying to grasp what Ben was telling me. "Do you mean that the FBI is going to arrest Bellows because of the golf match you played?"

Ben shook his head. "No, it has nothing to do with golf, the matches, or anything you or I are involved with. It's all about the crap Bellows and Marino are involved in with the track, the casino floor, and lying to the Gaming Commission. The money they make is being moved to other states which makes it a Federal issue. That means the FBI. The investigation has been going on for years."

I nodded, starting to understand what Ben was talking about. Still, there was something that didn't add up.

"Ben, why would Milly be telling me that these guys want to kill you if it has nothing to do with you?"

Now it was Ben's turn to sit quietly. I could see the struggle on his face. I let him think for a few more seconds, then I said, "Ben, why are you in danger?"

Finally, he looked at me and said, "I'll be leaving when it happens. And you should leave too. Marino wants something from me that he thinks I have. He thinks that by keeping me around earning for him, like I did against Monroe, eventually, I'd give in. He thinks I'd tell him where it is."

"What is it that he thinks you have?" I asked.

"Something from Kerry," Ben answered. "Something Kerry took from the Marinos, and they want it back."

"What is it?" I asked.

The tension on Ben's face was clear. He took a deep breath and slowly let it out. "It's money. Five million."

My eyes went wide. "Five million dollars? That's a pretty big number," I said.

Ben smiled. "A big number? You're starting to talk like you're from the desert. And you're right, it's a big number. And Marino thinks that Kerry gave the money to me and he wants it back."

I stared at Ben waiting for more information. Finally, I said, "Okay, so do you have it? Do you know where the money is?"

"In a way, I do."

I said, "So, why is it your problem that Kerry won't give it back? I don't understand how that involves you. And how did Kerry get all this money from Marino?"

Ben looked down and shook his head. "Mark, Kerry is dead. Marino killed him because of the money."

My heart stopped when I heard the word, 'killed'. I tried to say something but Ben held up his hand. "I should have told you about this, I should have never let Bellows let you get close to me. I'm sorry, I didn't think it would get this far."

Now, I put my hand up. "Ben, stop. I have no idea what the hell you're talking about. Why are... I mean... Shit. Ben, I need to know what this is all about."

He looked into the mirror and around the outside of the car. His paranoia was evident.

"I know," he said. "But you have to listen to me about getting out."

"Okay, I will."

Ben stared at me for a few seconds and then nodded. "Okay. Good." After a deep breath, he said, "Let's take a walk."

We started to walk into the night, out of the parking lot, and onto the course. When we got to the eighteenth green, Ben stopped. The only light was the dull glow coming from The Strip in the distance, and Ben was a dark silhouette. While I could not see his face, I could hear his breathing and see his shoulders going up and down. His stress was making me anxious, but I let him find his voice. He walked over to the flagstick and pulled it out of the cup. Dropping it on the green, he walked ten feet away.

"The last time I played with Kerry was many years ago. He called me out of the blue and said he wanted a match. He wanted to compete. I thought at first he wanted to set up a match with me and him against a mark, to maybe make some money. When I suggested we call up one of the casinos, he said he didn't want to play for money, he wanted to feel it. To feel the adrenaline. To feel it one more time. He scared the crap out of me the way he was talking, but I said okay. I hadn't seen him in about six months. He was in Europe doing crap for Marino. I thought that he was so sucked into that world, that he was gone forever. So when he said he wanted to play, I jumped. We met here at the Bridge, on the first tee. It was like the old days."

Ben walked back a few feet and faced the hole. He crouched down as if he were lining up a putt in the dark. I stood watching him. To me, it was not dark anymore. I could see his focus as he looked over the line of the putt. How he closed his left eye to see the line, and then closed both eyes to picture the putt rolling and falling. I expected him to stand up and walk up to his ball.

"This was the putt. I had this putt to beat him. I asked him on the first tee when he last played but he wouldn't answer me. That was Kerry. He would never make an excuse. All he said was he wanted me to play my best. I won the first two holes and then on three, he hit a four-iron to two feet. Just like that. He goes bogey-bogey on one and two. He looks like a weekend hacker. And after the swing on number three, it's a match. We never spoke. It was the old days, and on eighteen, I hit my second shot to right here. And the pin was right where it is now."

Ben took a deep breath and I could hear the emotion. When he turned his head, the light from The Strip reflected off of the tears on his face.

"He had the easier putt, straight up the hill. And he pulled the putt. He missed it. I played a thousand holes of golf with Kerry and never did I see him pull a putt. When the ball rolled by, he looked at me and smiled. Do you know what he said to me? He looked at me and said, 'Don't let me down. Not with this putt. Not with anything else'. I didn't know what he meant. Now I do, but at the time, I wanted to beat him. And I did. I made the putt. I acted like a selfish piece of shit and made the putt. I couldn't give him a win, and I didn't."

Again, Ben crouched down, and now he was crying. I walked over and stood next to him. After a few sobs, he stood up. Turning to me, he handed me an envelope.

"Here, Kerry gave me two envelopes and told me to never keep them together. I've never opened them. Don't you ever open it either. I don't want to know what you do with it but do me a favor and hide it. The next time we meet, you can give it back to me. We'll open them together."

"What are they? What's in this envelope?" I asked, holding it up.

"It's half of a European bank account number. My wife hid the other one. I told you that Kerry lost control. He was in Europe working for Marino. By the time we played our match, he knew he was never going to get away from him. So he did something that he thought would give him leverage. He almost pulled it off too, but he forgot about the one thing that guys like Marino place higher than money, and that's respect. And that's what killed him."

Ben started to walk back toward the clubhouse and as I walked with him he continued.

"In Europe, Marino asked Kerry to move money for him. A lot of it. The one thing that Marino didn't know about Kerry was that he was connected. All of those matches that we played against bankers, investors, and Wall Street guys exposed Kerry to a lot of smart financial guys. And not all of them were clean. One guy, in particular, told both of us that if we ever needed help hiding money from the government, he would be happy to help. And that's who Kerry reached out to. Marino told Kerry to move money from one bank to another so that he could keep ahead of the feds and the international banking law guys. He took it and hid it from Marino. Five million bucks. Five million dollars that belonged to Marino and the mob. All from drugs and gambling. And now Kerry had it, and he told them he would give it back if they let him go."

"Let him go?" I asked.

"Yeah, to stop using him. To give him his freedom. He finally realized that even in Europe, the desert had him." He waved his arm toward The Strip. "He realized that this place had swallowed him up. And he wanted out. Missing that putt proved to him that he was free. That he didn't have to be a player anymore."

"Did you know about the money?" I asked.

"Not until Kerry told me when our match was over. He told me he was getting out, and that he was leaving for Australia. He wanted to play with me one more time and then he was going. He was happy. He was changed. He had kicked the sand off of his feet and thought he could leave it all behind."

Ben took a deep long breath and let it out. "But he was wrong. Marino still had him. The desert wouldn't let go."

When we got back to the parking lot, Ben looked around.

"We're alone, Ben," I said, trying to calm him.

"Kid, don't ever assume that you're alone. It never hurts to be a little paranoid."

He took another moment to look at the parking lot and seemed to relax. "After he left, I stood right here, trying to figure out what he meant. To understand what was different about him. It was his smile when he hugged me that did it for me. I saw that he thought he was free. And I was still standing right here when Marino and Balito came for me."

"Balito?" I asked.

"Yes, Junior. The guy I told you to be careful with. They took me to see Marino's dad. I'm lucky I put the envelopes in my golf bag. If not, they would have found it. They took me to Marino's place, gave me a beer, offered me a massage and a whore, and then told me why I was there. The old Marino told me straight out, Kerry stole from them. They thought that I knew where the money was, and they said I had to tell them. When I told them I didn't know what they were talking about, the son pulled me aside. The money Kerry stole was mob money, not just his dad's. If they didn't get it back, Kerry was dead. He said they believed me that I didn't know where it was but he said I could save Kerry by telling him to give it back. And I could make a lot of money myself by partnering with Bellows. I didn't listen to the crap about partnering with Bellows, but I did think I had to do it to save Kerry. So I agreed. And the son vouched for me to his dad. He told me Kerry would be safe if he did what they wanted. I told him I would talk to Kerry, and I left there to find him."

"But you weren't lying, right?" I said. "Saying you didn't know where the money was."

Ben pointed to the envelope. "I didn't. So, I wasn't lying. At the time, I knew the info in the envelope was about the money. I was careful with my words and they didn't press me too hard. These guys can see through any lies. They knew I didn't know exactly where it was, but they thought I might have an idea. It's why they wanted me close. And that's why I never opened it, just in case they cornered me. I couldn't outright lie to them because they would know.

"So I went to find Kerry. I found out he was at one of the hotels called The Oasis. I ran to get to him before he left. I wanted to tell him they forced me to vouch for him, and that he should give it back. And that he would be alright. And when I pulled up to The Oasis there were cops all over the place. They found Kerry in the pool, dead from a gunshot. He thought that he had leverage, but when you disrespect these guys, you never have leverage."

I stood next to Ben unsure if he was going to continue or if I should say something. He stood looking down at his feet, kicking the dirt.

"Um, Ben, I am... I'm sorry," I said. "Who? Who killed him?"

Ben looked up at me. "Do you mean who pulled the trigger? Spano pulled the trigger. That bastard was probably picturing my face when he did it. If you mean who killed him? That was Marino. Both Marinos. I found out later that right after I left and the son vouched for me, he told the dad he would make me an earner, and eventually get me to tell him where the money was. So the dad made Kerry pay for the disrespect he showed. He told the son to kill Kerry, which Spano did."

"And do they still think that you know where the money is?" I asked.

"It's been a few years so they're starting to have doubts," Ben said. "And with the money I make them, they realize I'm worth more to them playing. That's why I'm still alive, or at least why I haven't been hung by my feet over the top of the highest building in the desert. Still, every time I go home, Marino has people check my travel schedule."

"But you're leaving?" I asked.

Ben nodded. "When they move to arrest the son, the father may want to strike out at me because they think I know something. I know Spano will. That bastard would love the chance to get to me, either with a bullet or at least to break my arm. I will give Bellows and the son one thing, they have protected me. That ends with them in jail. That's why I'm going to use this chance to take off. They look at me like Kerry. They'll never let me go, so I have an escape plan for my family."

"Where will you go?" I asked.

"Don't worry about it. The less you know, the better. Let's just say I have some help. After a time, when I think it's safe, I'll reach out to you. For now, go home. With Bellows in jail, the casino will stop all of his programs, including golf. Take your clubs, and get your ass onto the Tour. That way I'll be able to watch you play on TV. And take Melissa with you. She's a great girl and you two make a perfect couple."

I held up the envelope. "Where do I hide this?"

Ben smiled. "That's for you to know, and me not to know. Just don't carry it in your pocket. Maybe mail it to someone and ask them to hold it until you see them. Then put it away when you get home. Get a safety deposit box and forget it's there until I reach out."

I stood in the dark looking at Ben. "So you're leaving?" I asked him. "What the hell am I..."

"Stop," Ben said, putting his hand on my shoulder. "Mark, you're an incredibly talented and smart guy. And I'm not talking about just golf. I'm talking about life. And your game is good enough to go anywhere you want. Go back home, and start to live on the grass, not the sand." He kept his hand on my shoulder and nodded his head. "With you getting out now, and me getting out alive, I think that would make Kerry happy."

Then he turned and walked away from me. Without looking back, he said, "I have a ride out of here. I'll find you." He then stopped and stood still for a moment. Turning around, he said, "Mark, remember. Never miss a chance to show yourself that you can be great. You get a chance to go for it, no matter what the conditions, you go for it. And always remember you made that shot when things get tough. That is what will make you great."

That was the last time I saw Ben. He left me standing in the dark, holding the envelope. When I walked into the clubhouse, Milly told me Ben walked in the back, waved to him, and walked out the front.

He was gone.

I drove back to the apartment and found Melissa, Ken, and Kara. The four of us drove to the diner across town. I told them everything Ben told me, and that it would make sense for me to leave. Two hours later, I went to Melissa's house in Henderson for the first time. I moved my suitcase into their guest room and spent the night lying awake staring at the ceiling. What sleep I got was interrupted by the phone ringing at 6:00 AM. A minute later Melissa knocked on the bedroom door and stepped in. The call was from Kara. She got a call from work telling her to not come into the office, and that at some point during the day, she would be receiving directions from the casino lawyers about how she would soon be interviewed by the FBI.

After breakfast, Kenny called me to say that the FBI and local police were all over the office. As Ben said, there were several people arrested, including Kirk Bellows. Later in the day, the television news covered the arrests and said that along with several casino executives, a dozen people thought to be involved with organized crime were arrested. The only name they mentioned was Aldo Marino, Jr.

Melissa received a call from the HR department at the casino, telling her that she was being laid off. The news was not all bad since they would be paying her for six months to ensure she did not go to work for another casino. Her father took her to clear out her apartment and to fill out some paperwork at the office. She told me that Bellows' office was taped off and several FBI agents were sifting through piles of paperwork in the conference room.

The only time I left Melissa's parent's house was to go to the post office. I put the envelope from Ben into another envelope and sent it to Mr. Wittich at Water Edge Country Club with a request that he hold onto it for me. I tried to sleep the next night, but again I tossed and turned. I then spent the next morning sweating bullets as I prepared to have what I truly felt was going to be the most difficult conversation of my life. After finally getting the courage, I walked upstairs and found Melissa talking to her parents in their kitchen. I told her I needed to talk to her, and we went out onto her porch.

"I have to leave," I said. "I need to get back home, and try to get my old job at Water Edge."

Melissa did not say a word but I could see the pain on her face.

"I...I want to try and maybe make a go out of golf, and..."

"I know," Melissa said. "Mark, I don't want you to go, but..." She looked down and for the first time since I met her, she seemed to be at a loss for words. "Mark, you have to do what you think you need to do for... For yourself."

I put my hand up to her mouth and blurted out, "Stop. Melissa, I want you to come with me."

Her eyes went wide and she started to talk but stopped. After a moment she shook her head and said, "I can't... I mean, I don't..."

I could see her struggles. "Melissa, you don't have to come now, maybe you could come later, or...I don't know. Maybe later in the year?"

She saw my struggles and smiled. "Mr. Travers, are you attempting to continue the discussion we started at the restaurant the other night?"

"Well," I said, "I think I am. It's just that now with all of this crap, I don't know if it's the right thing to do, or even why you would want to go with me."

Moving closer to me, she said, "I told you that if you started the conversation with the question I thought you were going to ask that you should know what my answer will be. So? Are you asking?"

I stared into her eyes and saw nothing but how beautiful a person she is. The most beautiful person in the world.

"Yes, I'm asking."

She kissed me and then threw her arms around me. "And I'm saying yes."

For the first time since we stepped outside, I took a breath. I hugged her back and started to apologize for not having a ring, and for what can best be described as a lame engagement.

"Don't worry," she said. "It's who I'm going to marry that is most important."

"Thanks for that," I said.

"I just didn't know I was going to marry a mobster," she said with a laugh.

I also laughed, and after what was a surprisingly easy conversation with her parents, we started to plan out my travels back home and how we were going to start our lives together.

The next day, Kenny and Kara met us for dinner in Henderson. The feeling I had that I was hiding out from the mob was waning. Ken told me that my stuff was packed and ready to be picked up from the apartment, and Kara told us that things were getting back to normal at the casino. Ben was correct about one thing: all of the programs that Bellows was responsible for at the casino were terminated. There was no more golf ambassador program. Ken handed me a paycheck and told me I was out of a job.

Both Melissa and I thought that we would have to talk to the FBI but no one called us.

CHAPTER 15

Two days later I made plans to go home. I talked to Mr. Wittich on the phone and he told me my old job would be there. He also told me that he had already signed me up for the local PGA training courses that needed to be taken before becoming a member of the PGA.

As for Melissa and me, we decided she would be coming east the following month after I was settled. I took my last paycheck and went with her mom to her local jewelry store. Together we bought a ring and I proposed officially. We then spent the next two hours on the phone with my mom. Needless to say, she started a countdown for when I would be home.

The night before I was leaving, I was alone at Melissa's house while they were out shopping. Kenny called to tell me Rudy from Rosy's called the apartment and said someone had to come to get Ben. I asked Kenny if he was sure, and he said that some guy named Rudy wanted someone to 'get this drunk out of my bar'. I hung up the phone and sat back, wondering how Ben might be back. Was Rudy mistaken? Was Ben trying to send me a message and wanted to meet, but did not know how to get to me?

I got out my notebook and called the numbers I had for Ben, both in Vegas and California. Both numbers were disconnected. I tried the number at the Bridge, but the call went unanswered. I remembered that the clubhouse was closed while they replaced the old bar and added an actual grill. It seems that, believe it or not, the club was flagged for a code violation. I then called the last number I had for someone who could help, but Milly did not answer.

Left alone to decide what I should do, I figured I would drive over and see if Ben was at Rosy's. If he wanted to get in touch with me, having Rudy from Rosy's call was a logical way to do it. So I left a note for Melissa saying I would be back in a couple of hours and I naively drove back into Las Vegas not knowing what awaited me.

When I pulled into Rosy's lot, there were cars everywhere. Since it was a Friday, the place was hopping. I drove up and down the parking rows to see if Ben's car was there. Not spotting it, I drove around back but again did not see Ben or his car. So I parked and walked up to the front doors. The usual bouncer was there and he nodded at me as I walked in. I was going to ask him where Ben was, but he was too busy talking to a pretty girl. So I moved into the bar and right into hell. Literally. ACDC's Hells Bells was playing over the speakers, and people were pressed up against each other. When I saw Rudy at the bar, I raised my arm to get his attention and found myself staring at a gun, pointed at my stomach.

The bar was so full that no one noticed the man standing in front of me with a gun. He took two steps toward me and put his arm around my neck. Leaning in, he spoke directly into my ear.

"If you say anything I will gut your ass and you'll bleed out like a pig."

When I looked down the gun was replaced by a knife.

I looked up at him but with the lights pointed at the door in my eyes, I could not see who this was. I froze.

"Move your ass over the side door, and don't say a word."

When I didn't move, he pushed the knife into my stomach. I felt a stab of pain and tried to pull away, but he pulled me closer by the neck.

Again, speaking directly into my ear, he said, "I don't give a shit if

I gut you here, so you either move or bleed out."

Feeling the warm flow of blood down my stomach, I looked around for help, but no one was paying any attention to the man with his arm around my neck and a knife in my stomach. He shoved me to the side of the bar and walked directly behind me. Each time I slowed down to step around someone, his knife would cut into my back. By the time I stepped out of the side door, I felt blood running down my back. Looking down at my stomach, a bloodstain the size of a softball had formed. I started to raise my shirt to see where I was cut, but he shoved me into the side of the car that was parked right outside the door. He then pushed me down and into the backseat and jumped in next to me.

As soon as the car door shut, we peeled out of the lot. It took me a few seconds to realize what had happened, but I finally looked over at the man with the knife and asked, "Who are you?"

"Shut up," he responded. "Em, stay off The Strip, take the long way around."

"Yes, sir," the driver replied.

Again, I asked who he was and he replied by elbowing me in the ribs, doubling me over. I leaned forward and tried not to vomit from the pain. As I started to lean back, he backhanded me across the side of my face, driving me into the car door.

"You throw up in this car and I'll rip your stomach out through your asshole. You got it?"

I didn't say anything. The blow to my head may have hurt, but it also cleared my head. I got past the cuts and bleeding, and was able to block out the pain in my ribs. As I looked out the window, I started to analyze what was happening to me. Looking at the back of the driver's head, I could see he was a big guy. His shoulders rose above the car seat and he appeared to have no neck. As the lights from other cars reflected off of his head, I could see he had wet, slicked-back hair.

"Junior," I said under my breath.

Again, the man next to me elbowed me, this time on the back of my ribs.

"Talk again and I'll shove this knife down your throat, got it?"

I leaned into the door, doing what I could to move away from the man. Looking at the back of Junior's head, Ben's words came back to me: 'He wouldn't lose a second of sleep after putting a bullet through your head'.

We drove on backroads, and after getting onto one of the main drags, I started to recognize where we were. Pulling off the road, I saw that we were on a service road. It was the back entrance to The Bridge. When I looked out the passenger-side window to see if the clubhouse was lit up, I received another elbow, this one just a tap.

"Yup, asshole. We're at your favorite place. You and Newell's little playground. Too bad there's no one here."

He was right. It was all dark. As we pulled into the lot, there were no cars. In all my time in Vegas, there were always people at The Bridge. I thought to myself that it was my bad luck that I was being kidnapped on the only day no one was here, but I realized that was all part of this guy's plan. When the car stopped, I tried to sink further into the car seat, but he opened his door, grabbed me by the collar, and pulled me out onto the ground. In the process, my shirt was torn off my back and was on the ground in front of me. Looking down, I could see bloodstains all over the back where he had cut me.

Junior walked over and stood behind me as I cowered on the ground.

"Pick his sad ass up, Em," the man said.

Junior reached down and pulled me up and onto my feet. With

the light in the parking lot shining on the man's face, I could finally see who it was that was beating on me.

"Spano," I said. "You're the guy I saw with Ben."

He walked up to me and I noticed that he was no longer holding the knife. He again had a gun.

"You better show some respect, kid. It's Mr. Spano. Got it?"

When I didn't answer, he took the barrel of the gun and shoved it into my face. I turned away, but Junior grabbed me by the ears and held my head. This time Spano took the gun and pushed it into my mouth.

"Come on, kid, we're going to take a walk. And then, I'm going to ask you a question. You tell me what I want to hear, you'll walk away from this little party we're having with only a few cuts and bruises. If you don't answer, I'll stick this down your face and pull the trigger. Got it?"

When I didn't move or respond, he took the gun and moved it up and down making my head nod. "See, you got it, right?"

He took the gun out of my mouth and laughed. "I know how much you and Newell loved it here. I think finding your brains all over one of the putting greens will be perfect. Em, get the club out of the trunk, and don't forget a golf ball. Kid, let's go play some golf."

He slapped my cheek with the gun and shoved me into the darkness. I nearly fell over but he grabbed my arm, spun me around, and again pushed me. Not sure what to do, I stopped, but he put the gun into my back and said, "Walk."

After we had walked to the end of the parking lot, Spano told me to stop. I thought he was going to shoot me, and I looked at the ground in front of me. There was a small dry bed of dirt and rock. If I took two quick steps and jumped it, I knew I would be able to outrun both of them. I would need to serpentine so that he could not get a good shot, but that seemed to be my best chance at getting away. I took a breath and leaned forward, ready to go.

"Em," Spano said, "who do you think would win in a race between us three?"

I turned and looked at them, wondering why he was asking the question.

"Well, boss," Junior said, "I guess he would. He looks faster."

Spano's face was clear to me from the light at the edge of the lot. He was looking me up and down. "You're right, the kid is probably fast. He could take off, and although I'm a pretty good shot, I might miss him."

He stared at me and nodded his head. "So, kid, you can try and run. You might make it. Um, Em, what was the address again?"

"You mean in Henderson? Or the one back east? I got both of them in the car," Junior said.

Spano walked right up to me. "That's right, kid. I got the address of your pretty girl, and your mommy, right in the car. So if you take off, I could squeeze a shot off, but I'd rather save the bullet. Em and I would be back in our car and pulling up in front of... Em, what's his girl's name?"

"It's Melissa, boss," Junior said.

"Right, Melissa," Spano said. "Melissa. What a pretty name. I would be in front of Melissa's house before you could get to a phone. Trust me she would not enjoy my company."

I stood there as he got closer and closer to me until I felt like he was going to push me into the dry bed. "Alright," I said. "Enough. I won't run. What do you want from me? Why the hell are we out here?"

Spano smiled. "Look at you showing some spine."

Out of nowhere, he slapped me across the face. "The next time you talk to me, it better start with, 'Mr. Spano'. You got that?"

I didn't answer him. He was my height but seemed to be looking down at me. Even though I was more scared than at any time in my life, I didn't want to play games. I knew now that he wanted to know about the money, and I also knew I didn't know where it was. Ben said these guys could tell when you were lying. I hoped that was the case because I could honestly say I did not know where the money was.

Spano continued to stare at me. After a few seconds, he raised the gun and said, "Let's go."

I turned and walked off of the parking lot and into the desert. When we reached the first fairway, I turned and Spano pointed for me to keep going. The three of us walked without talking. We crossed the first and after tripping my way through a stretch of rocky, dark desert, we reached the seventeenth green. Spano grabbed me by the shoulders and pushed me toward the middle of the green.

"So, kid, I hear you're a good golfer. Is that true?" he asked.

I stood in front of them, not sure what I should say. By now my eyes were accustomed to the dark and I saw that Junior was holding a putter. I looked back at Spano and said, "You want me to hit a putt?"

This time I saw it coming, but still could not stop it. Spano slapped me, missing my cheek but catching me across the nose. I heard a crack and immediately felt the blood starting to flow from my nose.

"Mr. Spano," I said. "Do you want me to hit a putt?"

"That's better," Spano said. "But first, what I want is to know where your buddy is."

I felt nauseous, probably from the blood I was losing from my nose, stomach, and back. Starting to sway as I stood, I shook my head. "I don't know where he is. He told me he was leaving a few nights ago. That was the last time I talked to him."

Spano stood in front of me and crossed his arms. "Really? He didn't give you a hint? Do you know that he took his little family and is now no longer in California? I bet that he told you something. C'mon, you tell me where he is, and you walk. You'll be back with your little girlfriend in no time and you never have to worry about me or Em coming after you again."

I looked him straight in the eye, and said, "Mr. Spano, I do not know. He didn't tell me."

Again, Spano stared at me. The longer he stared and was silent, the more my heartbeat sped up. I decided that if he raised the gun, I was going to take off. I would beat them back to their car, and find a way to fight them. I would start to throw rocks if I had to.

Finally, Spano said, "You know what, I believe you, kid. Newell may be an asshole, but he's too smart to tell you where he's going. You did good, kid."

I took a deep breath and let it out. "You said one question."

Spano smiled. "Well, you didn't call me Mr. Spano there, so I get one more question. And on this one, I already know the answer, so it's more like a test. I think Newell told you where Miner put the money he stole from Mr. Marino. He told you right where it is. And you're going to tell me. You're going to tell me where the money is."

Again happy that Ben didn't tell me, I said, "I have no idea where the money is. He told me what happened, that some money was stolen. That's it. He never said where it was. He told me he didn't know."

"What?" Spano said. "Do you think I believe that? I don't."

"I swear, I have no idea where the money is. You think…"

"Shut up," Spano said. "You know what? I don't care if you know. This little meeting we have going here, it ain't about the money. It's about how Newell was able to get out of here. How he made me look bad. I think you helped him and I got to teach him a lesson. And I'm gonna do it by leaving him a little message."

When he paused, I looked over at Junior. He stood stoically with his arms crossed holding onto the putter. Looking back at Spano, I asked, "What message?"

"That no matter where he goes, he ain't safe. What do you think he'll do when he hears they found you splashed all over the green here at his favorite place? How his favorite little buddy got blown away where he likes to play. I know he'll come back. He'll want a piece of me."

My knees went weak and I felt the bile rising in my throat. I tried to say something but the thought that I was going to die here and now was too much. I tried to take a deep breath but I wretched and started to throw up.

"Hey, kid," Spano said, stepping back from me. "You get puke on my shoes and I'll make it worse for you. Besides, I'm gonna give you a chance. You ain't dead yet."

His words went over my head. I was bent over heaving and then I lost my balance. The blood loss, the broken nose, and now my impending execution were too much for me. I fell to one knee and started to spit out the remaining puke that was inside my mouth.

"Em, get this sad excuse back on his feet, will you please," Spano said.

Junior walked behind me and lifted me in one easy move. I took a couple of staggering steps forward but was able to regain my balance.

A handkerchief hit me in the face. "Here, wipe the crap off of your face," Spano said. "I told you I'm giving you a chance. I want

Newell to know that either you died because you failed, or that I'm a good guy because I gave you a chance. Then you'll tell him to get his ass back into Vegas before I do kill you."

"What chance?" I said through the spit and vomit in my mouth.

"Golf. A putt. If you can make a putt, you live. If you make the putt, you can go back to your little girlfriend. When Newell finds out I got to you, he's gonna do the right thing and come back. That's the type of person he is. A weak piece of shit. If you get him to come back, I'll make sure you get some of the money. That will be your incentive to get him back into Vegas. How does a million bucks in your pocket sound?"

I looked at him, not understanding what he was talking about. "So, you want me to make a putt?"

"That's right," Spano said, "and if you do, you walk away. If you miss, I'll kill you. Simple as that, kid. It's as simple as that. Em, give me the ball."

Junior walked over and handed a golf ball to Spano. He tossed it onto the green and it rolled to about forty feet from the hole.

"I never played this game," he said, "I think it's for pussies, but from what I know this is a kind of tough shot to make, right? You're going to have to be pretty good to make a putt this long."

I stood there looking at him, wondering what he was trying to do. And what he wanted me to do. He then walked over to Junior and took the putter from him. He tossed the club onto the ground next to the ball. He then raised the gun and pointed it at me.

"What do you want me to do?" I asked.

He shook his head and looked over at Junior. "Em, is this the dumbest person you and I have ever seen?" He walked over to me and pushed the gun into my ear, forcing me down to my knees. "This is what I want you to do. I want you to tell Ben Newell that

219

he better get his ass back into the desert. And you're either gonna tell him in person after you make this putt, or you're gonna tell him by me blowing your head off and him hearing about it from one of the losers that work here after finding your dead ass in the morning. Either way, I don't care. Maybe I still blow your head off if you make the putt. You don't get to know, kid. Hit the ball and let's see what I do."

When I didn't move, he leaned over to me and said, "If you don't get up and hit the ball, after I waste you, Em and I are headed to Henderson to fuck up your girlfriend's family. Got it?"

I did. Thinking of Spano pointing his gun at Melissa cleared my head. I took a few steps toward the ball but stopped. I turned and looked at Spano. He was no longer a tough guy to me. He was nothing more than a bully.

"I saw you that night you were at Ben's apartment," I said. "You were with two other guys. You acted so tough. A real tough guy standing behind two others. And now you threaten a girl? What the hell is wrong with you?"

Spano's expression changed, and he took two quick steps in my direction. "You little…" he said. He stopped and I could see he was fighting the urge to come after me.

I don't know why I said what I said, or why I stood up to him. I was in pain, and still felt like I was going to throw up, but when he threatened Melissa, I had enough. In some weird way, seeing him pissed and wanting to attack me gave me a sense of control.

"That's what I thought," I said. You're a bully. Nothing more. A cheap little bully."

He took a breath and smiled. "A bully with a gun, asshole," he said.

I smiled and said, "Thanks for making my point. You're not only a bully but a stupid bully as well."

From behind Spano, I heard Junior start to laugh and catch himself. Spano was not laughing. He raised the gun and said, "Hit the ball, asshole. Let's play."

With my thoughts now clear, I tried to figure out a way to get an advantage. I walked over and picked up the putter. I now had a weapon. Walking back toward the hole, I looked at the putter. It was a Zebra model with a large head that would do some damage if I could get a swing at Spano.

"Where the hell are you going?" Spano asked as I walked away from the ball.

"I need to read the putt, okay?" I said, stopping.

Spano turned to Junior. "You're a golf fan, right Em? Is there such a thing as 'reading a putt'?"

"Yes, boss," Junior said. "It tells you which way the ball will roll on the ground."

I looked at Spano and said, "That's right, I need to see how it will roll on the ground. Okay?"

"How are you going to see that in the dark?" he asked.

"I'll figure it out," I said. I walked to the other side of the hole. He was right about not being able to see the line of the putt. I did my best to use the light from The Strip to see the slope. The putt was straight, but downhill. I knew these greens well, and they were fast. The fact that it was a Friday was important. The greens were cut Friday mornings. Even at night, the ball would roll fast.

As I walked back to the other side of the ball, I forgot about the pain in my head, the cuts on my stomach and back, and even the fact that I was without a shirt. I focused on the putt. It was my only chance. Not making the putt, but at the very least, coming close.

I didn't think there was any way Spano was not going to shoot me. Whether the ball went in the hole or not, he was going to kill me. My only hope was hitting a good putt that would roll down the slope near the hole. While his attention was on the ball, I would try to attack him. I would have to get to him before he could change his attention from seeing if the ball went in the hole, to me. As I stepped up to the ball, he was standing behind me and a few feet closer to the hole. Junior was another few feet behind him. If I was able to move to his right and then start swinging, I might get a swing at his head. If I could knock him down, I would hit him again and then worry about Junior.

My only chance was to try and make this putt. If I hit a good putt and got the ball rolling, when it got five feet from the hole, I would attack.

As I took a practice stroke, I said a quick prayer asking for help, and asked that Melissa be safe. Stepping back again from the ball, I started my normal routine. I took two practice swings, closed my eyes, and pictured the line of the putt. I visualized seeing the ball rolling at the hole and falling in. I stepped back up to the ball and placed the club behind it. Taking one last look at the hole, I moved my focus back to the ball and took a deep breath.

"Good luck, asshole," said Spano.

"Fuck you," I said, and I hit the ball.

As soon as the ball left the putter's face, I regripped my hands to hold the putter so I could start swinging. I crouched and moved my right foot out so that I could strike. My heart was pounding through my chest, and the pain in my head was exploding as my entire body readied to attack. As I looked up at the ball, in my peripheral vision I saw Spano take a step toward the hole. His focus was on the ball, not me.

The ball was rolling to the hole. In the dark, I couldn't tell if I had the line, but I knew it was close. I felt my body go tense, and as I was about to strike, I saw Spano taking a step back at me. He was turning away from the hole. I saw the gun in his left hand and he was raising it. I can still remember thinking he was going to shoot before the ball reached the hole. He was going to attack before I had a chance. I took one more look and the ball was now a few feet from the hole.

It was now or never.

The gunshot was loud. The pounding in my head masked the fact that the three of us were outdoors and alone on a golf course. The silence of our surroundings was broken by the crack of the gunshot which exploded into my ears. The force of the shot knocked me down and away from Spano. I tried to escape by driving my face into the grass and covering my head with my arms. I took two quick breaths and waited for the pain. As I tried to crawl away from Spano, another shot exploded into the night. I felt paralyzed and waited for the last shot that would end me.

My ears started to ring when it hit me that I needed to move. I needed to run. I needed to do something. As I raised my head, I heard my name. Someone was calling my name. I thought it was Spano mocking me. He was going to laugh at me while he finished me.

"Mark!" the yell came, finally loud and close enough to drown out the ringing from the gunshots. "Kid, c'mon. We gotta go."

I felt hands grabbing my right arm and pulling me. Looking up, I saw Junior bending over me. I pushed myself up to my knee, raised my hands in fists, and looked at him. "What...?"

"We gotta go, Mark. You and me. Let's go."

He pulled me up onto my feet and firmly pushed me away from the hole, in the direction of the parking lot.

"Wait," I said. "What just happened? Stop pushing me."

Junior took a step back and raised his hands. "Sure, kid. Sorry. But we can't be anywhere near here when they find that."

"Find what?" I asked. I took a step away from him but stumbled. My head was still exploding from the stress and noise. "What the hell happened."

Junior stepped up to me. "Hey, kid. It's okay. Take a breath. You're okay. Go ahead. You gotta clear your head."

I did take a breath, and I took my hands and rubbed my ears, trying to squeeze the ringing and echoes out. After a few seconds, the pressure cleared. I looked at Junior and saw that he had blood on his arm.

"Hey," I said, pointing at his arm. "Are you alright?"

He smiled. "Kid, that's your blood. C'mon, let's go."

With my head clearing, it occurred to me that Spano was lying on the ground behind Junior. "What happened?" I said, pointing at Spano.

"Hey, Mark, I'm sorry I had to let him push you around a little. But Mr. Marino said I had to wait and see who Spano was siding with. He was gonna pop you just then. That ain't what Mr. Marino wanted. It's what Junior wanted."

"Junior wanted?" I asked. "I thought you were Junior?"

"Me," Junior said with a laugh. "I ain't Marino Junior. My name is Emilio Balito. Spano must have hit your head pretty hard. Call me Em."

"Okay, Em," I said. "Why was Spano playing all these games? Why did he want me dead?"

"C'mon, start walking and I'll tell you," Em said. He gave me a slight push and we started to quickly walk. "Mr. Marino didn't want this and he told Spano that. I'll let Mr. Marino tell you about it. Spano was more loyal to Marino Junior, and Junior wanted you dead to show Newell he couldn't run. You see, Mr. Marino trusted me to make the call. This is big for me, kid. I got the big boss telling me he trusts my judgment. I saw Spano pulling on you after you hit the ball. I popped him a few times like Mr. Marino told me to do if I thought he was gonna pop you."

I was getting confused but let it go. "Well, thank you for saving me. But, what do I do when you're not there next time?"

"Mr. Marino will tell you. We have to go see him now. Okay? Don't worry. But, hey, you got some big balls standing up to Spano like that. Calling him a bully? That was pretty cool. I'm glad I got him before he got you."

I looked at Em and said, "Yeah, me too." As we walked into the parking lot, I realized Ben was right. Em had just shot a man and looked like he was ready to have a good night's sleep. He wasn't phased at all.

As we got to the car, Em opened the door for me. Reaching in he pulled out a shirt and gave it to me. After slipping it on, I said, "Thanks."

"No, Mark," he said with a big smile. "If I lost my money clip in Arizona I would have had to hitchhike home. And now, you helped me look really good in front of the big boss. He's gonna move me up. So thank you."

He stuck out his hand and we shook. "I guess, congratulations," I said.

His smile widened and he pushed me into the car. We drove back into town and down The Strip. The entire ride Em talked about sports. He asked me about golf, about college basketball, and who I thought was going to win the Stanley Cup. When we pulled up at a light, he squealed in delight when a man on stilts walked by us on the sidewalk.

"Don't you love Vegas?" he said with the excitement of a child.

As we pulled around the back of the Green Emerald casino, I realized Em was just a big kid. If he played golf, he would be a lot of fun on the course. If I crossed him in a dark alley he would have no problem killing me.

Pulling into the parking garage, he reached over and patted me on the leg. "Listen, the big boss just wants to talk. He ain't gonna hurt you. He's gonna be happy to see you. Okay?"

I nodded and said sure. After the last hour, meeting a mob boss was not that intimidating an event. I was in pain, stiff, and my face was swelling up. When we got out of the car, I looked at my reflection in the window and shook my head. It looked like I went fifteen rounds with a pro boxer and did not do well. I also noticed that the shirt Em gave me to wear had the Olympia Casino logo on the front. The irony of ironies.

We walked to the elevator and when it opened, two men stepped out. Both were in dark suits, had slicked-back hair, and were as big as Em.

"Hey, Em, you good?" one of them asked.

Em only nodded. The other man walked up to me and twirled his finger telling me to turn around. He then frisked me. When his hands hit the cut on my stomach, I groaned. With no apology, he pointed to the elevator. Stepping in, a woman who was standing in the elevator's corner moved in front of me. She was older, maybe my mother's age. She wore a business suit and carried a notebook.

"Oh, my," she said, looking at me. "What happened to you? We need to clean you up a bit before going to see Mr. Marino."

"No," said Em, "I want the boss to see how tough he was. It will earn him some respect."

The woman stood back and said, "Okay, but do not let him near any of the furniture, got it."

Em nodded and winked at me. The elevator doors closed and we headed up. I noticed that there were no floor buttons on the control panel. Just 'Open' and 'Close'. We kept going up, and when the elevator stopped and the doors opened, we stepped out into a hallway with a shining marble floor and enough ornate art to fill a museum wing.

"This way," the woman said, walking out in front of me. Em walked behind me. When we turned a corner and stepped through an archway made of dark cherry, we were in a large living room. There were couches spread haphazardly around the room, and paintings hung on the wall of naked women and Civil War battle scenes. The lights were low, with the glow from The Strip below filtering through windows that took up two entire walls of the room. From the view where I stood, my guess is we were twenty stories up.

"Stay here and Mr. Marino will be right with you," she said. She walked over to a desk in the corner of the room and sat down. I turned around and saw the other two men standing in the archway. It was now just Em and me standing in the middle of the room.

Em tapped me on the shoulder and pointed to the far wall. A fish tank took up half the wall and was filled with tropical fish and plants. "I love those fish," he said.

I nodded and tried to smile, but the pain made me wince. I was starting to think I might vomit again, and was about to ask for a chair when a door opened across the room, and Mr. Marino walked in.

It was quite an entrance. Mr. Marino was older than I thought he would be. He was wearing a suit jacket with no tie, but his clothes were immaculate. He had closely cropped gray hair that was slicked back and wore glasses with dark frames that gave the impression he was an aged Hollywood star. He slowly walked toward me and Em, and his eyes never left mine.

Stopping five feet in front of me, he looked me up and down.

"Emilio," he said with a slight Italian accent. "Introduce me to this man."

Em stepped up and stood next to me. "Yes, sir. Mr, Marino, sir, this is Mark Travers. Mark, this is Mr. Aldo Marino."

I wasn't sure what I was supposed to do. The tension in the room was so thick, I thought that if I took a step at him to shake his hand, men with guns would drop out of the ceiling and surround me. I stood still, staring him in the eye and trying not to waver back and forth as he studied me.

"Mr. Travers, may I call you Mark?" he asked.

"Yes, sir," I said, my voice cracking as I tried to get the words through my dry throat.

"Deli, can we please get this man something to drink?" Marino asked. "Perhaps you would like water, something a little harder like a beer?"

"Water, please," I said.

We stood staring at each other until the woman walked over and handed me a glass of water. I thanked her and took a sip, pulling the glass away from my lips which were cracked and dry. After getting the first swallow down, I drank more and again thanked her. She took the glass and again we stood staring at each other until the woman sat back down at her desk.

"Emilio," Marino said, "please tell me why this man looks the way he does. It appears that he needs medical attention."

Em took a step forward. "Sir, I went with Mr. Spano as you instructed to ask Mark about Ben Newell. And as you instructed, I made sure that Mr. Spano did not hurt him too bad."

For the first time since he entered the room, Marino smiled. "Emilio, I do not know if what I see in front of me can be considered, 'not hurting him too badly'.

"Yes, sir," Em said, "but Mr. Spano was taking control. I did like you said and waited to see what he was going to do. He had me drive us to a golf course, and there he tried to kill Mark. So, sir, I made the decision that I needed to act. I shot Mr. Spano before he could shoot Mark."

Marino looked at me. "Mark, is that the way this happened?"

I nodded. "Emilio saved my life," I said. "For now, anyway."

Marino tilted his head. After a moment he said, "You have nothing to worry about, Mark. I want to apologize to you for the way you were treated by one of my men."

He turned and took a few steps toward the woman. "Deli, can you please ask Dr. Aria to come up here? Tell him I have a patient for him and describe to him Mark's injuries so that he can be prepared to help this man."

"Sir," Em said, "Mark is kind of beat up like this because he stood up to Mr. Spano. As you know, Mr. Spano was a tough individual, but he did not intimidate Mark."

Marino's eyes widened. "Is that true? I am impressed, Mark. Mr. Spano could be a rather intimidating and physical presence."

I continued to stand in front of him, starting to feel like I was being judged as part of a pageant. My head continued to pound, and I started to feel blood running down my back from the cuts that were reopened when I was frisked. I wanted to say something, but I figured it was best to remain quiet.

"Emilio," Marino said, "you have done a good job. I put my trust in you, and I feel my trust was well placed."

Em stood tall and smiled. "Thank you, sir." He turned around and walked out of the room leaving Marino and me standing together.

"I would like a minute alone with Mark," he said. Immediately the woman left via a side door and the archway doors behind me closed. Now alone, he said, "Please, come over here and sit."

"I don't want to bleed on your furniture," I said.

"I am sorry to say that you are not the first bleeding man to be standing in this room, Mark, It is part of the business. So please, do not worry."

We sat on two chairs in front of the fish tank that faced each other. It took me a full second to get my legs to bend as my body was stiffening up. I slowly leaned back, afraid my cuts would open up even more and I would bleed all over the leather cover on the chair's back.

"Mark, I do not usually explain myself to anyone," he said, sitting with his legs crossed. His eyes never left mine. "This is a unique case because someone that I indicated to my organization was an outsider, was impacted. In my line of work, I have no problem interacting with people that are directly involved. You were not. And someone went around me, and against my words. What makes it all the more difficult is that the insubordination came from my son.

"What I am saying is that you should never have been pulled into this mess with Kerry Miner, Anthony Spano, and Ben Newell. Because you did, I owe you an explanation. I do, though, want your honesty. Can you do that for me?"

I thought for a second, not sure what he was getting at, but I nodded.

"I know that you are aware of some of the details around Kerry Miner. He stole money. That money was not just mine but belonged to other partners that I deal with. Powerful partners. I worked to quell any issues and took the loss on myself. But my son saw things differently, and he went after Mr. Miner, Mr. Newell, and you, trying to find that money. He was wrong for doing that, and I allowed him to be arrested so that he can spend some time thinking about what he did."

He paused and stared at me. "I don't expect you to understand all of that. But you do need to understand that I must do what I can to find this money. So, I ask again for your honesty. I am very good at telling when a person is honest, and the people I interact with know that if they are honest with me, I am a very easy man to deal with."

I nodded at him, now knowing what he was going to ask.

"So, Mark, please tell me if you know where the money is. Notice I have not asked you if you know where Ben Newell is. I would not do that because I know you look up to him. But on the chance he told you where the money is, I want you to tell me. I know that the man that stole the money is now dead, and I do not believe either you or Ben have accessed the money. So if I get it all back, you both will not be approached. You have my word."

I maintained eye contact and tried to be convincing. "Sir, I don't know where the money is. Ben told me about the money, and he told me Kerry was killed. But he never told me anything more. Other than it being in Europe, I don't think he knows where it is either."

Marino stared me down for ten seconds. The longer he stared, the heavier my heartbeat became. It got to the point that I thought blood would start to shoot out of all my stab wounds and my nose.

Marino stood up, and I stood with him. "Thank you, Mark. Thank you for your honesty. I am impressed with you. You have been through a lot and come through on your feet. You can be proud of yourself."

"Thank you, sir," I said. "Am I free to go?"

Marino smiled and said, "Yes, son, you are free. I am not a monster who says one thing but means another. I do have my doctor out in the hallway. He is the best there is in Las Vegas. Please let him look at your wounds."

"I will, sir," I said, taking a deep breath and letting it out.

"Mark, there are two things that I need to tell you. Remember, whether I am giving good news, or bad, I mean exactly what I say."

I nodded. "I understand, sir."

"First, if you were to go to the police or the FBI about what you have learned or what has transpired with you and my organization, I would then consider you to be a participant. You would no longer be an outsider. I would be forced to find you."

"Sir," I said, "you don't have to worry about that. I just want to live my life."

"And a good life it will be," he said with a smile. "I can see that you have a good future in front of you."

"Thank you," I said.

"Second, I told you that the money stolen by Kerry Miner was not only my money. It belonged to others as well. Other men are feeling disrespected. Now, I have paid them back, and the death of the man that stole the money, although not what I wanted, did appease them as to their relationship with me. But seeing you in Las Vegas is to them, a further sign of disrespect. You need to leave and never come back. I can protect you as long as you leave. No one will ever come after you, your mother, your friends, Melissa, or her family in Henderson as long as you never set foot in this city again."

He might have been trying to make me feel better, but his words scared me to the core.

"Sir, if you can give me a couple of days, I will be heading home and never coming back."

He reached out and put his hand on my shoulder. "Because, Mark, if you do, what will happen?"

I shook my head. "Sir, I don't ever want to find out."

He now put his other hand on my other shoulder and shook me. With a big smile, he said, "I knew you would understand. There is no hurry to leave. My people will know when you fly out, and I will know that when your plane takes off, you will never be in the desert again."

CHAPTER 16

Marino's doctor was good. He took me into another room and cleaned all of my cuts and wounds. Between my stomach and back, I ended up with twenty stitches. For my nose, he took his hands and in one unbelievably painful act straightened it out. He gave me a bottle full of valium for the pain.

Em then drove me to get my car at Rosy's. When he dropped me, he told me Marino had already promoted him and made him in charge of some big accounts. I had no idea what that meant, but I was happy the man that saved my life was happy. When we got to the lot, it was pretty much empty. I got out of the car and someone from the bar must have thought I parked my car there and left it. He started to yell at me that this was not a public parking lot. Em floored the gas and drove over the man, who was standing outside his car. He jumped out and started to yell at the man to never raise his voice at me. I thought he was going to throw the man through the windshield of his car. After the man drove off, Em came back and with a smile, said, "Mark, I'll always owe you," and drove off.

As I sat in my car, I thought about my time in the desert. In my time here, I made a few friends and found the love of my life. I laughed when I realized that two of the best friends I met were Ben and Emilio. Ben was now on the run, and Em would not hesitate for a second to kill anyone, including me, should he be ordered to.

By the time I got back to Melissa's, they were ready to put out an APB on me. I thought quickly about how to explain myself.

Looking in the back seat and seeing an Olympia Casino gym bag full of shirts and golf swag, I had my plan. I emptied the bag, put on a sweatshirt and gym shorts, and headed into the house. When Melissa and her parents took one look at my face, they all jumped up and ran to me. I did my best to protect all the stitches as they hugged me. Melissa's mom, who was close to tears after seeing me, pulled me into the kitchen. While her parents were making tea, I whispered to Melissa to go along with my story. I told her I would explain later.

We spent the next thirty minutes drinking tea as I explained how I took an elbow to the face playing in the Las Vegas Casino Corporate Basketball League. I did my best to answer their questions and even had Melissa's dad feeling sorry for me when I told him I was hitting jump shots from all over the court before I got hurt.

Later, Melissa and I were able to sit outside and I told her the real story. I showed her my wounds, told her a dead body was lying on the seventeenth green at The Bridge, repeated verbatim what Marino told me, and said I would be leaving and would understand if she gave me the ring back and never wanted to see me again.

I believe the short scream I let out when Melissa hugged me woke up her parents, but I didn't care. While Melissa stopped the bleeding that started again from her hug, for the first time since Ben left, I was relaxed and happy. I was leaving Las Vegas, and Melissa was coming with me.

The next day, Melissa and I were eating breakfast when her father dropped the morning newspapers on the table. The headlines were about the mob hit at The Desert Bridge Country Club. I tried not to react and waited for him to grab one of the papers. When he finally chose one, Melissa grabbed the others and we moved to the backyard.

The stories were short as not much was known when the

articles were written. Each paper tied the murder to the ongoing battles between the mob, law enforcement, and the casinos. No names were given. More importantly to me, no witnesses were mentioned. The only thing I learned was that the Desert Bridge golf course would be closed while the investigation was ongoing. Much more than a dead body, I knew that was the one thing that would piss off everyone at The Bridge.

The day I left Las Vegas, I spent the morning driving around to say goodbye. Melissa and I had breakfast with Kenny and Kara. It was not a goodbye meal. Kenny and Kara were also going to be leaving. The four of us ended up living within a mile of each other in Texas. To this day, they are our best friends and the only other people that know all the details from my time in Vegas.

After I returned the car to the casino, Melissa drove me to the Bridge. We argued about whether or not that was a smart move, but I could not leave without seeing Milly. By now, the course was again open and the clubhouse was full of the usual lunch crowd. As I walked in, the usual cry of "Vlad!" went up. Not one person asked about my now two black eyes.

Milly saw me and waved me over. He was wiping down the new, wood bar.

"You're a real bartender now," I said, laughing.

"It's great to see you, Vlad. I was worried for a while. Especially when I heard about the murder and about what happened to you. Thank God you got out of there."

I shook my head. "How do you know I was there?" I asked.

He smiled and said, "Look around Vlad. There is nothing that the people in this room don't know. I will say one thing: if you did get hurt, I feel sorry for the mob guys. There are some pretty highly connected people here. Journalists, cops, businessmen and women, and even some connected guys. It seems a certain large friend of yours that was there mentioned to one of the guys here what happened. He filled me in."

"Who does Emilio know from here?" I asked.

Milly smiled and said, "Let's just say that Clip has a law background and knows a few people."

"Clip?" I asked. "How the hell does he know Emilio?"

Milly leaned over and said, "Clip is a lawyer and was a federal investigator. He knows a lot of people. He helped Ben with all the things he's been going through. It seems you made quite an impression on the Emilio guy. He told Clip everything that happened. He also said that you're leaving the desert. As much as I will miss you, that's the best news I've heard in a long time."

I looked around at the people in the room moving about, drinking and laughing. A few of them made eye contact with me and nodded. Gonzo gave a quick thumbs up and Clip smiled.

The emotions I started to feel were strong and brought a tear to my eyes.

"I feel bad. I couldn't tell you much about any of these people," I told Milly. "Our conversations never get past the ragging, the jokes, setting the stakes on a match, and playing."

"Oh, you do know them," Milly said. "That's why I'm a bartender. The best two ways to learn who a person really is, are to play golf with them or serve them drinks. I don't play, so I stick with the other way. You may not realize it, but these people here respect you. They all know why you came here, and what you're trying to do. And they all will be pulling for you when you go. Not just in golf, but in your life."

I wiped my eyes and nodded to everyone. Looking at Milly, I shook my head and again wiped away more tears. "You are a good friend. Ben once told me that you were a great guy, and he was right. Thank you for everything."

Milly reached over and grabbed my shoulder. "Vlad, thank you.

It's important that someone who lives on the sand like me knows that there's more in the world. Especially someone with as much as you have going for you. Knowing that you didn't throw it away gives me hope for all the others that are wandering down the strip."

I smiled at him. Taking one more look around the rook, I turned back to him. "Have you, um…"

"No, Vlad, and I won't," he said, cutting me off. "Ben wouldn't do that. He didn't say anything and I didn't ask. That's just the way it is."

"Yeah, I know," I said.

Milly turned serious and put his hand on my arm. "Ben thought the world of you. As a person, and as a golfer."

"Thanks, I wanted to be a player to impress him," I said.

"No," Milly said, "not a player. He thought the world of you as a golfer. He said that you get it, you get the game. The competition, the history, the practice, the work, the fun. I never heard him say that about anyone. He said he hoped that you would try to play. To give it a shot."

I exhaled. "I don't know, Milly. My head is so screwed up right now. I do now agree with one thing that he told me many times. A golfer needs a moment in his career when he comes through. When he makes a shot that he can remember, and puts that memory into what he called the 'brain bank'. Then when you need to, you can pull it out for confidence. If I had that confidence, well, maybe I could be successful. Maybe it would push me. But if not, I'm okay with that too. Right now throwing the clubs in the corner and starting a career and a family sounds pretty good."

Milly nodded. "Ben used to say that to me also. He would say how important it was to challenge yourself and always remember success. So you think you need that extra push of confidence?"

I laughed. "I don't know. Right now my 'brain bank' is empty. Hey, after I get out of here, I'll probably try. And maybe I'll hit that shot. Maybe it will be what I need."

"Vlad, tell me," Milly said. "Is it true that the guy that was killed made you hit a putt before he was gonna shoot you?"

The memory of Spano standing behind me sent a chill up my spine. I caught my breath and nodded. "He did. About a forty-footer. And that's when Emilio shot him. Right after I hit the putt. He ran me out of there as soon as he killed him. I never saw the body."

Milly put his finger up asking me to wait for a second, and he walked into the storage closet. Coming out with a copy of 'Vegas Live' magazine, he handed it to me. The magazine was known to be for advertising but did have serious articles about the city and crime. "Here, this came out this morning. It's got a lot of details about the murder. It doesn't mention you of course but has a lot of info from the police report. The writer was here a couple of days ago interviewing people. To tell you the truth, the murder is pretty good advertising for the course."

"I thought someone here might think that," I said with a laugh. "But, Milly, I don't want to read about it. I was there."

Milly pushed the magazine at me. "Vlad, take it. When you're looking for the memory. When you need to find confidence in your game, read the article. I mean, really read it. Okay?"

So I took it and shook Milly's hand. When I let go, I walked out of the clubhouse and started the next phase of my life. And now, thirty-six years later, I sat in the same room.

CHAPTER 17

The kid walked over to me and filled up my coffee. I thanked him and said this was my last cup. Golfers were now walking into the bar, their morning rounds completed. I looked at my watch. It was 11:50 AM. I had been sitting here for two hours.

The email said that if he did not walk in by noon, he would not be coming.

I took out my phone and read the email again. By now, I knew it by heart. I received it at work six weeks ago when it was an early morning like any other. After walking through the clubhouse and the practice grounds, I met with my team. Being the head superintendent of a golf resort was a dream job, but a busy one. I leaned heavily on my team, and they always came through. This day, like all the others, presented some unique challenges around the handling of the course, the guests, and business.

My favorite time of the day was mid-morning. I would retire to my office, sort through my email, and spend time thinking about the ways to make the resort better for the guests and my team. It was my quiet time.

When I opened my email inbox, the usual fare of daily, weekly, and monthly reporting filled the screen.

One subject line stood out: '*It's time to open the envelopes*'.

Immediately, thirty-six years disappeared. Without thinking, I stood up and locked my office door. Sitting behind my desk, I stared at the subject line for a full minute. I couldn't bring myself to open it. When I finally got the strength, I moved the cursor over the message and double-clicked. I don't know what I was expecting, but this was not it.

"Vlad, be at the Bridge. October 20. Between 10 and noon. I'll bring my envelope. Bring yours. If I don't walk in, I couldn't make it."

No one had called me Vlad since the day I left Vegas.

For the first few years, after I left, the events that ended my time in Las Vegas kept me awake and had me looking over my shoulder. I would get involved in something and I would forget, but a noise or a comment from someone would bring it all back. No one knew about my pain. I hid it all.

The one place I could get away from it was the golf course. It wasn't my success as a professional that allowed me to forget, it was my continued love for the game. I challenged myself to make a career in golf, and I thought that I could overcome the Vegas memories the same way. By challenging myself. One night when I was just starting to see success as a Tour player, I was on the road alone playing a tournament. To calm my golf nerves, I took a walk. All alone on the dark streets of a city, a man approached me and said something. I thought he had a gun. I reached down and grabbed a rock, ready to attack him but it turned out to be his keys in his hand, and he was asking for directions. I could not sleep for the rest of the night. In the early dawn, I decided I could not do it myself. I called the one person I could trust. I called my wife. I called Melissa.

After I asked for her help, Melissa helped me to control my emotions by convincing me that we were safe as long as I never went back to the desert. She helped me end the chills, sweats, and the 'desert nightmares' as we called them. While I occasionally found myself awake and staring at the ceiling, I was able to talk about Vegas without breaking down.

The reaction from reading the email was not so much from the nightmares, it was because of Ben. I had a chance to see Ben.

There was not a day gone by that I did not think about him. Several times I could swear I saw him in the crowds at a tournament with those piercing blue eyes looking at me from the masses. I looked for him at airports. I searched for him online. I thought about him whenever things got tough. I thought about strategy through his eyes. My pre-shot routine always started with a question: "How would Ben play this shot?" In an interview once, I was asked about my greatest teacher. I said there were two, and detailed how Mr. Wittich taught me to swing. When the interviewer asked about the second, I simply said it was someone that helped me remember.

When things got really tough on the course, or in my life, I thought about the memory. The memory from making the toughest shot in my life. The memory that told me I could make any other shot. That I could take anything life threw my way. The memory he told me to find and hold onto. The memory that made me who I am today, the good and the bad.

Now, after thirty-six years, the man that shaped me into who I am was no longer a ghost. I had a chance to see Ben.

On the day I received the email, I read it five times. I then did something I had not done in all my years at the resort. I left the office early.

Melissa and I sat for the next few hours talking about what I should do. While my thoughts went back and forth, she was adamant. I should go. She knew how important Ben was to me and that if I gave up a chance to see him, the regret would eat at me for the rest of my days. She also knew that until I went back to the desert, I would never completely rid myself of the nightmares.

I replied to the email with a simple, 'OK'. After hitting Enter to send the message, Melissa and I started to plan my trip. She tried to convince me that the threat was no longer real, but my racing heart said otherwise.

We decided I would drive and not fly. I would stay in hotels under the name of the resort and I would not use my personal credit cards. I also started growing my beard. While I did not think I would be recognized on the street, as a former Tour player the risk of being recognized at a golf course was real. Melissa laughed at my beard while I spent the next few weeks constantly itching my face. When it filled in, she admitted I looked different. She said I looked like an old man.

I came home from the resort one day and Melissa sat me down and handed me several pages of printouts from various websites. "I've been doing some research," she said. "I hope this will help you relax."

What she shared did help with my nerves.

Kirk Bellows, my boss in Las Vegas and the man that did more than anyone to stop me from being a smoker died ten years earlier. He spent three years in prison for his role in the relationship with Marino Junior. I knew about his sentencing but not about his death. I also knew about Marino Junior. He was sentenced to fifteen years in prison, got into a fight with another prisoner, and was beaten into a coma that he never recovered from. According to what Melissa found, the reason for the beating was a large sum of money stolen from multiple Las Vegas mob organizations. That was the only time I ever read about any mention of the money Kerry Miner stole.

The elder Marino lived until he was ninety. He died in bed with his thirty-five-year-old wife sleeping next to him. She was paid well for her five years of marriage to the old man. The article I was reading mentioned his estate was worth fifty million. Too bad for her the feds swept in and took it from her. The issue was still ongoing in the courts all of these years later.

The most interesting piece of information that Melissa found was an advertisement for the largest auto dealer in the desert. The ad read, 'C'mon down and ask for our manager, Emilio

Balito. He'll get you a great deal'. When I looked at the picture of the dealership team, standing in the middle was Emilio. The man who saved my life. I wondered if he took the same attitude toward shooting someone to the negotiating table when selling cars. I felt sorry for anyone thinking they could take advantage of him on a deal.

Melissa did help me feel better, but I remembered that the money was from multiple mob families. Were they all dead and gone too?

The day I left for Las Vegas, I went to the store and purchased a small briefcase with a lock. I then drove to the bank and accessed the safety deposit box for the first time in over thirty years. At first, I hid the envelope in my attic. My paranoia eventually caused me to think the mob would descend on the house, so I moved it to the bank. Now, it was locked in the briefcase, and sitting in the car seat next to me. I counted down the miles as I drove to the desert. The night before I went to The Bridge, I lay awake for hours thinking about seeing Ben.

Now, ten minutes before noon, I stared at the door. Every time it opened my heart jumped. Would I run up and hug him? Could both of us grab Milly and have the reunion that I played out in my head for three and a half decades? I wanted to see him, to thank him, to tell him about my children, to tell him about the memory.

Every time it wasn't him, my heart sank. As the clock moved to noon, the tears started to form. With the barroom now full of people walking in and out, I watched the clock over the door start the swing upward toward noon.

"Please, no," I said to myself. "Please…"

"Excuse me," a voice said, "are you, Mark? Mark Travers?"

I looked up at a man who was about forty years old. He stood with a pen in his hand. No one had asked me for an autograph in twenty years.

"Now?" I said, unable to hide my disappointment at his timing. I quickly realized I was not that type of person. "I'm sorry," I said, looking around the room. I quickly surmised it was not a problem to admit who I was. Since it was now noon, I needed to leave. "Yes, I'm Mark Travers."

"Oh, that's great," he said. "One sec."

He stepped over to another man and tapped him on the back. "It's him," he said, and both of them stepped up to my table.

I looked at both of them and started to stand up. I thought there was no way in this crowd of people they would try to hurt me, but I wanted to be able to get around them should they try. Looking at the second man, I stopped. His eyes were a deep blue. I had once before seen eyes that blue and intense. As my heart jumped through my chest I fell back into my chair.

The second man reached over and shook my hand. "You're Mark Travers. Wow, Mr. Travers, it's a pleasure to meet you."

"Please, call me Mark. You're Ben's son, correct?" I blurted out, unable to hide my excitement.

The men looked at each other. "Well," the first man said, "we are both his sons. He said that you would call him Ben. His name to us has always been Phillip."

"Or, Dad," the second man said. "Do you mind if we sit down?"

"No, please do," I said. I looked around the room behind the men. "Where is your dad? Is he here?" I asked, spitting out the words. In my brain, my voice was screaming: 'he made it!'

Both men sat down. "Um, Mark," the first man said. "Wow, this is weird to finally meet you. Since we knew we would be taking this trip, our dad told us a lot about you. Hearing everything he said, we thought maybe you two knew each other for decades."

"Yeah," the second man said, "he went on and on about you. He never mentioned you until a few years ago. After that, he never stopped. It was nice for me to know where my name came from."

My mouth fell open. "What do…"

"Oh, sorry," the first man said. "This is my brother, Marcus. My name is Kieran."

I looked at both of them and could see Ben. Kieran had Ben's face, and Marcus had his eyes. If you put them together you'd have a clone of Ben.

"It's great to meet you. Both of you," I said. "I can't tell you how much of an impact your father has on my life. It was only eight or nine months, but, well. That's the kind of guy he is."

They both smiled. "Yeah," Marcus said, "you don't have to tell us. He's special. And a great dad."

"Boys," I said, "did he tell you everything? Is that why he isn't here right now? Where can I meet him?"

Both boys looked at each other. "Well, um, Mr. Travers, I mean, Mark. Our dad died three weeks ago. I'm sorry to tell you. And, you see, we didn't know how to get in touch with you."

My mind went blank and my chest tightened. His words hit me like a hammer blow. I looked down and tried to breathe. My tears from the building excitement turned to tears of pain. I looked up at both of them, and whispered, "Ben is dead?"

Both boys nodded. Marcus put his hand on my shoulder. "I'm sorry, sir. When he reached out to you, he was so excited. He thought that meeting here was the perfect place and that you two would be able to start your friendship again."

I could not think of anything to say. Looking around, the expensive and stuffy room transformed into the bar and crowd that I remembered with Ben shouting that the drinks were on him. The roar in response shook the creaky wood floor. He was more at home here than anywhere else. With tears falling down my cheeks, I forced my attention back to Marcus and Kieran. "I don't know what to say and I don't want to make this about my grief." I wiped my eyes and face with a napkin and said, "Do you both have families?"

Marcus nodded and said, "Yes, sir, we both have two kids." He slowly smiled. "Dad was a tremendous grandfather."

"He left a great legacy," Kieran said. "We're both so proud of him. He was a great father, a great husband, and our kids loved him."

"How did he pass?" I asked. "What happened?"

"His heart," Marcus said. "We were all with him. Us, our families, and Mom."

I shook my head. "I'm so sorry," I said, again wiping my eyes. I took out my phone and brought up my photos. "Here, this is also part of his legacy. These are my children. My daughter Nancy, and my son. We named him Benjamin."

As both of them leaned in to see the photo, I worked to control my emotions. After they complimented me on the family I took a deep breath. I thanked them and asked if they knew about Ben and his time in the desert.

"Pretty much all of it, I think," Kieran said. "We knew that he was off the grid, but after we relocated to Montana, he felt we were safe. Not too many kids go through drills to be ready if the mob shows up, but I remember that as a little kid. Then Dad reached out to the FBI and we went into Witness Protection."

"Wow, I never considered that," I said. "So he was in Witness Protection until he died?"

"Kind of," said Kieran. "We ended up staying in Montana, but with new names. Dad testified against some people. He was a consultant to the FBI on the mob and gambling. That's the reason I do what I do. I'm an agent with the FBI."

"Hey, that's great," I said. "He must have been so proud. And how about you, Marcus? What do you do?"

"Well," Marcus said. " I kind of went into the family business. I'm a golf pro. I teach at a golf academy in Florida."

I looked at him and smiled. "He taught you to play? That's awesome. Did he still keep playing?"

"Oh, yeah," Kieran said. "He played all the time. He loved the game."

"Hold it," I said, "Your dad loved the game? Did he have fun when he played? Did he say he did?"

Marcus nodded. "He said it all the time. Golf was his release."

I sat back and shook my head. "Wow," was the only thing I could think of saying. Leaning back up to the table, I looked at both of them. "Do you have any idea how good your father was?"

Both boys sheepishly grinned. "Well," Marcus said, "he was pretty good. He never talked about it, but we always say we don't think we ever saw him try to play his best. He used to say it was fun just to hit the ball."

"Unreal," I said. "That is not the Ben Newell I knew." I took a breath and asked, "How much time do you guys have? I'd like to tell you a few stories."

They looked at each other and smiled. "We have a few hours until we have to be at the airport."

So I spent the next two hours telling them about Ben. About the golfer, the player, and the man. I told them everything I could remember, from the good things like his match with Monroe to the bad things about his drinking. I could tell that I was filling in a lot of holes in what they knew about their dad, and the questions they asked told me they were getting answers they thought they would never receive. I told them it was always my goal to see the real Ben Newell but that I never did. Hearing them talk about their dad, I at least had the feeling that someone did.

Finally, the brothers had to leave. I did my best to hide my disappointment, but I smiled when they told me they were flying back to Florida to spend a week with their mom. We hugged, they gave me their email addresses, and we walked to the door.

"Before you go," I said, "did your dad ever mention an envelope?"

They both looked at each other and shook their heads. "No," said Marcus. "When Dad set this up, he was sick. We spent a week figuring out how to get him here without raising any flags, and to make sure his heart could take the stress. He told us about you, but not much more. Nothing about an envelope."

"Okay," I nodded. "I understand. If you ever come across an envelope and don't know what it is, let me know."

They said they would, and after hugging again, they left. I watched them walk down the stone path toward the parking lot and then returned to my table. I reached over, grabbed my coat, and took a twenty-dollar bill out of my wallet. Throwing the bill on the table for a tip, I took a look at the barroom as I put my coat on. With a smile, I started to walk out.

"That's a pretty good tip, Vlad," a voice said from across the room. "I guess being a winner on Tour makes you a rich guy?"

I stopped and smiled. Without turning around, I said, "Well, now that you have a real bar here, I figure you're a real bartender. I have to tip you like one."

Turning around, Milly was walking toward me. "You thought you would just walk out?"

I put my hands up and smiled. "No, well, I don't know what I'm thinking. Except that it is great to see you."

He walked over to me and we hugged. When we pulled back, he looked me up and down. "Mark, I never thought I would see you again. The beard threw me off for a minute, but I knew it was you. I thought I'd wait to talk to you until after they left. You look good. I followed you when you played. We all did. We bought a big TV and put it in the corner. Anytime you were on, this entire place was filled. You made us all proud."

I smiled and thanked him. "I was scared to come back, Milly. Hell, I'm scared just standing here. But, he reached out to me. He wanted to meet. So, well, here I am."

"And now he's gone," Milly said. "When I heard, it hurt. It still does."

"Did you talk to him?" I asked.

"He reached out to me six months ago," Milly said. "Out of the blue, he called the phone behind the bar. I nearly fell over. But I had an idea of what was going on with him for a number of years. You know that Clip became a federal judge?"

"Clip? Are you kidding?" I asked. "I remember something about him being a federal agent. Now he's a judge?"

"Well, he retired a few years ago," Milly said. "Clip cleaned up well. When he wasn't being a player and wearing shorts and a t-shirt, he was in his robes or working with the law. And he worked with Ben when he went into Witness Protection. Ben gave a lot of info to the feds like stuff that Bellows wouldn't share, and mob organization info that Kerry left him. The bad guys from the desert wanted to find Ben. Right up to when he died there was some serious pressure to protect him."

"And me?" I asked. "I took Marino at his word that I was safe if I stayed away. I've been a wreck since Ben reached out. Am I safe here now?"

"Clip forced Marino to keep his word about you. So with the weight of Marino pressuring the other mob families, they agreed to not go after you to lure Ben. And I think they all knew you weren't in contact with him. So you were safe as long as you never came back. Now, with Ben dead, you're okay. "

I shook my head. "Given his age, I shouldn't be shocked that he's gone. But I've wondered about him every day since I left. I used to look for him everywhere I went. No matter what I was doing, whether it was golf or even being a dad, I thought about him.

"He had that way about him," he said. "Without trying, he would be the leader. I'm happy he could shake the desert off. And I'm glad that you did too."

I put my hand on Milly's shoulder. "You were right. I needed to leave. Thank you for that. I have always felt I owed you."

Milly smiled and nodded. "All that talent you have would have been a magnet for the scum of the desert. Turns out, you used it the right way. I'm glad for you. I take it you read the article I gave you?"

"I did. I had to read it about six times before I figured it out. He was right. One memory. That meant the difference for me."

We spoke for another hour. Milly filled me in on his family, about how The Bridge was torn down and rebuilt, and the whereabouts of some of the names from the past. We walked to the hallway where some pictures hung. I recognized faces from the group photos and laughed when he showed me the before and after photos of the barroom. When it was time for me to leave, we shook hands and hugged.

"Here," he said, handing me a business card with his home address on it, "you tell Melissa to send me a Christmas card with a picture of your kids. I'll send one back to you with a picture of my grandkids. Got it?"

I nodded and said I would. And I did.

CHAPTER 18

Driving out of Las Vegas helped to remove the burden of the fear I carried the entire time I was within the city limits. No matter what Melissa and Milly said about me seeing ghosts, the second I was out of the city I felt the tension release. Back in my hotel room, I called Melissa. When she mentioned Ben's name, it hit me again that he was gone. Melissa was patient as I struggled with the disappointment. I had so hoped to see Ben. I could have understood if he did not show up. Right up to the day I left Austin for Las Vegas I expected to get an email from him that he got cold feet. But finding out that he died ripped the dream of seeing him away forever.

Melissa did what she could to talk me through the pain. She reminded me that we would be celebrating her mom's birthday in a few days. My mom would also be there. Since Melissa's dad passed away a few years earlier, our mothers became best friends. Seeing them together was something to look forward to.

Even with the upcoming party, I had two days of driving ahead of me. Two days of thinking, mourning, and wondering about what might have been.

I was awake at 5:00 AM the next day and was on the road at 6:00. Before I left my room, I shaved the beard off. I didn't need it anymore. As I drove I did what I could to keep my mind on other things but the memories of Ben were like magnets pulling at my thoughts. When I stopped for breakfast, the food I ate was bland, the people sitting around me were loud, and the newspaper I read was boring. When I got back into my car, I looked at the trip app on my phone and saw I had five hundred more miles until I reached my hotel. That meant I was still eleven hundred miles from home.

I drove for four hours until it was time to stop for lunch, and then another five hours until I pulled into the parking lot at the hotel where I would spend the night. After checking in, I showered, called Melissa, and then walked down to the restaurant across the parking lot. I was hungry, tired, sore, sad, and ready for bed. As I walked through the restaurant's front doors, I felt the weight of disappointment on my shoulders.

The restaurant was fairly crowded. I asked the hostess for a table away from the people and she was nice enough to seat me in an empty section. I then did something I hadn't done in over thirty years. I sat with my back to the restaurant's entrance. Feeling proud of myself for doing it, I looked out the window and saw it was dark enough outside that the reflection still afforded me a clear view of the inside of the restaurant. "Okay," I said to myself. "It's a step in the right direction."

"What can I get you, sir?" my waitress asked, displaying way too much energy for my mood.

"A cheeseburger," I said. "I haven't had one in ages, and I'm in a nostalgic mood. I'll have a cheeseburger, fries, and a vanilla milkshake."

She smiled as she took my menu. I got out my phone, put on my reading glasses, and opened my PGA app. I liked to read the news about The Tour, the tournaments, and the latest about the business of golf. Finding a good article, I started to read. I sucked down half of the milkshake before my food came. I then pushed it to the far side of the table to force myself to save some for the meal and focused back on my phone.

Behind me, I heard the hostess talking to someone. "Is this okay?" she said. The person grunted and I heard some chairs moving. I looked up at the window and in the reflection, I saw the hostess walking away and a person was now sitting with their back to me.

When my food came, I realized that I was very hungry. I started to dig into my fries and was halfway through my burger in three bites. I closed the article I was reading on my phone and opened my photo app. Going through the pictures I found one with the entire family. Their smiles helped my bad mood. I swiped to a picture of Melissa and pushed the phone to the middle of the table. As I continued to eat, I stared at her beautiful face. Her smile was like a rope pulling me back to the surface. Her smile helped me realize that I had someone to share my pain with. Her smile made me smile.

I could not wait to get home.

"It really was a great shot."

I heard the words but paid no attention. I assumed somebody behind me was talking to someone else but the voice got lost in the noise from the restaurant.

"Wasn't it? Wasn't it a great shot?"

Again, I didn't know who was speaking. I only knew the voice was coming from behind me. I looked up at the window and noticed the person behind me, a man, was turned around in his chair. He was looking at me over his shoulder.

The man said, "That was the most fun I had on a golf course until the first day I played with my boys."

"I'm sorry," I said, looking the reflection, "are you talking to me?"

The man moved back from his table. "Can I have one of what he's drinking please, Miss?" he asked, speaking away from me.

He stood up and turned to face me. His body was a dark mass in the reflection so I looked over my shoulder to see who he was as he walked up to my table.

"I think it must have moved fifty or sixty yards left," he said as he walked up to me. "But, sometimes I think the drive was better. What do you think?"

I moved away from my table and turned in my chair. The man slowly walked up and stood over me. He was older with gray wavy hair. He was tall, perhaps six feet, and his shoulders were slightly hunched. Looking down, he had intense blue eyes that tore right through me. With a smile, he said, "Of course, the drive and approach aren't worth a thing if you don't make the putt."

I couldn't speak. I sat there with my mouth hanging open and stared at him. My eyes started to tear up, and my throat went dry. Three times I tried to say something, but no sound came out of my mouth. I finally gave up and fell back in my chair.

He stood looking at me and tilted his head. "I'm not a ghost if that's what you think I am."

Finally, I shook the shock from my head and swallowed hard. With a deep breath, I smiled. "I don't believe in ghosts," I said. "And in all the years I've had to think about it, I have decided that the drive was the best shot. Without a doubt."

I then flew up out of my chair and launched myself at him. For the next twenty seconds, I tightly hugged the man that for decades had been the focus of my thoughts, my dreams, and my profession, as well as the namesake of my son. When I pulled back and looked at him, I said, "Ben, it's been thirty-six years."

"Well," he said, "I've seen you a few times. I wanted to talk to you, to come up and at least say hello. To tell you how proud I was, and how much I support you. But, I couldn't risk it. There was always someone else there with me, and they would never allow it. So, well, here I am."

"You died. Your boys said you were dead."

He smiled and said, "Later, let's talk about that later. For now, I want to have a milkshake. Sit."

So we sat at our table and ate. Our conversation was mostly about family and sports. He got emotional when I showed him a picture of my kids. His son had already told him I named my son after him but seeing my Ben's picture brought out some tears. We both laughed when he asked if I named my daughter Mildred, after Milly. He appreciated that she is named after Melissa's mother, Nancy Lou.

Anytime I brought up the topics I wanted to discuss, the ones that I had in my head for years, he stopped me. "Wait," was all he said.

When we finished eating, he told me to go to my room and he would be right behind me. So I got up and walked out of the restaurant. Sitting at a table near the front of the restaurant were Ben's two sons. Both stood, shook my hand, and apologized for the deception.

Kieran said, "He moves a little slow, so we'll walk with him and get him to your room."

"Sure," I said, "it's room number..."

"We know it," he said.

I didn't ask how they knew my room number. Back in my room, I pulled the envelope out of the locked case and put it on the small round table in the corner of the room next to the window. When Ben arrived, his sons walked in with him, and Marcus placed a briefcase on the table next to the envelope. He took out a laptop which he opened and turned on.

Ben walked over and sat at the table. "We have some business to attend to, Mark. I'll leave it up to my lawyer to explain."

I nodded and Kieran reached over and opened the briefcase. "Mark, the biggest reason that we needed to tell you our dad was dead was to finally put an end to the risk that the mob would find him. There were several threats still open at the FBI. I know he told you about the money Kerry Miner took from several families. What he didn't tell you is that Kerry also gave Dad information that detailed each Las Vegas mob family's European organization."

"The mob found out, and that's why they killed Kerry," Ben said. "I never knew what the information he gave me was until I was in Montana. The FBI came to me and told me I needed to give them what I had. I agreed, but first I made a deal."

"A deal?" I asked.

"Yes, a deal," Kieran said. He reached over and took my envelope. He then reached into his briefcase and took out another older, browning envelope.

Ben said, "I told them I would share what I knew, and the information Kerry gave me, as long as they never pursued the money."

"And that is why you need to sign this," Kieran said, handing me what appeared to be a contract along with a power of attorney document.

I read through the two paragraphs in the letter. It said that I was 'person three of three' and that as long as I did not access 'funds' for thirty-five years after the original agreement, I was to have 'unfettered and complete' access. The second paragraph was full of legalese including mentions of the IRS, the FBI, and several other US Federal agencies.

"I'm sorry," I said, "what does all this mean?"

"Trust Kieran, okay Mark," Ben said.

"Here, sign this," Kieran said, passing the Power of Attorney document to me. "Besides being an agent with the FBI, I am an attorney. This says I am your lawyer, and that I can represent you in this matter."

I looked at Ben and he nodded, so I grabbed a pen and signed the document.

Kieran took the document and reviewed it. He then also signed it. "What my dad did was tell the FBI that he would help them, as long as he could do whatever he wanted with the money. The information he had was so powerful, they agreed. The only stipulation was that the money remains in the European account until this year. He agreed to that and went into Witness Protection. The mob never stopped trying to find him. Even today, there are a few people out there that want to kill him."

"So I allowed myself to be killed first," Ben said with a smile. "I've been Phil Barlow since Witness Protection. Ben Newell died a long time ago. We just got the word out to make sure everyone knew."

"And we needed to make sure you weren't being followed," Kieran continued. "If you were, they would have seen us telling you about Dad. But you weren't followed in or out of Vegas. Except by the FBI that is."

"I was followed?" I asked.

"We knew when you arrived, and when you left," Kieran said. "And there was no one taking any notice. It seems that when we got the word out that my dad died a few weeks ago, anyone that thought they could make a name for themselves by finding him stopped looking altogether."

"Death can be very liberating," Ben said with a smile.

"So, what about this?" I asked, holding up the legal document.

"It says you are agreeing to take ownership of an account that will sit in a European bank, and that you can bring those funds into the U.S. and do whatever you want. No questions will be asked by any federal or state agency."

"The money is all yours," Ben said.

I was confused about what they were telling me. "Money? Do you mean the money Kerry took? Wasn't that five million dollars?"

"That's what we believe it was," Kieran said. "Once I have the three signatures and we get the account number from you we can legally access it and find out. I have two of the three in my briefcase. You're the last one."

I looked at Ben and his sons. All three of them nodded. I then read the document again, took the pen, and signed it. "Who are the three signatures?" I asked.

"You, me, and Milly," Ben said with a smile. "I figured I owe you two guys, and I know Kerry would agree."

Kieran took out his phone and took a picture of the signed documents. He then used his phone to email the images to someone. A minute later he received a text message. Reading it, he nodded and told Marcus to go ahead.

"Okay, gentleman. It's been how many years?" Marcus asked as he typed on the laptop.

"Forty years since Kerry opened the account," Ben said.

"Well," Marcus said, "let's see what's in there."

He typed for a minute, then looked over at Kieran and slid the laptop to him.

"Dad and Mark," he said to us, "as the judge and the Department of Treasury have both agreed, I am acting as your attorney for this transaction."

Ben laughed and said to me, "I love it when he sounds so official. All that means is he can hit Enter on the keyboard."

"I'm just making sure this happens like the agreement says it should," Kieran said. "We are going to access this account, and I will transfer funds to the following four accounts."

He held up a piece of paper that contained four long streams of numbers.

"The first," he said, "is the US Government. As demanded, they are receiving half of the funds originally deposited into the account. If the amount Kerry took is what we think it was, that should be two and a half million. The rest will be split up into thirds."

"Hold on," I said. "You're telling me that we're getting a third of what's left?" I did a quick calculation, still not sure about what I was hearing. Signing the document was one thing. Getting this money was another. "That's what? Over eight hundred thousand each?"

The three of them smiled all at once.

"Give me a second, Mark, and I'll tell you exactly how much," Kieran said.

He typed for another few seconds, and then looked at Ben and me. "Okay, open the envelopes, and let's get into the account.

I looked down at the bag containing the envelope. "I finally get to see what's in here?"

"Trust me," Ben said, "it's only numbers."

I nodded. "I know but I've been holding on to this for how long? All those nightmares of having a gun to my head as they ask me where the envelope is."

Ben had a serious look on his face. "Mark, this money doesn't make up for any of that. I'm sorry about all of the pain I've caused you and Melissa."

I put up my hand and stopped him. "Ben, I've thought about this for years. None of this is your fault. If anyone, it's Bellows. With all the time we spent together the bad guys would still have thought I knew something. He's the one that hooked us up. I have never for a second blamed you."

He smiled and nodded. "Thank you for that, Mark. I want you to know how sorry I've been that you went through any of this."

"Well, you two," Kieran said, "if you open up the envelopes and give me the account number, I can tell you how much you're being paid for your troubles."

So, I finally opened up the envelope that I held onto for three and a half decades. And inside was a simple handwritten note that read, *'Part 1'*. A series of numbers and letters followed. At the bottom was the faded signature of Kerry Miner.

"It's kind of weird to see his signature," I said. "I guess I never realized that he wrote this out himself."

I handed over the note to Kieran, as did Ben with his note. I then sat back and watched as Kieran worked on the laptop. After a minute, his eyes widened, and he sat back.

"Okay, this account has only one transaction and it was a deposit for five million," he said. "I'm going to transfer the funds. First, two point five million to the US Government," He typed something and then hit Enter. After a few seconds, he nodded. "Okay, and now I'm transferring the remainder to three accounts." He looked up at us and smiled. "Because the amount won't divide by three evenly, who gets the extra penny?"

"Give it to Milly," Ben said with a laugh. "He works for tips at the bar, so he can use it more than us."

"Okay," Kieran said. He hit Enter on the keyboard and then typed for another minute. Making a show of again hitting Enter, he sat back. "All done," he said. "The original account, which was opened in 1978, is now closed."

He looked back and forth between Ben and me. Watching him type and work his way through the process managed to temper my curiosity. Now that he was done, I looked back at him. "So," I said. "Is it around 800K?"

"Um, Mark," said Kieran. "The account drew interest. It seems that the banker Kerry knew was pretty good with money. This account was turning over for forty years on average at more than eleven percent. That means after taking the government's cut, there is..."

He looked down at the laptop and took a deep breath before letting it slowly out.

"Son?" Ben asked.

Kieran smiled, aware that he was dragging this out to build some dramatic tension. "There is just over one hundred and seventeen million dollars."

I wasn't sure I heard him. "Did, um, you...um," I stammered. "Did you just say the account had over one hundred and seventeen million dollars in it? And you split it three ways? Unreal."

I sat back and looked at Ben who appeared equally stunned.

"Um, no," Kieran said.

I shook my head and looked at him. "Well, I thought I misheard you," I said. "That much would be ridiculous. What did you say? How much?"

Kieran smiled. "Mark, that's one hundred and seventeen million after splitting the account three ways."

The room was silent. I looked at Ben, and he looked at me. "I guess forty years of interest builds up," he said.

I stood and looked around the room. "This isn't real, right? I mean, how would the government let this happen? And how could there be so much money in an account that we can just..."

I stopped and walked over to the window. My head was filled with noise as I tried to understand if this was happening. I turned back to them and said, "How can this be legal?"

"It's perfectly legal," Kieran said. "The government got paid for its troubles. Back then they were unable to get the bank to tell them how much was in the account. So they decided that whatever the amount, they wanted half of the original balance. Then, ten years ago, a federal judge signed an order sealing these transactions in perpetuity. No one will be able to look at the details. Whatever you do with the money from now on, the government will allow it. You'll get the forms for controlling the account in the mail within two weeks."

Nothing made much sense to me. Perhaps the most perplexing issue was why the government would make such a deal. "What judge would sign something like that?"

"The Honorable Louis B. Clippard," Ben said.

"Who?" I asked.

"Clip," said Ben, a wide grin on his face. "I left Vegas pretty quick, and he owed me from a match. I guess he paid up."

Marcus and Kieran stood up. "We're going to head back to the restaurant for some food. You two guys can catch up," Kieran said. He gathered the documents and the laptop and put them into his briefcase. Both boys then walked over to me.

Marcus threw his arms around me and hugged me tightly. "I can't thank you enough for the talk we had at Desert Bridge. Both of us thought we knew our dad, but you told us so much more."

Kieran also hugged me. "A boy never gets to truly know what his dad is like. But you got us much closer. Thank you."

I smiled and felt my eyes start to fill up. I had no words to share with them other than to tell them they were welcome.

After they left, Ben and I sat at the small table letting the shockwave of the money settle down.

"It's only a number, right?" Ben said. "Something tells me that the type of family man you are understands there are more important things than a big number."

I nodded. "And something tells me that you feel the same way."

"You're right," Ben said. "Besides, this fell into my lap. There was no action so it wasn't that fun."

We both laughed and settled into a discussion about our lives. We were two old friends with a boatload of unique experiences to reminisce about but mostly, we were proud dads talking about our kids. We started to talk about golf after Ben asked me if my kids played.

"I believe Marcus told me that you now play the game for fun. Is that true?" I asked. "Because the Ben Newell I know told me he never had fun playing golf."

Ben started to laugh and nodded. "It's true. You know, I took my wife and Kieran to Montana after leaving the desert. After a year, Marcus was born. There's not a lot of golf played in Montana. I didn't touch the clubs for a long time. Hell, I worked in an office for five years. Fifty hours a week working, the rest was the kids. When they got old enough, I took them to the range. That's when it happened. Hitting the ball in front of them was rewarding. But I realized it wasn't the shot that was rewarding. It was their reaction. It was fun. Watching them learn how to play was great fun."

"Wow, I never thought I would hear you say that golf was fun," I said.

"Is it fun for you?" he asked.

"Yeah," I nodded. "It is. I still love the game. For a while, it was work. A lot of work. But, I guess I got out before I lost the passion. And now my job is helping other people that love the game have a chance to play at a great resort. And I've got the foundation Melissa and I started in memory of my old swing coach, Mr. Wittich. We're trying to help others."

Ben leaned forward and said, "Do you look at your donations every month?"

I nodded. "Yea, I do. It's not as much as when we started it and I was still on tour, but we do okay. The money goes to junior golf in the area."

Ben smiled. "So my five hundred a month is helping out?"

Now I laughed. "That's you? Wow. I never made the connection. We get a few donations each month from orgs like the PGA, but... Unreal. I never thought that might be you."

Ben pointed to his phone. "I got pretty good at setting up stuff on my phone. Now the donation is what they call, 'automated'. I think after what we just did with Kerry's money, I may be able to up my donation a bit."

I ran my hand through my hair. "Yea, I have no idea about how that money...." My words trailed off as my mind started to race.

Ben interrupted my thoughts. "I followed you all the time. Every Saturday morning I would check that week's tournament scores and look for your name."

"I used to think I saw you in the crowd," I said. "I used your pre-shot routine every time. I thought about how you would play a hole, how you would set up an opponent, how you would prepare." I looked him right in the eye. "You drove me. Even if you weren't there, it was you that pushed me. And it was you that helped me finally win."

Ben gave a slight nod. "Thanks, Mark. That means a lot. It does." He took a deep breath to control his emotions and then smiled. "You know, I was there in '89. I was in Texas."

My eyes widened and my mouth fell open. "Where? At the course?"

"I walked with you for the final nine. I was standing in the first row at the eighteenth when you made the putt."

I couldn't believe what he was telling me. "Why were you there? I mean, Montana is pretty far away."

"Because," he said, "I knew you were ready to win. I saw that when you missed the putt a few weeks earlier at Westchester. You looked lost when you were standing over that putt."

I stood and looked down at him "I was lost," I said. "I was playing better than anyone in the field that day, but I was lost. Were you at Westchester?"

He shook his head. "No, I saw you on TV on Saturday and thought you looked good, but not ready to win. You were missing something. Then, I saw you were two back going into Saturday in Texas. Watching the tournament, you made two long putts coming in. That put you one back on Saturday night. You were a completely different player than what I saw at Westchester. I booked a flight and made it to the course when you were teeing off on the tenth."

"Unreal," I said. "That entire back nine I could have played through a hurricane and not known it."

"Why?" he asked me. "What was different?"

I walked over to my suitcase and reached in. Pulling out a manila folder, I dropped it on the table in front of him. "This is why."

He looked up at me with a curious gaze. Reaching into the envelope he pulled out the 'Vegas Live' magazine Milly handed me on the day I left Vegas. He held it up and rifled through the pages. He then looked up at me. "I don't understand."

"Milly gave me that when I left Vegas. He said it had an article about the murder on the green at the Bridge. The writer seemed to know the police, and she included a lot of details about what happened."

"And how does this relate to you and your golf?" he asked.

"Ben, you always told me I needed to find that one shot, or that one hole that could tell me I could do it and put it into the brain bank. I never understood what you meant, but after I missed the putt at Westchester, I knew I needed to find it. To find something that gave me an edge." I poked at the magazine. "Milly told me that I would find it in here. He handed me this and said how you always talked about finding the edge. He told me to read the article and I would find it. And back when he gave it to me I did read it but nothing clicked with me. I threw the magazine in a box and forgot about it. After Westchester, I pulled it out of the box. I read it five times before I saw what he wanted me to. And he was right. I found it."

"Mark, I'm sorry to ask, but what happened that night at the Bridge with Spano? I never heard."

"Spano and Junior, or I mean Emilio, took me out onto the seventeenth green and told me to make a putt. He told me if I made it I would live, if not, well... So, I hit the putt, and when he pointed his gun at me, Emilio shot him. It scared the shit out of me. I fell on the ground like I was shot, but Emilio picked me up and we ran out of there."

Ben shook his head, "Spano hated my guts. He wanted me to know he killed you to get me to come back."

"And," I said, "he went against what Marino wanted. So, my friend from your match with Monroe saved me."

"You're lucky you gave him back the money he dropped," Ben said with a smile. Holding up the magazine, he asked, "So how does this tie in with you stepping up and making a thirty-footer to win on Tour?"

"Open it to the article and read the paragraph I highlighted," I said.

Ben put the magazine on the table and flipped it open to the page I folded over. Scanning to the highlighted part, he read through it. Looking back up, he shook his head. "I don't get it," he said.

"Either did I the first few times," I said. "I thought Milly was playing a joke, but then I remembered what you said. You told me, 'Milly knows everything'. So, I read it again, and then I saw it. I saw what he was talking about. And he was right. Go ahead, read it out loud."

Ben nodded and picked up the magazine. "Okay, it says, 'The police found the body of forty-three-year-old Anthony Spano of Las Vegas lying dead on the seventeenth green at Desert Bridge Golf Course. Mr. Spano, a known associate of several criminal organizations, was shot execution-style. He was found with a gun in his hand that police said had recently been fired. Blood samples found on the ground were taken by the Las Vegas Crime Lab. The only other potential evidence was a golf club found laying on the ground several feet from Mr. Spano, the flagstick of the seventeenth green found laying next to the hole on the green, and a golf ball found in the hole. Police say that this evidence has also been sent to the Crime Lab for analysis.'"

Ben put down the magazine and looked up at me. "Well, I bet the club was pissed that the flagstick was taken by the police. I doubt they had any extra ones. But...? What am I missing?"

I smiled and said, "The same thing I missed. I was pretty sure Spano was going to shoot me whatever happened, but just in case I wanted to make that putt. I hit as good a putt as I could and I was just about to take a swing at him with the putter when Emilio shot him. The noise scared the crap out of me. I thought I was shot. I fell over, and Emilio carried me out of there. I never looked back."

"Holy..," Ben said looking down at the article. "I see it now."

"You were right," I said. "When I missed the putt at Westchester, I knew I needed that one memory to tell me I could make any shot no matter the situation."

Ben read part of the sentence again. "'and a golf ball found in the hole'." Looking up at me, he said, "You did it."

I smiled at him. "Yeah, I made the putt."

Ben sat back and smiled at me. After a moment, he said, "You asked me after that Skins match against Clip and Gonzo if that's what it feels like to be a player. I think I told you something about having to feel what it is like to lose money to really know."

"I remember that," I said.

"I don't think I was totally right," he said with a deep breath. "What I realized after I stopped playing was that I missed the respect of the others. Not just the winning or losing, but the shared respect of other players. I feel it now for the first time in decades. You making that putt? I can't think of anything that is more like a player than to come through under that pressure."

Now it was my turn to smile. "I felt it too. Winning on Tour was a life's accomplishment. But more than that, when I finally saw what Milly wanted me to see, I think I finally knew what it was to be a player."

We spent the next two hours talking. He wasn't near eighty years old, and I wasn't near sixty. It was as if we were both back in Las Vegas, having conversations that we never had back then. We talked about golf the way two golf buddies do; with stories, laughs, and hollow challenges. It was the first time we talked about golf the way you should; as a game.

Two months later in Florida, we were teammates again, teeing it up together for the first time in nearly forty years. This time instead of rich casino gamblers or mob-supported desert players, we paired up and played against the younger versions of ourselves. We spent the week playing with our sons and my daughter.

This time there were laughs and digs at each other that, unlike the Bridge, I could share with Melissa. And when we were done, there were handshakes and hugs on the eighteenth green that I will remember forever. I got to see for myself, firsthand, what

Ben looked like having fun. Having fun being with the people that mean the most to him. Having fun hitting a ball and not caring where it went. Having fun playing the greatest game.

Finally, after all these years, I got to see the real Ben Newell.

ACKNOWLEDGEMENT

Many thanks to those that helped me with the book including Sammy on the graphics, and the pre-reading done by Melissa, Jason, Tony O, and Tom.

My love for the game was cemented by a shot I could barely see. Sitting in the projection booth at Interstate Theater in Ramsey, NJ while a movie was showing (where my sister and future brother-in-law worked), I watched the last round of the 1976 US Open on a small, black and white set (no sound, of course). Jerry Pate, up by a stroke and in the rough on 18, hit a 5-iron from 191 yards. The picture on the TV was so bad that I could not tell if it went in the water or not. After a few seconds, the camera focused on the ball that was 2 feet from the hole. I jumped up but did my best to stay quiet because the movie in the theater was playing, but I was hooked on this game for life from then on.

The game is for all to love and share with family and friends, so to all my golfing buddies, thanks for the great times.

ABOUT THE AUTHOR

Scott Chalmers

Scott loves to read, watch, and talk about all genres including Sports, Science Fiction, Technology, History, and Comedy.

Scott lives in New Jersey with his family. This is his third book, but not his last. The game of golf presents so many possibilities when it comes to writing that he plans to revisit the topic again.

BOOKS BY THIS AUTHOR

The Desert Player

The Desert Player takes you into the world of Las Vegas golf where birdies and pars take a back seat to wagers and winning bank. Where it's not the score but the dollars. Where setting up your opponent is more important than setting up your shot.

Faith After Death - Book 1:Hope Foresaken

In 2065, Trent Forrester is sitting on top of the world. He and his best friend, Ryan Griggs, have invented the single most innovative communication technology in history. Working with the President and his team, they are about to embark on an effort to connect the world, when people start dying. Trent and Ryan now find themselves in a race to save themselves so that they can save the world.

Faith After Death - Book 2: Hope Awakened

In this, the last book of the series, as the survivors cope with the new world that awaits them, a new threat is revealed. And their hope to save the human race lies in a most unlikely survivor, a most unlikely ally, and their ability to understand how their faith in each other and God is their only hope.

THE DESERT PLAYER

Made in United States
Troutdale, OR
11/24/2024

25256534R00157